Heart in my mou

only to stop dead in my tracks when I saw something furry wiggling in the faint light slanting through the window. *What the hell?*

I crept toward Carson's crib, mind frozen and adrenaline flooding through my body to deal with this unknown threat. Was a rat attacking my baby? Did a feral cat find a way into the house? A weapon—I needed a weapon, but my wild glance around the room revealed only baby paraphernalia. Every muscle in my body tense, I held my breath and stepped quietly, so I didn't frighten the strange animal into violence. Small whining noises, snuffles, and the scratch of scrabbling claws came from the crib.

I peered down over the crib rail and, at that moment, the clouds moved so moonlight clearly illuminated the creature in my son's crib. A wolf, unmistakably a wolf pup, with grayish-silver fur standing fuzzily askew, black nose questing in the air, tawny eyes framed by perfect black eyeliner. When the pup saw me, he gave a happy little wriggle and whined more loudly.

The wolf pup's gaze met mine and, in an instantaneous rush, I knew him and I understood somehow this was Carson. This wolf was Carson.

Dark Moon Wolf

by

Sarah E. Stevens

Calling the Moon Series

This is a work of fiction. Names, characters, places, and incidents are either the product of the author's imagination or are used fictitiously, and any resemblance to actual persons living or dead, business establishments, events, or locales, is entirely coincidental.

Dark Moon Wolf

Cover Art by *Debbie Taylor*

The Wild Rose Press, Inc.
PO Box 708
Adams Basin, NY 14410-0708
Visit us at www.thewildrosepress.com

Publishing History
First Black Rose Edition, 2017
Print ISBN 978-1-5092-1256-9
Digital ISBN 978-1-5092-1257-6

Calling the Moon Series
Published in the United States of America

Dedication

For Gary, Abby, Tyler, and Zack.
Our lovely, geeky family is the rock of my life,
and I would fight off crazed werewolves
for each one of you.

Chapter One

I couldn't identify the noise on the baby monitor. Alarm rang through my befuddled, sleep-deprived state and I felt one of those heart-stopping parental attacks, all too common in the last four months of single motherhood. Maybe Carson was dying of SIDS or stuck in the very-carefully-checked-for-safety crib bars or his toes were gangrenous from a loose bit of string in his footie pajamas.

Heart in my mouth, I rushed into his room only to stop dead in my tracks when I saw something furry wiggling in the faint light slanting through the window. *What the hell?*

I crept toward Carson's crib, mind frozen and adrenaline flooding through my body to deal with this unknown threat. Was a rat attacking my baby? Did a feral cat find a way into the house? A weapon—I needed a weapon, but my wild glance around the room revealed only baby paraphernalia. Every muscle in my body tense, I held my breath and stepped quietly, so I didn't frighten the strange animal into violence. Small whining noises, snuffles, and the scratch of scrabbling claws came from the crib.

I peered down over the crib rail and, at that moment, the clouds moved so moonlight clearly illuminated the creature in my son's crib. A wolf, unmistakably a wolf pup, with grayish-silver fur standing fuzzily askew, black nose questing in the air, tawny eyes framed by perfect black eyeliner. When the pup saw me, he gave a happy little wriggle and whined more loudly.

The wolf pup's gaze met mine and, in an instantaneous rush, I knew him and I understood somehow this was Carson. This wolf was Carson. Here was my Carson, here was a wolf pup, here was my baby, and he started to whine more desperately and paw at the crib slats. Everything else shut off—the questioning, the panic—in the face of my baby's need.

So I picked him up. He snuggled against me happily, nuzzling me with his wet nose, breathing in my scent, licking absently at the sleeve of my nightgown. My mind froze in panic, but my body functioned on autopilot. I walked around the room, bouncing him gently, singing a bit of a lullaby, just as usual. And, just as usual, his eyes grew heavier and his body soon felt lax with sleep. When he was well and truly out, I carefully laid him back in his crib and tiptoed from the room.

As I closed the door behind me, careful not to make the slightest noise, the pent-up adrenaline left my body and I started to shake, my muscles weak and watery, my head whirling. I slid down the wall, hugged my knees to my chest, and focused on not hyperventilating. I pressed my forehead to my hands, feeling my palms break out in a cold sweat. After a while, I stood up gingerly, opened the door to Carson's room, and looked in.

No, I wasn't insane. A wolf lay in Carson's crib. Carson was a wolf. Carson was a… I glanced up at the moon, framed perfectly in the window, and silently closed the door again.

I walked down the hall to the bathroom, poured myself a glass of water, and stared at my reflection in the mirror. Yes, still me. I picked up my glasses from the bathroom counter and the room snapped into clearer focus. My eyes stared back at me from within the green frames, looking about as shocked as I felt.

"Maybe..." I thought and went back to Carson's room with my glasses on. A sneak peek, however, showed me nothing had changed. I could just see the sleeping pup a bit more clearly from the door.

"Okay, Julie," I said aloud in the hallway. "You haven't gone crazy. Unless talking to yourself makes you crazy. But everything else seems pretty normal. You're not sick, no fever. You're not dreaming. So Carson is...Carson is..." I raised my hand to rub my forehead, closed my eyes for a moment, lowered my hand, and said it. "Carson is a Werewolf."

The words echoed in my head and I suddenly burst out laughing, the kind of laughter that has a sharp, maniacal edge—the kind of laughter that, if I didn't keep it in check, might yet convince me I *was* crazy. I couldn't control myself, though, and after several minutes I sat on the floor, gasping for breath, tears streaming down my face, unsure whether I still laughed or had moved on to crying.

A Werewolf. Carson. Me, Julie Hall, librarian, single mother of a Werewolf. Was it possible? An hour ago, I would have said no. As much as I loved the idea of the fantastical, as much as I devoured books about magic, Dragons, Were-creatures, Vampires, the Fae, as much as I spent time wishing such things were true and

I'd glimpse a Brownie or a Phouka creeping about the town, I now realized deep down, really deep down, I thought all such things were the stuff of make-believe. But it seemed I was wrong. At least about Werewolves, because clearly a wolf slept in the crib. The moment after Carson was born, my entire being flushed with pride and exhaustion, our bodies still connected by his umbilical cord, my doctor placed Carson into my arms. My baby looked right up at me with those huge blue-brown newborn eyes, alert, wide awake though silent, and in that instant, I felt a surge of insight and love, as if I'd known him all my life and had been waiting for this moment of revelation. Just now, when his eyes met mine in the crib, I felt the same thing. I had no doubt this was my Carson. Every atom of my being told me so.

Occam's razor: Carson was a Werewolf.

My God. Was this real? I checked on Carson one more time. No change, just a small gray wolf curled in his crib.

I went into the kitchen and put on the teapot. A few minutes later, I filled my favorite blue mug with a generous dollop of honey, a chamomile teabag, and hot water. My hands icy despite the warm June night, I warmed them against the mug as I sat and thought.

I knew nothing about Werewolves. That is, nothing about real Werewolves. Some part of me gibbered at the thought of making a distinction between fictional Werewolves and real Werewolves, but I told that part to hush while I thought about this logically. The gibbering part screeched again at the thought of logic and Werewolves, then fell silent, perhaps in exhaustion.

The fact remained: I knew nothing about werewolves. Obviously, that old bit about the full moon held true. I hoped that meant I wouldn't have to worry about Carson turning into a wolf at any old time, just once a month or so. But what else did I need to know? Would silver hurt him? Would he have uncontrollable rages and run through the woods like a wild animal? Would he be violent? Would he have any extraordinary abilities? Vulnerabilities? Were there medical ramifications? I thought back to his doctor's appointments so far, all of which had gone quite smoothly. Now that his Were-self had manifested, could he continue to get vaccinations? I stopped the cascade of questions running through my mind, aware I degenerated into the trivial as a way to avoid the central question.

Why was he a Werewolf? How had he become a Werewolf?

In all the tales I'd read, people became Werewolves after being bitten by another Werewolf. Carson was only four months old and I could vouch for the fact he had never been bitten. Not by a Werewolf, not by a wolf, not by a dog, heck, not even by a mosquito. I had absolutely no idea how this had happened.

But I knew someone who must. He must know something. If *he* didn't…

My tea sat there, cooling and neglected, as I stared out the kitchen window. My fingers absently traced the scratches on the old oak table I'd never refinished. Outside, clouds scudded past the setting moon, patches of stars visible where the sky was both clear and unobscured by trees. The inside of my kitchen was eerily superimposed on the outside world, reflected cheerily in the clear window panes: yellow walls, kitchen table, me sitting motionless in my old blue-striped nightgown, my grandmother's collection of ceramic chickens on a shelf behind me. It didn't look like the house of a Werewolf. The night grew darker, then lighter as the sun crept up. In the back of my mind, I was aware this was probably the longest stretch of time Carson had ever slept in a night. Perhaps once a month, when the moon was full, I would actually get a decent night's sleep.

Finally, quite suddenly, I stood up, walked to the phone, and dialed.

I shook again, this time from nerves instead of shock, and I didn't even register the message until the friendly automated voice repeated.

We're sorry. The number you have reached is out of service. Please hang up and try again.

We're sorry. The number you have reached is out of service. Please hang up and try again.

The grating beep-beep-beep-beep-beep sounded in my ear until I hung up. I dialed again. I opened my address book, pulled out a rather dog-eared business card, and dialed one last time, with the same results.

Shit.

I sank back in my chair, cradled my head in my hands, and yanked at my curls before pushing them behind my ears.

Shit! That bastard!

"How dare he change his phone number." I smacked the table for emphasis as my anger grew.

Okay, on one hand, I knew Mac probably had a good reason for changing his cell phone number. Lots of people changed their numbers when they moved—even though Mac never bothered to get a local Oregon number during the nine months he lived here in Jacksonville. But still, my rational side said it had nothing to do with me. On the other hand, the irrational bit inside me felt personally affronted I had no way to contact him now. I mean, yes, sure, he didn't even know about Carson. But I had always intended to tell him. Sometime. Soon. Yes, sometime soon, I planned to tell Mac he was a father. After I summoned the courage to explain why I hadn't told him in the first place. After I figured out for myself why I hadn't told him right away, why I let it escalate like this. For some reason, it never crossed my mind I wouldn't be able to find him when I was ready.

My relationship with Mac had been confusing, to say the least. We shared six months of some great times, a few screaming fights, and a lot of hurt feelings on my part. And three weeks after I ended it, I found myself pregnant.

Roger MacGregor. The first time I saw him, he'd been intently scouring the library shelves, pulling out book after book only to leaf through and discard them on the table. I noted him, of course, because we mostly saw regulars at the Jacksonville library. And few of our patrons rifled urgently through non-fiction books, except for the handful of high school kids who didn't plagiarize entire papers off Wikipedia. I re-shelved the books, making little sense of his mishmash of botanical guides, Native American histories, and tomes on eighteenth century migration.

The next time I saw Mac, he sat at a table in The Black Sheep with a pint of stout in front of him, appearing about as morose as I'd ever seen a person look. When I caught sight of him, I stopped short, causing my best friend Sheila to bump into me. I flushed, puzzled by my own reaction. He continued to stare into his beer with his brows drawn and my pulse pounded as we drew near. As Sheila and I passed him on the way to our table, I'd been unable to resist leaning over to say, "Hey, Happy McJoy-Joy, surely things can't be so bad." He raised his head to give me a sharp look, which turned quizzical as I gave him a wink.

"Jules?" Sheila raised an eyebrow at my sauciness and the only answer I had was a shrug. I didn't know why he'd attracted my eye, actually, because Mac wasn't my usual type: average height, slight build, hair as dark and curly as mine. Usually, I went for taller men and—having struggled with my own curls all my life—I didn't like the look on other people, either. But when he lifted his head to look at me, I saw blue eyes ringed with greenish gray and, somehow, I was lost from that minute on.

For the rest of the evening, as I chatted and laughed with Sheila and flirted mildly with the bartender, I was very conscious of Mac, still sitting at his table, nursing a couple of beers, and not looking terribly morose any longer. In fact, he mostly looked at me—something he didn't even try to disguise. Typically, when Sheila and I were together, she gathered the lion's share of the male attention, what with her long blonde hair and her flair for the dramatic. Mac didn't seem to notice, though. The intensity of his gaze raised the hairs on the back of my neck. When Sheila and I left the pub, we passed his table again. I kept my gaze down, a bit embarrassed, but then I couldn't help myself and looked up at the last minute. He watched me and I nearly missed a step. As I faltered somewhere between a blush and a smile, he rose, pressed a card into my hand, and said, simply, "Call me."

I think I was more surprised than anyone when I actually called him the next day.

And now? Well, if Mac didn't know anything about Carson being a Werewolf, then I was really lost.

I definitely needed to talk to him. But how?

The baby monitor screeched and I jumped to my feet, moving down the hall instinctually and relieved to hear Carson's normal cries.

When I opened the door, Carson lay in the crib, beating the air with his hands and feet, head turned to look for me. Upon seeing me, he screwed up his face and his cries redoubled in strength. He wore his little blue-and-green stripped pajamas, just like at bedtime. I wondered what happened to his clothes when he changed. Shouldn't they have ripped to shreds or something, like in the movies? This Werewolf business disobeyed the laws of nature in more ways than one.

"Shhhh, sweetie, Mama's here," I crooned and lifted him. His little body felt utterly familiar and my knot of anxiety loosened. He continued to cry, then stopped in anticipation as I sat in the rocking chair to feed him.

I looked him over inch by inch. My baby seemed perfectly normal. No fur, nothing to indicate the momentous events of the past night. In fact, if I hadn't checked so many times, I might have thought I imagined it all. I held his little feet in my hands, felt his perfect toes wiggle, and wondered how this Werewolf stuff worked. And how I might be able to get in contact with Mac.

When my baby was full, I tucked him into his little bouncy chair and put him in the bathroom so I could take a shower. Carson sat there in good spirits, kicking at the toys and sucking on his pacifier. I often wished anything in the world would make me quite as happy as a pacifier made Carson. Sometimes Carson managed to pull it out of his mouth and stare at it, as if memorizing every feature of the fantastic thing. Of course, when that happened, he more often than not dropped the paci and screamed bloody murder until I picked it up for him.

Thankfully, he didn't drop the paci during my shower, so I could actually relax under the hot water. After an almost sleepless night, I needed the shower to clear my head. And, I feared, I'd need a large amount of coffee as well.

Once clean, I faced the real post-baby challenge: finding something decent to wear that didn't look too frumpy and fit me. I wasn't too worried about losing the last ten pounds of baby-weight right away, but I was definitely ready to get back into my some of my clothes. With a sigh, I grabbed a pair of formerly-baggy jeans and one of my favorite shirts, purple with tiny black and white flowers. The shirt fit slightly tight across my chest now, but not indecent, I decided. In fact, perhaps that was one good feature of this post-baby body, I thought, studying myself in the mirror.

Carson reached his limit of alone time—well, not even alone time, but time not physically attached to me—and I lifted him out of the bouncy chair. I grabbed the baby sling and settled him in. He relaxed against my body contentedly, as I finished getting ready. Pushing my curls behind my ear one last time and scrunching up my nose, I frowned at myself before giving up.

The next order of business was coffee. Definitely coffee.

Then figuring out how to get in touch with Mac.

Chapter Two

After contacting every acquaintance of Mac's I could think of to no avail, I also blind-called all the private investigating agencies in southern Oregon. None of them had employment records for a Roger MacGregor, which didn't really surprise me, since Mac hadn't worked for anyone local, as far as I knew. I hoped he might have taken some freelance work during the months he was here in southern Oregon on his "real" case, but I quickly ran out of leads.

So that's why, six days after the full moon, I drove down North Fork Highway looking for the town of Greybull, Wyoming. A trip that, according to my phone app, should take eighteen hours and forty minutes lasted four and a half days, mostly because I had to pull over just about every hour for Carson. Diapers, feedings, general in-the-car-too-long crankiness: we'd dealt with it all. I made good friends with every coffee shop between Oregon and Wyoming and seriously contemplated the possibility of hooking up some sort of nonfat latte IV drip. It had been a long and weary trip, and I just hoped it wouldn't end in vain.

Mac was a pretty reserved guy, and I was amazed how much I didn't know about him after dating him for six months. I'd attributed his reserve partly to his personality and partly to his profession—tact and discretion were obviously important components of an investigator, or a "private eye" as I joked to his not-so-much amusement. He was mum about that aspect of his life, but his taciturn nature also carried over into all things personal. I knew Mac's parents were still alive and he had a brother quite a bit younger, still in his late teens. I also knew he'd grown up in Greybull, Wyoming—a fact he'd mentioned once, in passing, while joking with me about small town life. Certainly, everything in Jackson County, Oregon qualified as small town life. I would like to say I was surprised I remembered the name of the town, but that would be a lie. Sometimes, I felt like every detail of my time with Mac etched into my long-term memory. Heck, I remembered his toothbrush was blue and the deodorant he used was scented "Cool Fusion," whatever that means. Perhaps I was a bit obsessive, I couldn't deny it.

At any rate, here I was, about to drive into Greybull, and hoping to track down Mac. An internet search for MacGregor in Greybull, Wyoming turned up no leads, so either the family had an unlisted phone number or they had moved. Out of any other options, I bet on the former—perhaps Mac's odd sense of personal privacy was a family trait.

While hunting for Mac, I'd also spent a bit of time trying to find real information about Werewolves. My research confirmed not only that I knew nothing about Werewolves, but also no one else did. At least, no one on the internet. And neither the fiction books nor the works on myths I checked out of the library helped much. I still had no idea why my baby turned into werewolf. He wasn't bitten by a wolf. He didn't drink water from a wolf's footprint during the full moon. He didn't wear a belt made out of a wolf pelt. And yet, he had definitely turned into a wolf.

During the last four and a half days, I tried to keep my hopes down by telling myself it was extremely unlikely I'd find Mac himself in Greybull. The most I could expect, I reminded my racing heart, was to find his parents or his brother. Somehow, though, I had a hard time listening to myself. My hands shook and my heartbeat thudded loud in my ears as I saw a highway sign announcing I entered Greybull. I drove slowly down the main town thoroughfare, such as it was. At every minute, I expected to catch sight of Mac walking into a store or getting out of his battered red truck. After I drove the length of the downtown and came once again into a residential area, I turned around, drove back, and parked in a bank lot.

Leaning my head against the steering wheel, I closed my eyes and settled my breathing. At that moment, Carson decided to wake up and scream—one of his ear-piercing, glass-shattering, pick-me-up-NOW-Mama screams. I jumped out, unhooked his car seat harness, and picked him up.

"Shhhh, now, Carson, little fella, shhh," I murmured as I bounced him. Looking around, I spotted a nearby bench in front of a local hardware store.

Carson struggled in my arms, trying to bite my shirt and making it otherwise quite clear he was going to starve to death in the next three minutes. Not known for his patience, my Carson.

Giving a bit of a mental shrug, I grabbed my purse and went over to sit. I wasn't a hundred percent sure what folks in Wyoming thought about breastfeeding in public, but there weren't many people around and I didn't have any other options. So, I sat on the bench, settled Carson to nurse, and pasted a smile on my face, channeling my inner diva in case anyone gave me a disapproving look or—worse yet—said something rude.

The proportion of pickup trucks to cars was definitely high in Wyoming, I noted while watching traffic and checking out the parked vehicles. I didn't see Mac's truck anywhere, though. Not that I expected it, I told myself again.

The bell on the hardware store door tinkled merrily as it opened and a middle-aged man in an honest-to-goodness cowboy hat stepped out. He paused sharply and darted a glance at me and the baby. Then, touching his hat brim, he said, "Ma'am" and hopped into a large green truck. Before pulling away from the curb, he popped open a cell phone and dialed, looking at us one more time. I continued to beam a smile into the vicinity, thinking my first experience with a rancher could have been much more traumatic. The rancher talked for several minutes, stealing glances at me the whole time, then nodded, snapped his phone shut, and drove away, with one last lingering look in my direction.

Weird.

Across the street from the hardware store were a realtor's office, a pizza place, and a drugstore, which I decided would be our next stop. After a few more minutes, Carson decided he had enough to eat and wanted to look around this new place. He started waving his little fists and making funny little squawks.

"Hey, Coo-coo Carson, you funny fella," I sang, making a face that always earned a baby grin. Carson smiled, grabbing for my face at the same time, and we played for a bit.

My cell phone rang and when I fumbled it out of my purse, I saw a picture of Sheila sticking her tongue out at me. It made me smile—here I was, in the middle of Nowhere, Wyoming, but I still had cell phone reception.

"Hey," I said, happy to hear my best friend's voice.

"Hey yourself. Did you find him yet?"

Sheila didn't waste time on non-essentials when busy fixing people's lives. She never understood why I broke up with Mac, and she gave me some serious grief for not telling him I was pregnant. She even threatened to tell him herself, but never carried through with it. When I called to say I was headed to Wyoming in a possibly futile search for Mac's family and his whereabouts, she sounded joyful. She knew about the problems Mac and I had, but she was also a firm believer in love conquers all. She was crushed she couldn't come with me, but she taught communication courses in the summer session at Southern Oregon University until the end of July. Of course, she didn't know about the whole Were pup thing—I hadn't told anybody, partly because verbalizing might make it even more real somehow. Mostly because I was afraid everyone would think I was crazy. During our five years of friendship, I'd kept few secrets from Sheila, and I felt awkward during our conversation.

I explained we'd reached Greybull, but hadn't had a chance to find the MacGregors yet, and I reminded her I did *not* expect to actually find Mac here in Wyoming. I reminded myself at the same time. We chatted for a few minutes about the drive, Carson, and some new guy named Bryan who Sheila was dating, before we said our goodbyes.

Feeling much more relaxed, I stood up and told Carson, "Okay, sweet boy, let's go across the street and see if they know the MacGregors, hmmm?"

As I looked both ways to check traffic, I noticed a clerk in the hardware store staring at us. I hovered at the curb for a moment, my attention caught by the voyeuristic clerk, who looked about seventeen and surely had better things to do than watch me and my baby. A coworker must have noticed his distraction, finally, and said something, because the clerk jumped slightly and turned away. Huh. Must be boring, living in Greybull, if Carson and I were the highlights of the day. First, the rancher, then the clerk. Didn't these people have anything else to do?

I crossed the street, inwardly shaking my head at the thought that living in Greybull really might be more small town than Jacksonville. I guess Mac hadn't exaggerated.

Opening the door to the drugstore was like opening the door to the past, when superstores and chain pharmacies didn't exist in every town. The several aisles contained all sorts of toiletries and medicines, racks of magazines, and a generous display of candy at children's eye level. Dirty marketing ploy, that. The cash register was to the right side of the store, where a bored-looking teenager stood cracking gum. At the rear of the store, I saw an older man busy with bottles and pills in a raised pharmacy window.

"Hi," I projected cheer and approached the cashier. Crap. Now what? Somehow, my plan hadn't extended further than "go to Greybull and find people who know the MacGregors." Sorry-ass plan.

I asked, "Do you have a phone book I could borrow?" I balanced Carson with one arm while I pushed my curls out of my eyes with the other hand.

"Yeah, somewhere." The teenager stopped picking her nails, and bent to rummage behind the counter.

I noticed the pharmacist had approached the window. I half turned to give him a smile and a nod, at which his narrow look cleared somewhat. He stood there watching me for a moment, then walked the length of his counter, opened a half-door, and stepped down to approach us. He had a fringe of short brown hair on the sides and a bald pate. His frame was broad and muscular, though he carried a small paunch near his belt.

"Hello, miss," he said, his mellow tone at odds with his assessing gaze. "Can I help you find something?"

Weighing potential help versus discretion, I said, "Yes, perhaps. I'm looking for the MacGregor family? Roger MacGregor's family. Do you know them?"

"Liam and Erin MacGregor?"

"Um…yes. Yes. Roger MacGregor's parents."

"Yes, I know the MacGregor family." He paused and then proceeded in a genial voice. "Where are my manners? I'm Don Reid, the pharmacist here."

Carson squawked slightly as I adjusted my stance to shake his hand.

"Julie Hall."

"Fine boy you have there," Don said. "What is he, about four months old?"

"Yes, four months last week. Thanks." I smiled down at Carson. "I think he's pretty fine, too, although I happily admit to being biased."

"Did you still want the phone book?" the teenager asked, plopping it down on the counter.

"Yes, thanks." I juggled Carson, wishing I'd brought the sling from the car, and flipped the pages looking for the MacGregors. I made what I hoped was a convincingly disappointed moue. "Oh dear. They don't seem to be listed."

"So, Mrs. Hall—"

"Ms. Hall," I corrected the pharmacist automatically, then looked up quickly to soften it with a smile.

"Ah, Ms. Hall." Don Reid cleared his throat. "Excuse me. I don't think I've seen you around here before. Have you traveled far? Liam and Erin didn't mention they expected visitors…"

I hesitated a moment, not sure how to deal with this small town curiosity.

"Yes," I said, "All the way from Oregon. I, um, I'm friends with their son M—Roger."

"I see." He looked at me for a long minute, then gave a decisive nod. "Well, I happen to be friends with Liam and Erin, so I can give you their phone number. Here." He pulled out a small piece of paper and wrote down a string of numbers.

Jackpot! I could hardly believe how easy this was. I guess Greybull *was* small town America.

"Thanks so much for your help," I said to both the teen and Don Reid. "I really appreciate it." Shoving the paper in my pocket, I took a better hold of Carson and left the store. As the door swung shut behind me, I heard the pharmacist say, sharply, "Tracy, hand me the phone."

Great. Perhaps the MacGregors would hear about me before they heard from me.

****

As I crossed the street, Carson fussed loudly, announcing to the world he was in need of a diaper change. Just about done changing him on the passenger seat—a skill I had quite perfected in the last few days—I noticed a car pulling into the lot. Snapping the last snap on Carson's outfit, I taped the dirty diaper around itself and looked for a trash can. As the car parked next to me, my eyebrows rose at the bright red convertible about the half the size of my trusty sedan. Sitting in the driver's seat was a woman who might have been Miss Wyoming thirty years ago: long blonde curls, exquisitely made-up baby-blue eyes, and shiny pink lips. She wore a white western-style shirt with rhinestones on the trim and skinny white jeans. I saw the toes of white crocodile-skin cowboy boots peeking out. Mentally, I revised my impression from Miss Wyoming to cowgirl fashion doll.

As I picked up Carson and the dirty diaper, she rose from her car and clicked her high-heeled boots in my direction. At first, I thought she headed for the bank, but she fixed me with a white-toothed smile and walked straight toward me.

"You must be Julie Hall," she said, holding her hand out. Her perfectly shaped pink nails matched her lipstick.

She was even shorter than my five foot four. I bet without her heeled boots, she'd be lucky to claim five feet. I juggled the diaper in order to extend my hand. Her firm handshake belied her dainty stature and, as our eyes met, she exuded a sense of strength utterly at odds with her appearance.

"Yes?" I said, guarded, wondering if this was some member of Mac's family tipped off by the pharmacist.

"This must be your son." The woman nodded at Carson in the crook of my arm.

"Yes? And you are?" I drew myself up to my full height and attempted to look stern, inwardly wishing I wasn't still clutching a dirty diaper.

"Lily Rose. Mayor of Greybull."

"The mayor comes to meet every visitor to Greybull, Wyoming?" I knew a note of sarcasm crept into my voice, but this entire encounter was surreal.

"No. Not every visitor. Only the visitors who come into town with a Were pup and ask about Roger MacGregor."

Correction. *Now* this encounter was surreal.

"Wha—How…" I clutched Carson a bit harder and took half a step backwards, only to bump into my car.

"I think we need to talk, Julie Hall. Privately. Let's go to my office."

I looked at her a moment, mind whirling. Was this some kind of trick? How did she know about Carson and what was her relationship to Mac?

"Julie." Lily smiled and spread her hands wide, rings sparkling in the sun. "I'm not going to hurt you. You have questions, I have answers. I have some questions, too. It benefits us both to share information.

"My office is just down the street, take a left on Cottonwood Road and you'll see the town hall. You can follow me in your car, and we'll talk."

I nodded, feeling cautious, but thinking the town hall would be a safe, public space to talk.

"Okay then." Lily flashed her million-dollar smile once more. As she click-clicked back to her car, she turned and said, "There's a garbage can right in front of the bank for that diaper." I smiled at her in return, though it felt more like a grimace.

After visiting the trash and strapping Carson into his seat, I got in the car, furious at myself for feeling anxious and defensive. If anyone should feel defensive, it should be this Lily Rose. Who names their daughter Lily Rose, anyway? And who elects someone named Lily Rose as mayor? She should definitely be an aromatherapist. Or a stripper. I followed Lily's red convertible, regaining my mental equilibrium by imagining her as a cowgirl stripper.

The town hall didn't look like much, especially compared to those Midwestern towns always pictured in movies, the ones with large grassy squares and limestone buildings decorated with carvings. Instead, it was just single-story square of brick with white trim sitting in a row with all the others on Cottonwood Road. A western-style wooden sign out front read "Town of Greybull" with smaller lettering announcing Mayor Lily Rose, Clerk's Office, and Notary Public. Right next door was the local police station, a small, plain brick building with stone steps, double glass doors, and two police cars parked in front. A large American flag and, I assumed, the Wyoming flag flew on poles set in front between the two buildings— actually, after a closer look, I realized the two buildings joined at the rear, forming a municipal complex. Lily's red car zipped down a side driveway, presumably to park in a back lot. After thinking for a second, I opted to park on the street. Easier getaway, if I needed to leave in a hurry. I checked myself in the visor mirror, frowning at my freckles as usual. I added a layer of lip gloss and called it a day.

As I opened Carson's door, I saw he had fallen asleep in the approximately two and a half minutes we'd been in the car. I debated whether to transfer him into the sling, which was more comfortable, but meant a chance of waking him up, or detach the baby seat from its base and schlep that into the building. Schlepping would be heavy, awkward, and uncomfortable, but nearly guaranteed sleep continuity. After weighing the decision a minute, I decided to value sleep over ease and detached the car seat. I balanced the handle on my forearm and the side against my hip.

As I pushed open the glass door, a bell jingled. I saw an empty receptionist desk and a few token chairs for people waiting. I doubted much of a crowd ever entered the Greybull town hall. Hallways led back into the building on either side of the reception area and, as I balanced the car seat on a chair to wait, I heard footsteps coming down the left-hand hall. Not the clicking of Lily's boots, the footsteps instead turned out to belong to a police officer, one of the tallest men I'd ever seen. Standing at least six foot six, he looked even taller because he was so thin—like someone had taken a guy of average height and stretched him an extra eight inches. He appeared about my age, probably in his late twenties, with his brown hair in a military-inspired cut. If I hadn't been looking closely, I would have missed the slight widening of his eyes as he approached me and Carson.

"I'm Officer Hardy, ma'am," he said, making it sound like he addressed one of his mother's friends over for tea. "Can I help you?"

"Yes, I'm here to meet with Mayor Lily Rose."

The officer nodded, obviously expecting that answer. He opened his mouth to speak, but was interrupted by the arrival of the mayor herself, down the opposite corridor.

"Julie, thanks for coming. Right this way," she gestured. "Bill, please wait out here." Lily's implied "in case I need you" caused me to narrow my eyes briefly, but I followed Lily down the hall.

Lily's office turned out to be a very formal room indeed. Facing the door, a broad cherry-toned L-shaped desk held a large flat screen monitor and several stacks of papers. Full bookshelves lined the left-hand wall. On the right, two large windows with sage curtains drawn back and an oblong table matched the desk. Lily pulled out a chair from the table and motioned for me to do the same.

"Please, have a seat."

I put Carson's seat down on the floor gently, positioning him near my foot so I could rock the seat if needed. I sat straight in the chair, focused on Lily, who lounged across from me and flashed her perfect smile once again.

"Go ahead," she said, just as I opened my mouth to speak.

"How did you know Carson... How did you know about Carson?" I asked.

"Obviously, because I am also a Werewolf." Lily flared her delicate nostrils. "And Carson smells like a Werewolf. It's unmistakable."

"You're a... And you smelled him, all the way from your office? No," I interrupted myself. "The pharmacist. He must be one, too, and he called you."

"Yes. And a few others in town. You created quite a stir," Lily said. "And it's okay to say the word, you know, especially to me, especially here. Werewolf."

"How?" My voice rose an octave. "How is this possible? How can Carson possibly be—how can you be—a Werewolf?"

Lily looked at me for a moment, considering. Without segue, she asked, "Where are you from, Julie? Where does your family live?"

"Oregon. Southern Oregon, Jacksonville, actually. Although, my parents now live in Arizona. Why?"

"And before then? Were your parents raised in Oregon?"

"No, my mom is from the Midwest, from Ohio, near Cleveland. My dad's family is from Indiana." I shrugged, "Why? What does that have to do with...this?"

Lily said, "I don't know of any wolves in southern Oregon. Any werewolves, that is. But there are some packs in the Midwest and one in particular near Cleveland. So perhaps that's your familial connection."

"*My* family? Carson's a Werewolf because of *my* family? That's not possible."

"It must be, Julie. For Carson to be a Were, he must have inherited the gene from both his parents. You're here in Greybull, obviously, to find his father's family—I assume Roger was the father?" I nodded. "And you must also bear the recessive gene."

She paused for a moment, but I just stared at her.

Lily continued, "Roger would have been very proud to know his son had already changed, at such a young age."

Suddenly, something clicked.

"Why are you talking about Mac—Roger in the past tense?" I asked, bolting out of my chair. Without intending, I leaned over the small mayor, practically shouting in her face.

Lily's brows rose in surprise. A look of chagrin passed fleetingly across her face, although she showed no distress at my standing over her.

"Julie," she said, gently. "I think you need to sit down. Roger MacGregor is dead."

****

Several minutes later, I still sat numbly in Lily's office. A cup of coffee appeared after Lily stepped to the door and spoke to Officer Bill Hardy in a hushed voice. The cup sat untouched in front of me. Carson slumbered on at my feet, oblivious he'd just lost his father—a father he'd never even known. It seemed so unreal to me, even more so than the whole Werewolf business which, after all, I actually witnessed. One minute, Mac was alive and I had every opportunity to contact him, to introduce him to his son—maybe even reconcile with him. Yes, now, at this point, I finally admitted part of me, a large part of me, had expected we'd end up together again. Yes, I was angry. Yes, I'd felt betrayed. And so I had acted with utmost immaturity, hiding my pregnancy and our baby from Mac. I think deep down I knew Mac would have been full of joy to know about Carson. I'd been spiteful, spiteful and unfair not to contact him earlier. And now it was too late. I'd never see him again and he'd never, ever meet Carson.

Lily placed a box of tissues in front of me, and I blindly reached out to wipe my face. I blew my nose, loudly, and then dissolved into tears again, as I remembered Mac teasing me about how blotchy and snotty I became when I cried. I took off my glasses and blotted my eyes.

Dammit.

"When did..." I cleared my throat. "When did Mac die?"

"About three months ago." Lily sat back down, next to me this time. "Actually, I hoped you'd have some information about it, but I...I guess not."

Three months ago. Carson was one month old.

"What do you mean? How did he die?" Every time I uttered the word, another dagger stabbed my heart. Yes, a melodramatic metaphor, but that's really how it felt.

"We're not sure, exactly." Lily looked at me, her doll-blue eyes assessing. "He was murdered."

"Murdered," I echoed. "Murdered? How does someone murder a Werewolf? Don't you have, ah, superhuman strength and stuff? Vulnerable only to silver and garlic and..."

Lily smiled. "Kind of. We heal quickly, and we're stronger than humans. It's true silver weapons affect us more strongly than steel. Not the garlic thing, though, thankfully, since I love a good shrimp scampi. Anyway, don't they say garlic is for Vampires?"

Her voice turned serious. "We're not immortal, though. And whoever killed Roger knew full well he was a Werewolf."

"How do you know?"

Lily looked down, not meeting my gaze. "Let's not go into the details right now, Julie. I promise you, I'll tell you the full story later, once the news has settled in a bit."

After a few moments of silence, Lily leaned across the table and took my hand.

"It's good you're here, Julie. It's good you knew to come to us. Roger's parents will be happy to meet you and Carson."

I nodded, silent but grateful.

Chapter Three

I let Lily walk ahead of me as we approached the farmhouse and forced myself to loosen my nervous grip on Carson. The modest two-story home sported a fresh coat of white paint with dark green trimming the windows, the lawn and flower beds meticulously maintained. The house sat on several acres of land; mostly scrub grass, sage brush, and reddish dusty soil. I saw a hen house in back, but it didn't seem the MacGregors had an operating farm—more like almost everyone had some sort of livestock in a place like Wyoming. We'd taken a narrow road off the highway and then followed a gravel lane for nearly a mile before arriving. I couldn't see any neighbors and wondered what it would be like to live somewhere this remote. Seemingly oblivious to the momentous occasion, Carson looked blearily up at the blue sky and opened and closed his little hands as if grasping for the sun.

Before Lily could even knock, the door flung open to reveal a middle-aged woman who practically pushed the small mayor aside as she stepped toward me.

"You're... And this... Oh, my, oh my..."

The woman closed her eyes, swallowed hard, and then looked at me with one of the most generous and sincere smiles I've ever seen.

"I'm sorry, excuse me. I'm Erin MacGregor and you are most welcome here. Please, come in."

As I stepped inside, the coolness of the air conditioning met me and the contrast from the strong sun left me momentarily blinking in the tiled entry way.

"I'm Julie Hall and this is Carson. Um, Carson Roger Hall."

"Carson Roger?" Erin swallowed once more and shut her eyes for a split second before continuing. "He's beautiful."

"Isn't he?"

We exchanged a smile.

Impulsively, I offered, "Here, why don't you hold him?"

"Oh! Oh." She took Carson gently into her arms. "Hello, sweet boy. Hello, Carson."

Lily moved restlessly in the doorway, breaking Erin's reverie.

"Oh, Full. I'm sorry, come in, come in." Erin ushered Lily into the house. "Full, Julie, let's go into the living room where it's more comfortable."

"Full?" I echoed, as we followed her into the house. Erin still cradled Carson, who grabbed hold of her thick, graying braid.

"Full. My title, as head of the pack."

I stopped short. "Head of the pack?"

Lily turned toward me and raised a perfectly-shaped brow.

"You're the head of the pack? The pack of Werewolves? The local group of Werewolves? You're the head?"

"Yes." Lily's mouth quirked. "I'm the pack's Full. As in: full, waxing, half, waning, crescent, dark. And the head full moon wolf is *the* Full. Which is me," she said, slowly and clearly, as I stood looking at her.

"Oh."

"Expecting someone—hmmm, let me guess— someone bigger, taller, stronger, *male*-er? Some burly, hairy brute of a man?"

"Well. Yes. I guess."

Lily shook her head. "Julie Hall, you have a lot to learn about Werewolves."

****

In the next two hours, I didn't learn much about Werewolves, but I did learn a lot about Mac and his family. Mac's mother and I clicked instantly, and we both soon cooed to Carson about "Grandma Erin." She pulled out piles of baby pictures, and we happily engaged in the game of Who Does Carson Look Like. We agreed, with the curls Mac and I both shared, Carson's hair would only get curlier as it grew. Right now, he had that baby male-pattern baldness look, where his hair was worn away on the sides. At the nape of his neck, though, were a couple undeniable curls. Erin thought Carson's eyes might end up blue like Mac's and hers, but I thought they tended toward the brownish side. Or maybe green. We both agreed he had Mac's mouth and chin, and we blinked away watery eyes. At some point during all of this, Lily made her excuses and left us to it.

As the afternoon drew on, Mac's brother Ian came home. Ian was seventeen, almost ten years younger than Mac. He slouched into the house and barely met my eyes. After a halting exchange of awkward social pleasantries, he escaped up to his room and turned on some very loud music.

Erin sighed.

"He's been having a very hard time since Roger's death. Ian's always idolized his older brother. I hope we don't lose him."

"Lose him? Are you worried he's suicidal?"

"No, not exactly. But he spends a lot of time as a wolf. And sometimes I worry he won't…come back."

I rocked back on my heels. For a brief moment, I had forgotten.

Carson lay on top of a blanket on the floor, kicking and flailing his arms. Erin and I sat on the carpet next to him.

"I don't know much about all of this, about Werewolves," I admitted. "When I saw Carson had…changed…I freaked out."

"I bet you did." Erin shook a rattle in front of the baby.

"Um, so, are you a Werewolf, too?"

"Yes, and so is Liam. And both boys. Although none of us manifested this early. You're going to be a strong little full moon wolf, aren't you, Carson?"

I was disconcerted to hear her coo to Carson about being a Werewolf.

"What exactly does that mean? A 'full moon wolf'?"

"Well, let's see. We classify ourselves in five categories, depending on strength. A full moon wolf is the strongest, then waxing, half moon, waning, and crescent moon wolves."

"And what about dark moon wolves? Lily said something about that?"

"You're a dark moon wolf, dear. Someone who bears the gene, but cannot change or call the moon. I forgot you basically don't know anything." Erin sat back and started again. "As you know, Werewolves respond to the full moon by changing shape, from human to wolf. Folklore has that much correct. Almost all Weres must change at the full moon; it's only a choice for the very strongest of us. Most can change voluntarily at other times, as well, all except for the weakest, the crescent moon wolves. Weres are also stronger than humans, and we heal very quickly, unless injured by silver. Or unless the injury is too severe." A frown briefly crossed her face.

"Okay. I follow you so far."

"Now, when I refer to 'strong' and 'weak' wolves, I don't mean physical strength, I mean strong or weak in their ability to call the moon."

"Call the moon?"

Erin nodded. "Yes, this is the part I don't think any of the lurid Werewolf stories depict. Our identity as Werewolves is tied to the moon—our own individual abilities even wax and wane with the moon in the sky. The moon is the catalyst for our shape-changing, as I said. In turn, we have the ability to call on the moon, to call on the power of the moon. I guess you might call it magic? Moon magic?"

"So what can you do with this moon magic?"

"Our powers depend on the strength of the Were, but calling on the moon means invoking its powers— powers of shifting light, tides, madness, illusion, creativity—most cultural associations of the moon have some basis in actual moon magic."

"What can you actually do?"

"Hmm, an example will help most. So, let's say there's a drought and the crops suffer. A strong Were, a full moon wolf, might call on the moon and make the waters rise from the ground, similar to the way the moon affects the ocean tides."

"Wow." I digested that information for a moment.

"Yes. And Carson will be a very strong Were, definitely a full. The earlier the shapeshifting manifests, the stronger the Were. Most Werewolves don't shift until they hit puberty, although some shift for the first time even in their late teens."

Erin smiled. "Roger, he was also quite strong. He shifted when he was six. He was a full moon. Ian is a waxing moon, fairly strong himself."

"What are you?"

"Waning. Liam, my husband, is a crescent moon wolf, not strong at all. He has never successfully called on the moon for anything other than shifting the light a bit in order to stay hidden. The strength of a Were isn't inherited directly."

"But being a Werewolf is somehow genetic? Some sort of recessive gene the child must inherit from both parents?"

"Yes. We haven't isolated the gene—or genes—yet, although I know there are some Weres in genetics research trying to do just that. Our power seems mostly hereditary, although the recessive gene can also sometimes be awoken from dormancy."

"How?"

Erin looked surprised at my question. "Why, by being bitten, of course. A dark moon wolf bitten by another werewolf sometimes becomes a Were."

My heartbeat quickened with excitement. Become a Were?

"Wait. Only sometimes?" I said, after her qualifier registered in my brain.

"Yes. Sometimes the dark moon dies."
****

Mac's father Liam came home shortly after our conversation. If I hadn't known ahead of time he was a "crescent moon wolf," I would have thought *he* was the pack leader. A bit over six feet tall, he was broad shouldered, muscular, and had a mess of unruly curls that matched his in-need-of-a-trim beard. Unlike both boys, his hair was on the reddish side of brown.

"Liam." Erin stood as he walked into the living room. "Did you get my voicemail?"

At Liam's blank look, she continued with a flush, "This is Julie Hall. She was Roger's girlfriend. And this is their son, Carson. Carson Roger Hall. Our grandson."

Erin dabbed at her eyes once more. Liam's eyebrows rose.

"An ex-girlfriend shows up with Roger's child and you leave me a voicemail?"

Erin gestured widely. "I'm sorry, Liam. I got distracted..." She crossed the room and took his hand, squeezing hard. He looked down at her for a moment, and they exchanged a small smile.

"Pleased to meet you," he said, and extended a hand to envelope mine. "I apologize, but I'm a bit taken aback. We didn't know Roger had a son."

"Yes." I looked down at the floor before meeting his eyes. "Actually, Roger didn't know, either. We were—estranged—before I found out I was pregnant."

"I see."

The moment of silence seemed to last forever.

"I'm sorry, dear heart, I should have tried harder to reach you as soon as the Full told me...I don't know what I was thinking, I was just so..." Erin shook her head and shrugged. She held Liam's arm and smiled up at him. "Isn't he the cutest baby you've ever seen?" Erin picked up Carson, who promptly started to scream.

Erin laughed and handed Carson to me. Liam's expression was unreadable.

"Um, I think he's hungry," I said.

"Well, by all means, make yourself at home," said Erin. "And, speaking of being hungry, I need to check on dinner. You'll stay to eat, of course, won't you, Julie?"

I sat down on the couch to feed Carson.

"Yes," I said, slowly. "If you're sure it's not an inconvenience. Also, I hoped you could recommend a hotel in town; I haven't made a reservation yet."

"Hotel?" cried Erin. "Julie Hall. You're practically family, Carson *is* family, and I won't hear of you staying in a hotel. You'll stay with us and I won't take no for an answer."

I looked at Liam, and he nodded after a long moment. Erin bustled out of the room, leaving Roger's dad and me alone. Whereas I had felt comfortable with Erin right away, Liam's less-than-genial scrutiny made me horribly aware of my failings. An unwed mother without the human decency to inform Mac I was pregnant. And now I'd descended on the MacGregor household. An interloper.

I focused intently on Carson, smoothing his downy head.

"So, Julie. What do you do for a living?" Liam asked.

"I'm a librarian. I'm on extended maternity leave right now, but I'm going back to work in about a month."

Silence.

"And what about you? What do you do?"

"I'm a CPA, an accountant."

"Oh, an accountant. That's, um…"

"Interesting?" Liam's mouth quirked in a smile I returned in relief. "About as interesting as being a librarian to most people I suppose. But I enjoy it."

"Well, that's what's important. That you enjoy it, I mean."

We lapsed into an awkward silence. Just as I desperately wracked my brain for something to say—*anything*—Erin called to tell us dinner was ready. Ian slunk down from his room to join us, but didn't participate much in conversation. His hair hung in his eyes, and I couldn't tell whether or not he ever glanced in my direction. The meal was hectic because Carson had taken it into his mind to become difficult-screaming-baby, which sometimes happened at this time of night. My mom always called it the "witching hour" and made some laughing reference to "payback." I managed to eat my salad and enchiladas while standing up and bouncing next to the table. Carson nestled against me in his sling, but nevertheless regaled the table with occasional screeches that stopped just short of shattering glass. I dropped only a little bit of food on his head, definitely not my worse show.

"I remember when Roger was a baby," Erin said, "I don't think I ate a hot meal for six months. Somehow, whenever the food was ready, he needed to be held or nursed. Liam, do you remember?" She sighed. "Ian, on the other hand, was a dream: sleeping through the night by six weeks and hardly ever crying. You were such a happy little fellow, Ian, always cooing and smiling at everyone."

I thought I caught Ian's eyes rolling under his hair.

"How does Carson sleep, Julie?" Erin continued.

"He sleeps. Sometimes. He's doing the best he can, right little fella?"

"Will he be happy sharing your bed tonight, Julie? Or shall we make up a small bed for him in a dresser drawer? That's what my grandma used to do—I think my mom and all her siblings had a drawer for their crib. He's not rolling over yet, is he?"

"No, he can't quite roll over. He tries, though. I think he'll be fine in bed with me. That's actually his preference, even when we're home," I said. "But…are you quite sure it won't be any trouble? I really am happy to find a hotel."

"Absolutely not. You and that sweet boy—" The so-called sweet boy shrieked, so Erin raised her voice as well. "Will stay in this house as long as you're in Greybull."

"Speaking of which." Liam's baritone cut in. "You need to have a hard think, Julie. It may be better for you to move to Greybull. Permanently."

"Liam—"

"Have you given real thought to what it means to raise a Werewolf? You need to be around a pack. You can't handle this on your own."

"Liam—"

"What are you going to do when he changes next time? How are you going to teach him to hunt? To use his abilities? He'll be strong, very strong. How will you cope when he calls the moon?"

"Liam!"

"If not this pack, you need to move somewhere with another functional pack. But since Carson is part of our line, he really should be here with us. That's how Roger would have wanted it." Liam finished. I flinched.

"*Liam!*" Erin shot her husband a dirty look as he finally stopped talking. "Julie, we don't need to talk about this now. It's been a long day for you, a long day for all of us. At the very least, you'll stay here for a while, and we'll have plenty of time to talk things through. Right, Liam?" she said, pointedly.

Carson started screaming in earnest, this time protesting my frozen stance. I closed my mouth, took a deep breath, and started bouncing my baby again.

Move to Greybull. Greybull, Wyoming? Population 1815? Unless there'd been some birth or death since the highway sign went up. Me, Julie Hall, move to Greybull, Wyoming? Did they even have libraries in Wyoming? Did ranchers read? Move here to the middle of nowhere? Impossible. Although…How *was* I going to raise a Werewolf all by myself in the middle of Jackson County, Oregon?

The shrill ring of a phone cut through my troubled thoughts and Erin jumped up, seeming equally relieved to have the moment broken.

"Hello? Oh, Full, hi. What? Oh, no! How? Where was he? Do Miguel and Elise know yet? Do we—Yes. Of course. Yes. Tomorrow at moonrise, I'll tell them. Moon guard you, Full."

Erin hung up and stood for a moment with her back to us. When she turned around, she met Liam's gaze with a grim face.

"Carlos Sanchez has been killed. The Full's called a pack meeting tomorrow, moonrise at the old Beswick ranch."

"What?" Ian exploded from his chair, no longer slouching, but stretched to his full height. Energy spilled off of him, and I felt the hairs on my arms rise.

"Ian." Liam's voice was flat. "We don't know everything yet, and we shouldn't jump to conclusions—"

"*Bull*shit. This is *bullshit*!"

Ian slammed out the kitchen door. For a moment, we remained motionless, then Liam jumped to his feet to follow his son. As he pushed open the door, I saw it—or, rather him—a wolf as tall at the shoulder as my waist, dark fur glinting in the slanting sun, tearing through the grass away from the house.

"Ian!" Liam called. "*Ian!*"

No response from the wolf as he raced out of sight.

Liam smacked the door jamb with his hand, then leaned on it heavily with his eyes closed.

"Should I…" His toneless voice trailed off.

"No. No, don't go after him. You can't change at this time of the moon anyway. Just let him run it off, and he'll be back. He'll be back." Erin sounded as if trying to convince herself as much as her husband. She moved to stand beside him, placing a hand on his shoulder in comfort. Liam shifted slightly and took her into his arms.

I stood there, feeling awkward in the face of their grief, not understanding what just transpired. I took a few steps toward the living room with a half-formed notion of giving them some privacy, but then Carson let loose with an ear-piercing shriek. I shushed him, as

Erin turned to me. Liam turned the other way and stared out into the early evening.

"I'm sorry, Julie. This must all seem very strange to you," Erin said.

"No, no, no. I mean, yes, this whole thing," I gestured expansively, "is still strange to me. I'm sorry to intrude at such a private time. Ian—all of you—just experienced another loss and maybe it's best if Carson and I leave, give you some privacy."

Erin sighed and rubbed her forehead. "Ian is overwrought, but perhaps for good cause. Carlos Sanchez—the Werewolf who just died—was sent to investigate Roger's murder. It seems the murderer caught up with him first. I'm not sure how to react myself. Two pack members murdered within a few months? Believe it or not," she gave a small, wry smile, "we're usually not a violent bunch."

Liam turned around and came to her side. They clasped hands and Erin leaned into him, gratefully.

"We'll know more after tomorrow's meeting," Liam said to his wife. "Did she say if—Was Carlos killed the same way?"

Erin's blue eyes turned storm-cloud gray. "Yes."

A moment of silence followed.

I started to speak, then cleared my throat before I could continue. "How was Roger killed?"

"He was beheaded," Erin said.

Chapter Four

In the last few months, I'd found Carson was a great excuse. An excuse to indulge in chocolate—a nursing mother needed the extra calories, after all. An excuse to turn down unwanted invitations. An excuse to sing silly songs and watch *Sesame Street*. Sure, he didn't even pay attention to the television yet, but personally, I'd never stopped enjoying Grover. And he loved it when I sang "I Don't Want to Live on the Moon" along with Ernie.

Right now, he was an excuse to get me out of the house alone for a minute. Carson needed diapers, so after careful directions from Erin—and turning down her offer to accompany us—we were back in the car on the highway driving toward Ron's Grocery. I hoped. Carson finally stopped screaming, and he actually fell asleep within 15 seconds of me starting the car: a new record. I drove slowly, obeying the speed limit for once. Originally, I thought I needed to get some time away to think, but I found myself trying *not* to think—trying very hard to keep my mind in a Zen-like state of nothingness.

Beheaded.

My stomach lurched and I veered onto the gravel at the side of the rural road. Leaving the car sprawled diagonally, I pushed open the door just in time.

After several minutes of absolute misery, I wiped my mouth with the back of my hand and realized sharp rocks dug painfully into my knees. I sat back, hugging my legs to me, glanced into the car to make sure everything was okay, and gave in to my thoughts.

I couldn't get the picture of Mac out of my mind. Mac, beheaded. I tried to hang onto my real memories of him: Mac sprawled across my bed and whistling as I came out of the shower; Mac laughing when he first saw my inherited collection of ceramic chickens; Mac one brow raised in mock confusion as I confessed I hated dark beer. But my imagination kept sending me grisly images of Mac's head flying through the air, of his eyes glazed and fixed on nothing. The pictures were pure Hollywood, since I'd never actually seen such a thing. Intermixed with it all were flashes of headless chickens, of blood spurting from an empty neck. I considered the brute force required to cut off someone's head. Some sick, morbid part of me wondered what it sounded like, chopping through someone's spine. What it felt like. My stomach rolled again, and I wished fervently to turn off these obsessive thoughts.

I cast back in my mind, trying to latch onto a happier memory.

Like the day we picnicked at Applegate Lake. I put together a delicious spread: fresh strawberries, triple-cream brie, sourdough bread, roasted red peppers, and an assortment of olives. Mac loved olives. He could eat a whole container in a sitting; black, green, pitted or not, stuffed with pimento, garlic, feta, whatever. His favorite, stuffed with jalapeno peppers, came from a little roadside stand in northern California. And, of course, I'd brought wine, a bottle of chilled white wine.

What kind of wine was it? I scrunched up my eyes, trying to bring back every detail. A local pinot gris, maybe from Weisingers. Yes, that was it. We spread out my old picnic blanket, its multi-colored plaid soft with age and many washings. I remembered Mac lounging on one elbow, popping olives into his mouth. His hair had been on the long side, ready for a trim. I leaned over and brushed it away from his eyes. He caught my hand and pulled me down with him, to lie against him. God. I remembered the warmth of the sun on my back, the smell of lake and green things growing, the taste of olives and wine and berries and Mac, the sound of a woodpecker somewhere nearby. I'd craned my neck this way and that trying to find the bird, but gave up and just listened. I remembered at the time trying to lock every element of the afternoon into my mind so I could always feel the vividness of that moment. That perfect moment.

Followed by a less than perfect night, which, unfortunately, remained more vivid than all the rest of it. After our picnic, after returning home to impatiently shuck off each other's clothes, after lying together in twisted sheets and talking about everything and nothing, Mac got up to leave. To work, he said. On a Saturday night. After a Saturday afternoon like the one we had spent together. Oh, I'd been so mad. I felt the anger, the hurt, even now. I yelled. I cried. I accused him of not caring, of being utterly selfish, of being cold. Of using his job as an excuse to shy away from intimacy. Finally, at the end, I practically pushed him out of my house, telling him to get the hell away if he couldn't be there with a whole heart, if he'd rather work on God-knew-what.

And I remembered waking up the next morning, eyes swollen, parched and lonely, wishing to take it all back. Wishing I didn't always have to push and push and push. Wishing I could respect his boundaries and his needs. That I could love him without trying to cage him. I called him over and over and over again on his phone until he finally picked up.

Now, I wondered: had it been a full moon?

The Wyoming desert was quiet, except for the skitter and pop of grasshoppers moving through the brush. I stood up, brushed off the seat of my jeans and ran fingers through my curls. Mac. God, it hurt.

****

The long summer evening drew to a close as I drove home from Ron's Grocery, diapers and baby both safely ensconced in the backseat. The two-lane highway was nearly empty, and the setting sun turned the brush into long, slanting shadows. I kept the windows down to smell the sharp tang of dust and sage. Behind me, a lone car approached and I automatically slowed a bit to allow the car to pass in the other lane. The road stretched out straight in either direction, no other vehicles in sight. The car—a blue sedan—swung out to pass. Then suddenly it veered and crashed into my fender.

Metal shrieked and the steering wheel bucked in my hands. The car spun with the impact and I fought back, instinctively trying to regain control. Before I could straighten the car, before I could even understand what happened, the other car hit again. My car jerked violently as the other car crashed into us, this time against the side of my poor car. My tires left the road, hit the gravel, and skidded into the dirt before the front end hit a shallow depression and the car jolted to a sudden halt. I slammed against the steering wheel, then the seat.

Heart pounding in my ears against the silence, I finally found my voice enough to yell, "Shit," and then found my head enough to scream, "Carson!" I jerked my rigid arms from the steering wheel and turned around, straining against the seatbelt before unlatching it, half climbing into the backseat to inspect my baby.

Carson opened his mouth in a terrific scream and my pulse skipped, then hammered away in sheer panic.

"Shh, shh, it's okay. Are you okay?" I fumbled into the seat next to him. I ran my hands along his arms and legs, checking for injury, moving him gently. No obvious breaks. No blood. He thrashed about, a good thing, I told myself. Sobbing now, I unlatched his belt and carefully lifted him out, cradling his head and neck carefully, using one hand to poke and prod a bit.

"I think you're okay." I closed my eyes and sank my nose into his hair. "You're okay. Thank God you're okay. Holy shit. What the *fuck* was that?"

Shaking, I opened the door and got out, holding Carson tightly. He continued to voice a few hiccupping sobs, but quieter now. He butted his small head into my shoulder like a kid goat. I rubbed his back and bounced him on rubbery legs, looking around and trying to get my thoughts in some sort of order.

Off the road ahead of us, the other car loomed ominously in the fading light, and a jolt of adrenaline ran from my core to my fingertips. The blue sedan's engine suddenly stopped, and I took a step backward. For a frozen moment, I was only aware of myself, my frightened baby, and the dark shadow of the man behind that wheel. I glimpsed something metal, a flash as something reflected the setting sun, some movement in the car. Then our standoff was interrupted by a distant susurrus that at first sounded like the ocean and quickly resolved into a pickup truck approaching on the highway. The blue sedan came to life, spun its wheels, and bolted down the road to disappear into the distance.

I came out of my daze as the pickup truck approached. I had an irrational flash of panic as it slowed, before I registered the concern on the driver's face. For the first time, I turned to look at my little compact. My car was in sad shape: the back end smashed, a huge dent in the driver's side, nose down in a small ditch, entangled in brush. It looked like at least one tire was toast.

"Fuck. Fuck! Holy…shit." I took a deep breath, trying to gain some measure of brain activity—not to mention a less profane vocabulary.

"Are you okay?" A lean, weathered man jumped down from the red pickup. "Ma'am, are you all right?"

"Yes. I mean…yes. I think so." I focused on breathing.

"Here, why don't you sit down?" He gestured to the passenger seat of his truck and then guided me there with a warm hand on my shoulder.

As soon as I sat down, I started shaking uncontrollably, suddenly freezing. Carson twisted in my arms to watch the rancher as he walked around my car.

"Whoo-ee," he said, as he came back over. "What happened?"

"I'm n-not sure," I said, "A c-c-car h-hit me. Us." I was afraid my shaking arms might drop Carson.

The rancher walked to the back of his pickup and came back with a blanket, slightly worse for wear. "Here," he said, "I think you're in shock." As I nodded, he settled the blanket around us.

"Ma'am." The rancher's eyes squinted in concern. "Can I call someone for you? Do you want me to call 911? Do you need an ambulance?"

"N-no, not an ambulance. I'm sta-staying with Erin and L-Liam MacGregor. Um. I have their number in my cell phone." I gestured to my purse, still in the front seat of the car, and he brought it to me. He took the phone from my shaking hand.

"Okay, don't you worry about a thing." He smiled kindly, then took a few steps away and made the call.

****

Erin and Liam arrived in under ten minutes.

"Julie," Erin cried in dismay, leaping out of their SUV almost before it came to a full stop. "Are you really okay? What happened?"

I explained to the best of my ability, and their faces grew grim.

"Describe the car again?" Liam said.

"A dark blue sedan, kind of medium-sized. That's all I noticed—I really wasn't in much of a state to pay attention to the details and I'm not much of a car person."

"You didn't see the driver at all?" he asked.

I screwed my eyes shut, trying to remember. "Male. I'm pretty sure it was a man. Dark hair, I think. But that's all from glancing at him in my rearview mirror...and from a distance, when he stopped over there." I pointed, then shrugged in apology. "I'm a bad eyewitness."

Liam walked over to where I had gestured and cast about in the dirt at the side of the road. After a minute or so, he shook his head and walked back over to us.

"Don't worry about it," Erin reassured me. "No one would have gotten a good look in those circumstances. I just wonder…" She trailed off, with a quickly averted glance at the man who'd stopped to help me.

I sat up a bit straighter and smiled at the rancher. "I'm sorry. I'm afraid after all of this, I didn't even get your name. I'm Julie. Julie Hall."

"Thom Gardiner." He nodded. "I'm from Worland; headed back there tonight. Do you folks need any more help? If not, I'll take myself off."

"Thanks, Thom." Liam shook his hand firmly. "I think we'll take care of things from here. We appreciate all of your help."

After sincere thanks from all of us, Thom headed back down the road. The three of us—four, counting Carson—sat for a moment in silence, letting the emotion of the moment subside.

"Should we move Caron's car seat into the SUV? We can send a tow-truck to pick up your car and bring it to a shop. I think it's going to need some work." Erin put an arm around my shoulders.

I nodded. "Yes. I need to get a new car seat, though—I don't think you're supposed to use it if it's been in an accident."

"We'll do that tomorrow. We can drive into Sheridan."

"Right." A haze of exhaustion blanketed me.

"Julie, I think it would be a good idea to have a doctor make sure you and Carson are okay." Liam's brow creased in concern. He reached out to touch a rapidly rising bump on my forehead. I flinched, feeling the injury for the first time. I must have hit my head on the steering wheel when the car stopped in the ditch. Various other minor pains started to surface, mostly muscle aches from being wrenched about in the car. Poor Carson, did he feel the same way?

Erin nodded in agreement. "There's a hospital in Basin, about fifteen minutes away."

****

Two hours later, Carson and I left from South Big Horn County Hospital. The smallest "hospital" I'd ever imagined, by the way, with only a dozen or so patient beds. After clean bills of health, an admonition to come back if I felt dizzy or nauseated, a prescription for muscle relaxers, and both adult- and baby-strength painkillers, out the door we went. I'd already prophylactically dosed Carson and taken a double dose of ibuprofen myself. I'd also made a report to the Greybull police, though I couldn't give much information about the man or the car that forced us off the road. I was bleary-eyed as we drove back to the MacGregor's house. The combination of high emotions and the car accident had depleted my energy.

When we reached the house, Erin showed me to a room and I used all my remaining strength to put Carson into his pajamas and to make sure the bed was safe for co-sleeping. The bed rested against one wall, so I made sure Carson couldn't get stuck in the crack, moved the pillows and blankets away from his side, and gratefully climbed into bed, still wearing that day's t-shirt. I fell asleep without even brushing my teeth.

Chapter Five

Although Carson woke up frequently in the night, I dealt with him while half asleep so morning dawned before I looked around the room and realized I slept in what must have been Mac's childhood bedroom. Carson continued snoozing away, sprawled on his back like a green-striped starfish. I sat on the edge of the bed and looked around, feeling a lump rise in my throat. Erin and Liam must have removed some of the detritus of Mac's childhood in order to make the room into a guest bedroom. Nonetheless, on a shelf high on the wall sat a couple of football trophies, a model car, and three framed pictures. Above the shelf, hung his old Boy Scout sash, full of badges. A pennant proudly proclaiming "University of Wyoming" hung above the mirror. I stood up—groaning a bit as my muscles screamed at me—and crossed the room toward the shelf to examine the pictures. In the first, a young Mac carried a preschool-aged Ian on his shoulders. The camera had caught Ian in the act of yanking on Mac's curls, and Mac's face was twisted up to look at his brother. Both boys were laughing, with a clear kind of rough-and-tumble love. The look on Ian's face, the ease with which Mac's hands held his ankles; all of this made me understand some of the desperate ache Ian must feel at the loss of his brother.

The second picture was much more stilted: a tuxedoed Mac at what must have been his senior prom. His wrists stuck out of the jacket cuffs and he looked like a gangly puppy dog, not yet grown into himself. His curls tightly sculpted to his head and his ears seemed to stick out. I snorted softly at his powder-blue vest, which *exactly* matched his date's long, ruffled dress. As well as her eye shadow. The dress hung asymmetrically off one shoulder. Ah, prom fashion. I stepped even closer, searching the girl's face. Who was she? Had she been Mac's girlfriend? I tried to read into their pose and frozen smiles, wondering if they looked awkward from the scripted moment of professional picture-taking, or if they had been uncomfortable and nervous with the date itself. These small glimpses into Mac's life shouldn't hurt, yet I ached with the reminder of how much I didn't know. I hadn't had enough time with him, and now I never would.

The third picture wasn't Mac at all. In the forefront, grasses and sage brush spotted the reddish dirt and led my eye toward what must be a creek, hidden by its banks and lined by cottonwood trees. I searched a minute before I saw the figure standing in the dappled light. She looked perhaps fifteen, caught in that moment between being a girl and claiming her womanhood. The girl stood poised, silent, contained in herself. Mac—for it had to have been Mac who snapped this shot—photographed her from behind, with one hand resting on the cottonwood next to her, the line of her spine as graceful as the tree trunk, her fawn-colored hair cascading in a straight stream down her back over a plain white t-shirt. The picture captured an essential sense of tranquility. An utterly private moment.

I looked back and forth between this and the prom picture. No, definitely not the same girl. Who was this, then? The picture—both the moment captured and the place of prominence in Mac's room—bespoke intimacy.

Carson stretched, opened his eyes, and squealed. He craned his head around, then relaxed as he saw me standing across the room. His little feet kicked in unison. I let loose a deep breath and smiled at him.

"Good morning, sweet baby." I climbed onto the bed next to him and gave him zerberts until he screamed with laughter. I gingerly untangled his hands from my hair, pushed back to kneel at the side of the bed, and frowned in mock seriousness.

"Now, now, Carson, you crazy imp," I scolded, "I am a very serious Mama and I expect you to be a very serious baby."

I accompanied my words with lots of tickling, causing Carson to squirm and squeal.

We played Serious Mama a little longer. Then I stretched a bit, trying to loosen my sore muscles. Actually, I was surprised I didn't hurt more and reminded myself to indulge in a few more ibuprofen, just to head things off. Carson seemed in fine fettle himself. I felt like a bit of a *real* Serious Mama, though, as I thought about my poor car. What the hell had that been about? Car terrorism?

Well, first things first definitely meant a shower and—I hoped—coffee. Or perhaps coffee first. I dressed Carson in one of his little rompers, pulled on some pants myself, and headed downstairs to the kitchen.

Almost 8:00—pretty much a miracle when Carson slept that late—and the Wyoming June sunlight implied another hot day. I found Erin holding a cup of coffee and staring out the window over the kitchen sink.

"Good morning," I said.

Erin turned and gave me a preoccupied smile. "Good morning, Julie. I hope you and Carson slept okay? How do you feel? Are you in a lot of pain?"

I rolled my shoulders. "We slept fine and I'm actually better than I feared—sore, but that's all. Carson seems okay, too."

As I spoke, Erin looked out the window again, before snapping back to me.

"Good, good… Would you like some coffee?"

What a silly question.

I helped myself to a large mug of black gold, snobbily eschewing the cream and sugar, and sat at the table. I balanced Carson against one shoulder and sighed blissfully into my mug. After a moment, I noticed Erin's hands clenched on the counter.

I cleared my throat. "Did Ian come home yet?"

"What? No." Erin turned to me and smiled weakly. "Sorry to be curt. No, he hasn't come home yet, Julie, and I'm trying not to be too anxious." After a pause, she asked, "May I hold Carson?"

"Sure." Carson transferred happily, wrapping his fat little fist around Erin's braid.

"Is it unusual for Ian to be gone for so long?" I asked.

"Yes, it's unusual, but not unheard of. I really don't need to be so worried. I just don't know—I just don't know what I would do if something happened to him, too." Erin finished in a near whisper, then swallowed hard and turned a bright but wavering smile to Carson.

"Oh, Erin." I crossed to her and gave her a hug. "I'm sure he's—well, I mean, I'm not *sure*—but I'm sure—he's probably fine. Just blowing off steam. You know how teenagers are. He probably hasn't even thought you might be worried."

Erin blotted her eyes with her sleeve and nodded.

"Did Liam leave for work already?"

"No, Full asked him to go over to the Sanchez's house, to be with them for a bit. Since we've recently been through this same type of loss, we all thought he might help. I'll be fine, Julie, really. You're right, I'm sure Ian will be home soon." She visibly collected herself. "Do you want to take a shower? I'd be happy to watch Carson."

The idea of taking a shower without worrying about Carson screeching as my hair was full of shampoo sounded heavenly, so I didn't take much convincing.

****

Half an hour later, feeling like a new woman, I went back downstairs, tucking slightly wet curls behind my ear. I was very ready for a second cup of coffee. I was not ready for the sight of Ian, sitting at the kitchen table, balancing my son on his knees, and cooing in a high-pitched, animated voice. Carson chortled and waved his feet.

I stopped short and Ian started, falling silent in mid-coo.

"Hi, Ian, good morning," I said and tried to seem nonchalant as I crossed to the table.

Ian mumbled something and glanced at me from underneath his bangs. He started to hold out Carson in my direction, but I waved him aside.

"No, no, Carson seems really happy with you. It's fine." I tried not to laugh as Ian rather awkwardly resettled the baby in his arms. "Do you want some coffee? I thought about getting myself another cup."

"Um, sure," said Ian.

Wow! An intelligible word from Ian. I busied myself with two mugs and the coffee maker.

"Milk? Sugar?" I asked.

"Um. Yes. Both. Please."

I thought about how much I dreaded the day Carson would turn into a teenaged boy—oh, for Pete's sake, a teenaged *Werewolf*—when Erin and Lily Rose walked into the kitchen.

"Ian," Lily said. "Outside, now."

Eyes momentarily widening, Ian stood up and handed Carson to Erin before following Lily. The door closed loudly in his wake.

"Full's going to rein him in a bit," said Erin. "He needs to hold it together better, for his own sake and for the well-being of the pack."

"And his mom," I added, and we exchanged a smile.

Suddenly, Carson squawked and rolled his head around to look for me. I enjoyed the moment to sit quietly, drink my coffee, and snuggle my baby. Erin sat across from me with her own mug and perused the newspaper. I felt a brief pang as I imagined what it would be like to have Mac sitting here, too, just like a real family. Would Carson have brought us together? Would things have been different, if Mac had known?

My cell phone chortled at me, and I pulled it out to see Sheila sent me a text. *Well?* it said. I swallowed hard, feeling the gulf between me and my past life—dammit, my *real* life—widening. I texted back, *Mac's dead. I'm with his family. I can't talk about it yet. I'm ok.* I imagined Sheila's arched brows raising higher and higher, then furrowing with worry over me. After a minute or two, she texted, *I'm sorry. I'm here, whenever, however. Love you.*

How was I ever going to explain this?

Lily spent fifteen minutes or so talking to Ian and then walked back into the kitchen. Today, she wore a sleeveless lemon-yellow blouse and chunky turquoise jewelry set in gold. Ian stayed outside. When I glanced through the window, he stared toward the tree line and kicked at the dirt with one toe.

"Good morning, Julie," said Lily, accepting a cup of coffee from Erin's proffered hand. "Tell me about your accident last night."

All business, she leaned forward, eyes narrowed as she listened to the story. She then proceeded to interrogate me: Did the car have round or square headlights? Two doors or four? She asked me about ten different questions about the shape of the sedan and the exact shade of its paint. By the time she finished, she'd wrung every scrap of memory from me. Then she made me tell the whole story from the beginning for a second time. Only at one point, when I described the helpful rancher Thom Gardiner, did she turn to Erin.

"Worland?" she asked.

"Yes," Erin confirmed. "And, no, I've not met him before. I didn't notice anything unusual about him or his truck." With a glance at me, she added, "By sight or smell."

I made a mental note to find out more about what Werewolves might be able to smell.

"Any scent from the car that hit her? Or the driver?" Lily asked.

"No. I bet the windows were closed," said Erin.

Lily sat back and looked at me for several minutes before she spoke.

"Julie," she said. "I don't think this encounter was an accident or random. I believe you were targeted."

I shook my head and frowned.

"Targeted by whom? And why?"

"That's what we need to find out," Lily said. "I suspect the same person—or group of people—that killed Roger and Carlos Sanchez."

"But why? Why me? None of this makes sense. Why was Mac murdered?"

Lily and Erin exchanged glances.

"Julie," Lily said, in a voice akin to what you'd use to comfort a skittish horse, "Right now, you just need to trust us. After the pack meeting tonight, I may be able to tell you more."

Small comfort.

I looked down at Carson, who turned his head and gave me a smile. With or without the help of the pack, I was damned well going to protect my baby. That was certain.

****

The remainder of the day passed quickly. Erin and I took two hours to drive into the bustling metropolis of Sheridan, population sixteen-thousand-and-some. The sign off the highway proudly proclaimed, "Sheridan,

Wyoming: The West at Its Best!" and I hadn't comparison shopped around the state enough to disagree. Sheridan had a historic downtown, lots of Western shops, and plenty of attractions vying for the attention of tourists. Well, plenty considering the size of the town. Sheridan also had a superstore, our real destination since the first order of the day was a new car seat for Carson. I'd called the manufacturer's 800-number this morning and received a strict warning: "The impact and force of a collision can cause unseen structural damage to the interior of your car seat." Carson was close to the length-limit of his baby bucket seat anyway, so I needed to get him one of those plush rear-facing/front-facing convertible ones.

Half an hour later, I picked out a seat from a reputable company with, almost more importantly, an adorable Holstein cow print. Erin did some shopping of her own, so we met up at the check-out, paid for our purchases, and left the store.

Half an hour after that, I had not managed to safely install the now-very-annoying-and-not-so-cute car seat. Erin jiggled and danced Carson around the car in a baby-soothing two-step, while I sweated profusely, knelt on the damned seat and pushed with all my might, trying to get the seat belt tight enough. For icing on the cake, there was supposed to be some type of floor latch to anchor the top of the seat when rear-facing, but Erin's older SUV didn't have such a thing. The company provided some weird piece of belt with metal loops to wrap around a stable portion of the car in order to make my own top anchor. Yeah. Not as easy as it sounds, believe me.

By the time the seat was finally strapped and anchored to my satisfaction, lunchtime had come and gone, so Erin suggested we drive into downtown Sheridan to eat at Sanford's Grub Pub. After a pretty decent chicken Caesar salad for me and a tuna sandwich for Erin, we were ready to head back to Greybull.

Or almost ready. As we walked to the car, I noticed a coffee shop around the corner. I know some people hate the proliferation of coffee chains with over-priced drinks and trendy menus. Me? I'm overjoyed I can get a great cup of coffee no matter where I am.

"Erin, can you put Carson in the car while I grab a latte to go?" I asked, gesturing. "Do you want anything?"

"No, I'm fine." She held out her arms for the baby, already cooing to him.

On my way out of the coffee shop, latte and espresso brownie in hand, I noticed the dark blue sedan across the street. I missed a step, nearly falling, and my heart started to race. Almost as suddenly, however, I realized this couldn't be The Blue Sedan: it showed none of the dents or scratches my mystery hit-and-runner must have accumulated. I stood for a moment on the sidewalk and stared at the car. For a brief moment this morning, I forgot the recent happenings, distracted by this trip to Sheridan. But this car brought it all flooding back. Someone had really, truly tried to injure me—or kill me—last night.

I walked to Erin's SUV, deep in thought. What was going on? Why would Mac have been a target for murder? Was this about an investigation he'd been involved in? Was this directed against the pack at large? Why was I now a target? I grimly resolved I would get some answers tonight, one way or another.

Chapter Six

As Erin, Liam, and Ian prepared to set off for the pack meeting, a knock sounded at the kitchen door. Liam rose to open the door as Erin shot a semi-apologetic glance in my direction.

"You might not be safe alone while we're all gone, Julie," she said, "So Full sent someone to stay with you."

I lifted my brows, torn between amusement at the thought I needed a babysitter and relief I wouldn't be left alone to worry about someone skulking around the house.

"Julie Hall, this is Eliza Minuet. Eliza, Julie."

Eliza was tall, tall and slim, with fawn brown hair pulled back in a ponytail, and brown eyes, somehow fierce and warm at the same time. The woman in the third photograph in Mac's room. All of this registered in the first glance, as I automatically stood, shifted Carson to the side, and offered my hand. We exchanged greetings, me trying not to sound stilted, even as I sensed her assessing every aspect of the situation. Apparently, I passed muster, because she responded with a genuine smile and sat down at the table with me as we said goodbye to the MacGregors.

"So, tell me how you met Mac," she said, her tone inviting. "May I hold Carson? What a cutie."

"I met Mac at a bar, actually, although I know that sounds cliché. He was nursing a pint of stout and glowering at the world. Not the most auspicious beginning, I suppose," I paused, then continued in a rush, "I'm not sure why I was so drawn to him. But I was."

Eliza nodded. "Mac was like that. Intense about everything, including glowering at the world over a beer."

"I haven't heard anyone else here call him Mac. It's jarring to hear everyone say Roger."

We exchanged smiles before Eliza continued.

"I remember when we were about ten these high school kids gave him a hard time because he was afraid of rattlesnakes. I mean, everyone's cautious of rattlesnakes, but he was particularly jumpy. Whenever we were outside and he heard a bush rattle in the wind, he was convinced a snake would emerge. Anyway, on this day, there actually was a rattler hiding under an overhang, and the older kids taunted him about it, daring him to poke it with a stick. You have to understand, older kids in the pack knew Mac was a full. He was already shifting, and it caused quite a bit of tension. And the ones who didn't know anything about pack didn't understand why this ten-year-old kid had such a sense of...poise and depth. Intensity. Anyway, they teased him about this snake and he set his jaw, you know," Eliza aptly imitated one of Mac's common expressions, "and he took that stick and, with one motion, flipped the snake out from under the rock. And then he grabbed it—actually grabbed it with his hand, right behind its head, just the way a snake-wrangler would—and he held it up toward the teenagers and said, 'What, this snake?'"

Eliza shook her head slowly, as if to show the disbelief she'd felt at the moment. "Those high school boys never messed with him again. I'm the only one who saw what happened afterward, after the boys sulked off to do whatever obnoxious teens do. Mac flung that snake as far away as he could, then he sank to his knees and threw up. That was Mac, even at ten. Intense. Strong. Determined. Not many people knew more than that."

Her lips tightened for a minute before she met my gaze.

I cleared my throat before trusting my voice. "I still can't believe he's gone. I always thought—I always expected—to see him again. To be with him again."

Eliza nodded and I continued, the words tumbling out.

"I think what you just said was part of it, you know? Part of the reason things were rocky between us. I saw his strength, his forcefulness, and that's what drew me in. He let himself relax around me—I saw him playful, saw his capacity for joy was as deep as any other emotion—but I don't think…I never saw him vulnerable. I never felt he let down his guard completely. He could be so…distant."

"He was pack and he was a full," Eliza said.

The simple statement rang with significance, like she thought it answered everything.

"Yeah. I know that now."

Eliza leaned toward me, her eyes dark as if she sensed my hurt. "He couldn't tell you, you know. First of all, you wouldn't have believed him. If he'd proved it to you, you probably would have freaked out and who knows what you would have done. Second of all, if the pack—or any pack—found out he told you, he would have been in big trouble. I don't mean slap-you-on-the-wrist trouble, but possibly executing-the-Were-and-the-humans-he-told trouble."

"Oh." So much for Erin's comment that Werewolves aren't used to violence.

"So don't be bitter. Don't let that color what you and Mac had."

What Mac and I had.

"I think I should get Carson ready for bed. This is about the time of night I try to get him to sleep." I stood up abruptly, softened it with a smile, and took Carson upstairs.

****

About half an hour later, I came back down to the living room. Carson slept a little bit better these days. I wasn't going to count my chickens, but I hoped he'd have a good three hour stretch before needing me.

Eliza had cleaned up the kitchen and sat on the couch leafing through a magazine. She looked up as I came in and gave me a smile.

"Well, Carson's sleeping," I said. "I wanted to say thanks for listening, before."

"I miss Mac, too," she said, simply.

"Yes. So, you and Mac…" I waited, but when Eliza didn't finish the sentence, I filled in awkwardly, "you and Mac grew up together?"

"He was like my brother. I can't remember a time when I didn't know him."

Like a brother, that was good to hear. Yet, somehow, even before I knew how to characterize their relationship, I felt strangely unthreatened by it, even though surely if there were anyone I was likely to envy, it would be someone like Eliza. But instead, I'd felt an instant kinship with her, finding her incredibly easy to be around.

"I wish...I wish I'd known him longer."

"How long did you and Mac date?"

"About six months. Only six months. I found out I was pregnant a few weeks after we broke up. Right after he left Oregon. His case was over, I guess. I was so bitter...I told him if he left, then he should never come back."

Eliza nodded, and I continued in a rush.

"I didn't even tell him, you know? He never even knew I was pregnant and he would be a father. I was so angry, so hurt... I was going to tell him, though, I really was. I just wanted to prove to him—or to myself—I could do this on my own and I didn't need him any more than he needed me. I can't believe I didn't tell him. I can't believe I was so stupid and stubborn."

Eliza laughed, an unexpected lilting sound. "Stupid and stubborn, huh? Well, that sounds about right for Mac. You two must have been quite a pair."

I snorted. "Yeah, well. I'm the one who broke up with him, you know, but I think...I still think...maybe he was *it*. The only one for me. If I hadn't been so stubborn, so demanding, things might have turned out differently. Maybe he'd still be..." The rest of my sentence hung in the air, and I shrugged awkwardly. "I'm sorry. I barely know you and here I am unloading all this crap."

"Julie, we just met, but we know each other. We loved Mac. We're grieving for him. I understand."

"Yeah, but...you knew Mac his whole life and me? I'm just some interloper who knew him for six months and got pregnant."

"Julie!" Eliza voice was fierce. "If you know anything about Mac, you know he never did anything casually. And that includes dating. If he was with you for six months, then you were important to him. Now you're important to me and so is Carson."

She held my gaze until I nodded, then she leaned back against the cushions with a sigh. "It's a hard life, being part of the pack. It's hard to have relationships with humans."

I raised my eyebrows in shock at her phrasing. After a moment, I said carefully, "Do you not consider yourself a human, then?"

"No." Eliza frowned. "I'm a Were."

"Tell me. What does it mean to be a Werewolf? How are you different? How does it change your life? I need to know a lot more to support Carson. More than the fact that he'll probably go furry once a month."

"Well, I'm not sure where to start."

Abruptly, Eliza sat up straight, eyes flashing, and motioned me into silence. I looked around the room, feeling tension shoot up my spine and into my muscles. Eliza remained motionless for several moments, then stood in a fluid motion and moved silently toward the front door. She turned and pointed at me, a gesture that unmistakably said, "Stay where you are and don't make any noise." As she neared the door, she paused and the shadows in the hall seemed to writhe and swallow her. I caught my breath, staring intently, but wasn't able to see her. I felt as if my eyes couldn't focus or somehow couldn't see through the otherwise very normal light in the hall. I stood up, balancing on the balls of my feet, hands clenched at my sides. My gaze darted between the front door and the stairs behind me.

Unable to stay still any longer, I made my decision and darted up the stairs, down the hall, and into Mac's old room where Carson slept. My baby lay on his back, arms flung wide, one knee crooked. Even at that moment, something inside me loosened when I saw his little form, sleeping so sweetly. I padded to the side of the bed and gave him the lightest kiss. Then, I lifted my head and saw the window. Without thinking, without letting myself think, I crept over to kneel by the window and I cautiously peered over the sill. I scanned the front yard, not knowing exactly what I hoped to see.

In fact, I saw nothing. Except...was that Eliza, there in the shadows near the driveway? And was that a person near the cottonwood?

As I squinted, trying to focus better, a knot of shadows leapt toward what-might-have-been-a-person. A rush of motion confused my eyes, then a tangled shape rolled onto the gravel drive. I took a step toward the door, following some instinct to rush out and help, then realized I didn't know what the hell I was doing and would be only a liability. I watched the knot of indistinct shadows, and reminded myself to breathe. Suddenly, the night tore open with a flash of fire and a loud noise, like a car backfiring. Shit—a gun. An actual gunshot! I moved so quickly I had to grab the wall for balance and sprinted down the steps to the front door.

Once I reached the door, though, I hesitated. I peered through the little peephole when the door yanked open from the outside and I nearly fell into Eliza.

"Crap! Eliza," I blurted, never more articulate than when my heart pounded a mile a minute. "Are you okay? What happened?"

My question was answered as soon as my brain registered the sight in front of me.

"You've been shot. Holy hell, Eliza."

Somehow graceful even with blood running down her right arm, Eliza lifted one eyebrow and pushed her way into the hall. I followed her, babbling who knows what.

"Julie. Julie." She reached out and shook my arm. "I'm fine, okay? Look, it's already healing. The bullet went right through." She pulled up her short sleeve to show me a gaping red wound in the fleshy part of her upper arm. The bullet hole almost visibly closed as I looked.

"Julie, I'm fine. Okay?"

I closed my mouth and nodded, then followed her into the kitchen where she wet a cloth and washed the blood off her arm.

"God, I *hate* getting shot," she muttered.

I shook my head. "This is a regular thing? No big deal?" I cleared my throat, realizing my voice came out shrill.

"No, no, of course not. No, I've only been shot once before and it was an accident. Kind of."

I closed my eyes, tabled the zillions of questions that jumped into my mind from her answer, and focused on the point at hand.

"What the hell just happened? And would you sit down and at least pretend to rest a minute?"

A minute later, we sat at the table, Eliza still dabbing her arm with a damp cloth. She explained what happened from her perspective.

Apparently, Eliza had heard footsteps outside, or noises that might have been footsteps. She called the moon, cloaking herself with shadows, and sneaked out the door to investigate. Once outside, she caught the intruder's scent and easily located him. She chastened herself for not immediately smelling the gun, but claimed it was an easy scent to overlook when the gun hadn't been fired recently and when one was near other metal machinery like a car. She pounced on him, intending to capture him, but during their tussle, he pulled a small gun from his waistband and shot her at close range. When she fell back, startled, he darted away. Quickly.

"And you're really okay now?"

Eliza lifted the washcloth to show me a small puckered scar. "Even that will be gone soon enough."

"Holy crap."

"Julie, are *you* okay?" Eliza asked me, her voice seemed to come from far away.

I tried to answer her, but my ears rang too loudly and she seemed to retreat farther and farther down a long tunnel—a tunnel?—and I fell into the darkness.

****

"Julie? Julie?"

Eliza's voice registered softly, and I became aware of something cold on my forehead. I lay on a hard, smooth surface. When I opened my eyes, I realized it was the kitchen's linoleum floor. Eliza knelt next to me and peered down at me.

"What?" I mumbled.

"Shhh, it's okay. You fainted."

Events flooded back to me, and I abruptly tried to sit up. The cold washcloth fell off my forehead as I moved. Eliza held my shoulders down, telling me to take it easy for a minute.

"Let me get this straight. You got shot. And I fainted." My voice rose. "*You* got shot and *I* fainted?"

"Yep, guess so."

Eliza had no reason to sound so merry, I thought with some pique. Although—my mouth twisted wryly—I guess it was kind of funny. I snorted, Eliza laughed, and pretty soon we were giggling on the kitchen floor. After a minute, Eliza pushed herself back and wiped her eyes.

"It's not funny," I said, before we both dissolved into laughter again.

"All right, all right." I sat up gingerly and collected myself with some deep breaths.

"So, could you tell who he was? The guy who shot you?"

Eliza lost her smile. "I didn't know him. But I'll know him next time," she said, a low growling note in her voice.

Which reminded me. "Why didn't you change when you pounced on him? You know, into a wolf?"

"I didn't want to hurt him, just restrain him."

"But." I looked at Eliza's slim frame dubiously, and my thoughts must have been clear.

"Move your arm," she said.

"What?"

Eliza reached out, pinned my left wrist to the table, and repeated, "Move your arm."

I tried, oh, believe me, I tried. I'm not the weakest person in the world, even if I am short. But I absolutely could not move while Eliza held me.

"Oh."

Eliza released me and sat back.

"Then how did he get away?"

She shook her head slowly. "Just lucky. He moved at the very instant I jumped him, so he had one hand free, and I didn't have great traction, and then, well, then he shot me."

"Ah." I swallowed hard, remembering the gaping red wound slowly closing up. I raised a hand to forestall her question. "I'm fine, really. You know, I'm a *librarian*. Usually, when I see carnage it's…a binding ripped to shreds or some toddler with a crayon who's gone to town… This…this is just a bit beyond me."

"For a librarian, Julie Hall, you're doing okay."

I smiled back at her with real warmth.

****

Eliza wouldn't let me go back outside with her, even though she was pretty sure our mystery intruder high-tailed it. She returned after fifteen minutes and announced he'd run partway down the driveway and then gotten into a pickup truck. Initially, I was impressed she could distinguish a pickup just from the smell, but she explained something about tire tracks and axle length. I remained impressed, actually, because no way could I figure out anything from a set of tire tracks. Anyway, he was long gone, but Eliza was absolutely sure she'd know his scent again—and probably the scent of his truck. I was surprised it hadn't been a blue sedan. Maybe that vehicle had been too conspicuous, after last night's accident, and our enemy had changed cars. If it was even the same person. Maybe a whole passel of people was out to get me. I found myself preoccupied by that discomforting thought.

"I should probably call Lily, even though the pack is in the middle of meeting," Eliza mused out loud.

"By the way, why did Lily choose you to miss the meeting, to protect me? Not that I'm complaining," I added, "since you obviously proved yourself an apt protector."

"Lily and I already conferred," Eliza said, pulling out her cell phone, "so there'd be nothing new for me at the meeting."

She walked into the other room, dialed, and after a short pause I heard her relaying recent events. She listened for a minute and spoke in a low voice, then hung up.

When she came back into the kitchen, I asked the question occupying my mind the whole time. Especially since I tried not to think about how many people might lurk in the darkness, intending me harm.

"You and Lily confer closely about things? Are you also a 'full'?" I tried to throw in the pack vocabulary casually, but didn't miss Eliza's quick quirk of the mouth.

"Yes, I'm a full and we work closely together. Of course," Eliza's voice turned serious, "she also knows how personally invested I am in finding out who killed Mac."

I nodded in grim agreement—though what help I could be, me, Ms. Fainting Librarian, I wasn't sure. If only I were more than a dark moon wolf.

"Are there many fulls in the pack?"

"Lily, me, and a high school student named Dave. He's one of Ian's friends. We're the only fulls right now. And, of course, Dave's still a pup."

"And how big is the pack? And what do you mean, a 'pup'?"

"Fifty-three. No, fifty-two." Eliza's brow furled as she corrected herself and I realized she had forgotten, momentarily, they'd had another pack member murdered. "Dave and Ian are pups because they're not eighteen yet, so they haven't reached adult status within the pack."

"Huh," I said. "I bet Dave and Ian just love being considered puppies."

Eliza shrugged. "Anyway, Lily said she and some of the other Weres will come over after the meeting to catch this guy's scent."

"How long will Guy's scent stick around? Strong enough to be useful, I mean."

"At least 24 hours, maybe longer. 'Guy.' " Eliza snorted and I smiled back.

Chapter Seven

When Lily and the Weres arrived, the house seemed full of roiling energy and tense bodies. By my count, seven Weres had joined us, including the MacGregors and Lily, so it wasn't an actual *crowd* of werewolves, but I sure felt that way. Lily was visibly in command and made quick introductions. One of the new werewolves was Dave Blythe, Ian's high school friend and the other full. The others were introduced as Claire Bernard, a middle-aged woman, and Miguel Sanchez, whose drawn visage and name led me to assume he was the father of Carlos Sanchez, the pack's latest murder victim. Dave stared at me without regard to rudeness, and I found myself wondering what Ian might have told him about me and Carson.

Lily gathered everyone into the living room to listen to Eliza retell the details of our encounter. At one point, she turned to me and asked for my version, although I had little new information for the group. I left out the part about me fainting.

"Dave, Eliza, Ian, Erin, Miguel. Outside and change." Lily gestured and the others moved quickly. Dave stopped to give Lily a long, level look before proceeding out the door.

By the time the rest of us stepped out, five wolves ranged around the driveway. The differences between the wolves surprised me. Ian, whom I'd seen in wolf-form before, albeit briefly, was the darkest, his black coat nearly invisible in the night. Two wolves were shades of gray—similar to Carson, I remembered, shaking my head a bit as I once again confronted the fact my son was truly a Werewolf—one several inches taller than the other, one reddish-brown and lanky, and the last wolf was buff-colored. The buff one trotted up to me and pushed a wet nose into my hand, causing me to jump slightly before I awkwardly petted it on the head. It canted its head at me, tongue lolling in what must have been laughter, and I felt certain this one was Eliza.

The wolves communicated with each other in snuffs and jostled a bit, tracing the path of the struggle around the tree before they loped down the driveway— Eliza in the lead—presumably to the site where the truck parked. A pure white wolf leaped from the front stoop behind me and pounded after them. When I looked around, I was entirely unsurprised to find Lily wasn't there. Of *course* she'd be a sleek, white wolf with enormous blue eyes. What else would I have expected?

Liam and Claire Bernard walked around the driveway and the tree, apparently taking in what scent was perceptible in human form. I joined them under the tree, not sure of my place in this whole investigation.

"So," I said, "Does anything…smell familiar?"

Liam quirked his eyebrow at Claire before shaking his head for the both of them. "No. We're definitely not working with someone local. After all, Roger and Carlos were both killed in Las Vegas."

"Las Vegas?"

Liam frowned. "Yes, Vegas."

I was shocked, though I realized a moment later I'd never asked where Mac was killed. I hadn't asked for many details of his death—and the one detail I asked for, I regretted hearing. I wasn't sure I would ever stop seeing Mac beheaded in my morbid mind's eye. Now, I realized I needed to learn more, because whatever threatened the pack also impacted my safety and, even more importantly, the safety of my baby.

"Is there a pack in Las Vegas?" I asked Liam. Claire knelt in the dirt near where Eliza and Guy had scuffled, though I wasn't sure what she could see in the dark.

"Not that we know of, although there have been rumors of a rogue or maybe two—that's why Roger went there to investigate in the first place."

"A rogue?" I prodded, though I thought I understood the term.

"A rogue is someone who isn't part of a pack, who's not subject to pack authority, and who disobeys general pack law." Liam sighed, then turned his attention to me. "Sometimes Weres don't get along with their native pack for whatever reason, and then a Were may become a 'lone wolf' and leave the pack. As long as he or she still lives by the same strictures as the rest of us, that's no problem, and sometimes the Were finds another pack to join, eventually. But if the Were breaks pack law and endangers the rest of us, well, then the Were is dealt with. That's what we mean by a rogue."

"And that was one of Mac's—Roger's—roles, wasn't it? As a private investigator, he checked on lone wolves. And rogues."

"Yes, among other things," said Liam.

It all clicked into place. "But this time, he was killed. The rogue got to him first."

"Except he wasn't killed by a rogue. Or any other Were."

"You're sure?"

"We're sure."

Our conversation was interrupted by the return of the other wolves. Lily loped off across the driveway. She called on the moon to pull shadows across her body, emerged in human form with not a hair out of place, and opened her hand to reveal a bullet, caked with blood and driveway dirt.

Eliza ran up to sniff it, hackles rising, and gave a low growl. She shook herself vigorously, then pulled on the nearby shadows as if they were blankets. She stepped out of their midst and smoothed back her hair.

"Can I have it as a souvenir, Lily?" she asked, peering down into the Full's hand.

Lily raised one eyebrow. "Ballistics, Eliza." Her voice expressed curt disapproval. "The police may be able to find something helpful."

"But how will we explain it to the police? Eliza's already healed." I wondered aloud.

Lily ignored my question, but Liam answered, "The sergeant is pack, Julie."

****

After the Weres compared notes for a few minutes, they dispersed. Ian and Dave disappeared up the stairs into his room, after a warning from Erin not to play their music too loud and wake up Carson.

"I don't think they'll bother the baby, Julie, and it's good for Dave to be here. Ian needs the company and

Dave needs... Well, Dave needs a home." Erin sat down at the kitchen table with a sigh.

As the rest of us settled, Liam brewed a pot of decaf. Heck, I'd take the coffee anyway, and he had a point: it was waaaay too late to get caffeined up, even though I wasn't so sure of sleep anytime soon, given the events of the day.

I frowned at Erin. "What do you mean Dave needs a home?"

"Oh, he has a home, of course. That is, he lives with his older sister, now, but she's not the most stable influence," Erin said.

"What happened to his parents?" I asked.

After a brief moment, Erin sighed again. "I'm not sure why I started this story. Surely we've had enough sadness for today."

She shifted in her chair again and looked at me. "Dave's parents died when he was twelve. Almost five years ago, now. His older sister Rebecca is a dark moon, but both his parents were half moons."

I shook my head, not following. Eliza stared out the kitchen window; Liam messed with the coffee pot.

Erin continued, "You can imagine the consternation when his sister never changed—when it became clear she was a dark moon. Their mother had had an affair and Dave's father, well, wasn't Rebecca's father. When his father discovered the truth, he went after the—the other man, the lover, who wasn't pack, of course. The other man ended up dead. Dave's father returned home to find his wife had committed suicide. Which isn't easy, for a Were. It...it wasn't a pretty sight."

That poor boy. "And...Dave's father?" I asked, not quite sure I wanted the answer to my question.

"He drove off a cliff," Liam said from behind me, his voice causing me to jump.

"My God."

Eliza turned back to the rest of us. "Rebecca hasn't fully recovered from it all, but she's of legal age and Dave insists on staying with her. Full has tried many times to convince him to move in with another pack family. But he feels—well, who knows what he feels. Full hasn't pulled rank on the issue."

Erin's quiet voice spoke again. "Dave's older brother Tony went wolf. Tore off the day after it all happened and hasn't been seen for five years. He was strong, too. Both boys are—were—full moons, which is very unusual in one family."

Erin rubbed her eyes and let out another sigh. "It was the worst tragedy our pack ever faced."

"Until now." Once again, I jumped at Liam's voice. Perhaps because I didn't expect it. Perhaps because of what I heard in his tone.

"Didn't Dave's sister—did she ever think of—of becoming a Were? Of being...bitten?" My voice cracked on the question, so strongly did I want to know.

Erin's deep blue eyes caught my gaze and I couldn't look away. "No."

"Because..."

"Partly because she resented the pack. Still resents the pack, I suppose. She believes we should have known what was happening, that someone should have prevented it all."

"Oh," I said.

"Partly because she values her life and the risk is too great."

I had never heard Erin sound so stern. She was right. Of course, I knew she was right and the cost would be too high. I opened my mouth, then closed it again, unsure what to say.

"Right," said Eliza, suddenly all business. "Let's—"

As she spoke, I heard Carson squawking from the upstairs bedroom.

"Hold that thought," I said and darted up the stairs, counting on my if-I-reach-him-quickly-he'll-settle-right-back-down theory. As I reached the hallway, I stopped in mid-stride, surprised to see Ian's friend Dave at the door to Carson's room.

A look of discomfort fleeted across his face. These boys, what, did they think it criminal to care about a baby? I gave him a warm smile, even warmer than it would have been if I hadn't just heard his story.

"Oh, thanks, Dave," I said, voice lowered as I moved past him. I squeezed his arm in gratitude. "I'll go in, though, he's probably hungry."

****

This time, at least, my quick response theory worked and Carson settled down almost immediately. When I walked back into the kitchen, conversation halted mid-sentence.

"All right, that's enough." Eliza pushed her chair away from the table and looked at both Erin and Liam. "Julie's involved as much as any of us and she needs the full story. Now."

Liam took a sip of coffee and Erin nodded, mouth set grimly.

"You're right, Eliza, and Full said as much herself at the meeting. I'm sorry, Julie, and please don't take it personally. We have a fairly ingrained habit of keeping secrets from humans." Erin patted the chair next to her.

Again, an offhand comment proved Weres didn't consider themselves human. Strange, by that time, I'd seen several Weres in wolf form, I'd seen Eliza and Lily draw upon the moon to move shadows and distort light, I'd witnessed the incredible speed of Eliza's healing, and I'd felt the strength concealed in her slim figure. And yet, I found it impossible to sit at the kitchen table with them and actually understand they were entirely other—they were somehow not human. Did Mac feel such a large gulf between himself and me? Was that part of the reason he couldn't quite open up to me? If I'd told him I was pregnant, would he have told me he was a Were? If he'd known I was a dark moon, would he have opened up to me? Or would it have never worked out between us, because I was still…human? Not pack? The sadness of that thought welled up within me, and I fought hard to push it down. I couldn't afford to get emotional over Mac. I needed to discover exactly what had happened to him and to find the people responsible. And make them pay. I set my jaw; oh yes, somehow they would pay.

Without further ado, Eliza began.

"Liam said you and he already talked about some of this, but I'll start at the beginning. As you know, Mac was a private investigator. At times, he worked for human clients on normal cases, but his primary business was Were. Sometimes individual packs hired him, but more often, his business was at the request of the pack council. The council is comprised of the Fulls, the individual pack leaders, from all U.S. packs and it guards the general interests and well-being of the Weres, makes policy decisions, and sets pack law. Since Mac was a full, he was in high demand for...sensitive council cases. That's actually what brought him to Oregon, too."

"What was he doing there, anyway? You said there's no pack in my area," I said.

"I'm not sure. Lily might know, but she couldn't tell you anyway. As I was saying, after working on the case in Oregon, he came back to Greybull for a few months." Eliza smiled. "A bit of a vacation for him, lots of hunting, bonding with the pack, training the young ones. In January, the council met and asked him to take on a new case in Las Vegas and he left right away. The details I know from Lily are these: two murders occurred in the city within the last year, both chalked up to dog attacks. Both victims were found near the Strip, locals, not tourists. The Vegas police downplayed the two incidents, presumably because they didn't want to hurt the tourist business and perhaps also because they occurred almost ten months apart. Both on the full moon, by the way. At the same time, the local news reported numerous sightings of a large wolf in nearby wilderness areas and the council worried a rogue was responsible. One registered lone wolf lived in the area, but she claimed complete ignorance of any other Were activity. She's a waning moon, hardly able to conceal the truth from a stronger Were. Mac was instructed to make contact with the lone wolf—her name is Suzy Zhang—to verify her story and her innocence. From all reports, he met with her and did not believe her involved. The council then asked Mac to infiltrate the local scene and investigate."

Eliza sighed and rubbed her forehead in a weary gesture. Liam and Erin stayed silent, drinking their coffee.

"None of Mac's reports indicated anything unusual. He hadn't caught any scent of a fellow Were—well, besides one or two on vacation—and there had been no further wolf sightings or 'dog' attacks. In fact, the council considered recalling him and closing the investigation, when Mac missed filing a report. Lily tried to contact him—as did Erin and Liam, of course, once alerted there might be a problem—to no avail.

"Four days later, the police found Mac's body in the same alley the first murder had taken place. And," Eliza's eyes burned fiercely, "they found his head in a motel parking lot, the site of the second murder."

I swallowed hard and set down my coffee mug before I dropped it. Meeting Eliza's gaze, a moment of clear understanding passed between us. I pushed my curls behind my ear.

Eliza nodded in grim approval and continued. "They sent a message. Mac's murderer knew his exact purpose. The method of his murder also proved they knew he was a Were: beheading is one of the only sure-fire ways of killing us. However, that said, his murderer was *not* a Were. We had pack on the scene within twenty-four hours—Carlos Sanchez—and the body and the scene...scenes...revealed no evidence of Were.

"So," Eliza leaned back in her chair. "Carlos and two investigators sent by the council have been in Las Vegas for the last three months. And, as you know, Carlos was found yesterday in a local park, also beheaded. Signs near his body indicated a struggle, nothing like the staged crime scene where Mac was found. And that's where we are now."

"Was Carlos sent by the council?"

"Initially, he was sent by the pack, to report back any details about Mac's murder internally. The council knew his location, though, and asked him to coordinate efforts with their own investigators."

"So," I thought aloud, "anyone associated with the council would have known about both Mac and Carlos. Is it possible someone on the council is in league with…the responsible party?"

Eliza shrugged her shoulders, while Liam remained stone-faced.

Erin gave a huge sigh. "I certainly hope not," she said.

"Hmm. The other two Weres sent by the council are still in Vegas?"

"Yes." Eliza nodded approval at my line of thinking. "Tim Rogers and Kayleigh Anderson."

A werewolf named Kayleigh. What was this world coming to?

My thought must have been transparent, because Eliza laughed and elaborated.

"Yeah," she said, "Kayleigh is from a pack in California, near Yosemite. I've never met her personally, but I know Mac worked with her on a couple of cases."

I nodded curtly, trying to take this in as new information and nothing more. Bitter thoughts boiled up in the back of my mind, though. A California werewolf—probably a tanned, long-limbed beauty, a sleek, gorgeous blonde who was also pack, who knew Mac. I think I hated Kayleigh.

Eliza leaned forward and tapped me on the hand. "Focus," she said sharply.

"Right." I pushed the crazy jealousy aside. "Kayleigh is from California. And Tim Rogers is the other council investigator."

"From upstate New York."

"And they are both fine, with no clues as to who killed Mac and Carlos?"

"Correct, as far as we know. I'm sure they're investigating the scene of Carlos' murder to find any scents of Weres or humans, especially human scents that might correlate to where they found Mac's body, or, uh," Eliza glanced at Erin before continuing, "or his head."

I unclenched my jaw. Leaning back in my seat, I broadened my attention to include all three Weres.

"Wait a minute." I paused to catch a fleeting thought before I lost it. "You said Mac was found about four days after he went missing. Where was he during those days? Were there any clues? Any physical traces or scents?"

Eliza shook her head decisively. "Carlos arrived on the scene about twenty-four hours after Mac's body was discovered, but he reported the scent trail on the body itself had been completely overwhelmed by the morgue. He said Mac smelled sterile, like chemicals or antiseptic, like a hospital. Or maybe just like the morgue."

A hospital. I thought about it for a minute before asking, "Tell me, how reliable is your—a Were's—sense of smell?"

Liam spoke first, surprising me. "Our sense of smell is comparable to a wolf's, even in human form, about 100 times stronger than yours. It's quite easy to pick out the scent of an individual and to differentiate between those scents, much as you can distinguish between rose and lavender. When a person wears a large amount of scented product—perfume, lotion, things like that—it's harder to catch his or her natural scent, but even in that case Weres trained as investigators are unlikely to make a mistake. And it is absolutely impossible to miss the scent of another Were; that's why Don Reid, the pharmacist, knew about Carson as soon as you entered his store."

"Does a scent linger at a scene for quite a while after the person leaves?"

"Depends on the weather and the climate, but we can reliably identify scents for several days. Not quite like a bloodhound, though, from what I understand they can pick up scents even after 300 hours."

I digested the information. "Since it seems our enemies know they are dealing with Weres, do you think it's possible they found a way to mask their scent?"

Eliza shook her head. "I think it's much more likely we are dealing with a larger group of people, well-coordinated and knowledgeable enough not to give us any advantage. The investigators have identified at least five distinct scents."

That didn't sound good.

Erin broke in and laid a hand on my arm. Her gaze met mine, welling with an ocean of sympathy, yet somehow still stern.

"Julie," she said, "these are not *your* enemies. You are *not* involved in this and you shouldn't be involved in this. I agreed with Full when she said you had a right to know what happened to Roger, because I know he was important to you. But I do not want you—or Carson—dragged into these pack matters. I don't want you playing 'detective,' sitting here and coming up with theories as if this were some…some mystery novel from your library."

"I'm already involved—I've already been dragged in. *My* car was forced off the highway. They threatened your house when Carson and I were here."

I looked around at each of them in turn, seeing faces just as serious and earnest as my own.

"I don't know why. I'm not sure if I'm a target or a victim of circumstance. But I do know I'm well and truly part of this, even if I'm not part of the pack."

Chapter Eight

Sleep came slowly that night as my thoughts continued to whirl. After his latest wake-up, Carson somehow turned himself horizontal in bed and his little feet nudged against my side as I lay there, staring alternately at the ceiling and at the pictures of Mac across the room. In some ways, everything that happened in the last two weeks seemed like a dream. Was it really possible my son was a werewolf? That Mac had been a werewolf? That I was at this very minute the only human being in a house full of Weres? What did it mean that Weres didn't consider themselves "human"? Was my own son so different than me? Somehow removed, though my own flesh and blood? I was a so-called dark moon wolf, one with recessive genes but no manifestation of Were-nature. Did that make me "normal"? Human? Were there any differences between me and someone who didn't bear the Were gene? Why did I have this strange genetic legacy?

Right then, I resolved to find an answer to that last question, as soon as these unknown enemies were dealt with. Perhaps if I traced my family tree, if I talked to other relatives, I might figure out when the Were gene was introduced to my family. I wondered if I had ancestors who were full Were or if it was it some past love affair between a member of my family and a Werewolf.

As the house settled into utter stillness around me, I realized musing over such matters—important, but hardly relevant at this precise moment—was actually a way of diverting myself from the pressing questions keeping me awake. I needed to find out who these people were. They killed Mac, endangered the pack and my son. I needed to know why they targeted us.

I stood up and ran my hands through my hair, yanking on the ends of my curls. Tension snaked its way down my back and I felt jittery, even though it *had* been decaf. I gazed down at Carson, his mouth half open, pacifier fallen onto the sheets, his little eyelids delicate and translucent as eggshell, cheeks flushed. I locked the image in my mind, but failed to feel the sense of relaxation my sweet boy usually inspired. Instead, my stomach clenched and worry flared in my gut. In mama bear fashion, I would allow nothing and no one to hurt my Carson. No matter what it took.

As I stood there, consumed by thoughts of protecting my baby, I heard the lightest of sounds from my window—small feathery taps, nearly as muted as a moth brushing glass. I jumped up and whirled around wildly, caught my foot on the corner of the bed somehow, and went sprawling onto the carpet. Out of the corner of my eye, I caught a brief image of Eliza at my window, her mouth opened in a silent O of astonishment as she watched me flail and fall.

I lay on the ground, closing my eyes in rue. Some mama bear I was. First, I fainted when Eliza got shot. Then, I fell over my own two feet when trying to identify a potential threat. Good job, Julie. So much for being human.

Eliza tapped again. I picked myself up and walked over to the window, hoping my dignity hadn't been too compromised. As soon as I raised the window, Eliza whispered, "Geez, Julie, you look like a cat that just fell off a table. You know, fur ruffled, yet stalking haughtily away as if to say 'Who, me? You must be mistaken. I meant to do that.' "

"Yeah, thanks, very funny," I grumbled.

"Well," Eliza's eyes still sparkled merrily, but I saw she would drop the subject. "Are you going to let me in or what? I'm pretty sure you can just raise the screen."

"Don't you want to rip it through with your fierce Werewolf strength?"

"Ha. All right, I'm sorry about the cat jibe. Now let me in."

Silently, Eliza climbed through the window and—I admit—I watched her graceful movements with a teensy bit of jealousy. Drawing me as far away from Carson as possible, she sank down on the floor to sit crosslegged and beckoned me to join her.

All teasing dropped as she leaned toward me and spoke in a low voice, "I need you to cover for me, Julie," she said with no preamble.

I tilted my head in invitation for her to elaborate.

"What Erin said today—this is not your fight, you shouldn't be involved—I have a chance now. Tomorrow morning, I want you to tell Liam and Erin you've decided it's all too much and you're returning to Oregon. No, wait, hear me out." Eliza held up a hand to forestall my interruption. "I'll drop by for breakfast and you can tell them your decision. Then, I'll volunteer to come with you to Jacksonville for a while, so I can help you with Carson, and make sure you're prepared for being the mom of a Were-baby."

As I opened my mouth, Eliza cut me off me once again.

"We'll leave together and you will return home, but I'll actually go to Vegas. I'm not sure who to trust right now, but I'm determined to figure out who killed Mac—and Carlos. And I don't want the council to know my intentions."

Incorrectly interpreting my forthcoming objections, Eliza hurried on once again.

"Don't worry. I *will* come to Oregon as soon as I can. I'll come and help you learn about Carson. I just need to spend some time in Las Vegas first."

I shook my head. "It's not that, Eliza. I'm not worried about going back to Oregon alone, because I'm not going. I'm coming to Vegas with you."

Our whispered argument was heated, but short. Eliza pointed out she, a full moon werewolf, was well-qualified to deal with whatever we might find in Vegas. She said I, on the other hand, had not quite proven myself physically capable of dealing with any violence we might encounter. I glared at her not-so-veiled reference to my unfortunate fainting and retorted Eliza would be in as much danger as I. After all, being Were hadn't helped Mac or Carlos avoid their fate. Eliza countered that I needed to keep Carson out of harm's way and the surest way to protect him was to return home. I said danger seemed to have no problem finding us, thanks very much, and whoever was responsible could hunt us down in sleepy little Jackson county.

Plus, in Oregon we wouldn't have the pack to protect us. Besides, I claimed, if Carson was part of the pack, then as his mother I was, by default, responsible for protecting the pack in any way possible. Eliza said I didn't have any idea what I was getting myself into, but I retorted angrily that she didn't either. The pack had never been threatened like this before. Not by some rogue wolf, but by some seemingly organized group of humans who nonetheless knew the Weres' vulnerabilities. None of us knew exactly what it meant. We reached a standoff, staring at each other angrily with a common bond of stubbornness.

"Julie," Eliza said. "Don't you understand? I'm not sure I can protect you and Carson, and I'm not sure how I'll live with myself if what happened to Mac happens to the two of you."

"Eliza," I said, proud to hear my voice steady. "If Carson and I end up beheaded on the streets of Las Vegas," I inwardly squelched the vision that arose inside my head, "it will be through no fault of yours. I'm willing to take this risk. I feel compelled to help, regardless of the danger, regardless of the fact that, yes, I'm a mere human. Those beasts—sorry—those people killed Mac. They killed my Mac. They took him away from me and from Carson forever. I may not be as physically strong as you. I may not be used to this type of intrigue and violence and danger. But, hell, I've read my share of Agatha Christie. I think if these enemies are not Were and they expect only Weres to come after them, then perhaps I might actually have some type of strange advantage in this whole situation. I need to go with you. Carson won't be safe until we've figured this out. Like you, I'm not sure I trust anyone else to do it. Except you. I do trust you."

Eliza sank back on her haunches and captured my gaze for several long minutes. Finally, she sighed deeply and turned her gaze across the room. She rose in a fluid motion and moved lightly across the room to stand in front of those three pictures. Her fingers traced across the frames slowly, ending on that picture of herself, that younger self. She turned toward me and nodded, her lips narrowed with determination.

"All right," she said, crossing the room to join me. "How are we going to pull this off?"

****

The next morning dawned way too early after a kibitzing session that lasted half the night. The other half of the night, Carson had been restless and half awake.

Coffee. Coffee would help. At least Eliza and I had a plan. A plan I might be able to carry off. If I had some coffee first.

Such were the rudimentary thoughts I was able to form as I stepped quickly into the shower, leaving Carson happily kicking on a folded blanket on the bathroom floor. I toweled off briefly, stepped into some clothes, and stumbled downstairs

Returning my greeting, Erin held her arms up for Carson and I handed him off on my way to the coffee pot. I took a large sip, winced as it semi-scalded my mouth, and dropped into a chair beside her.

"Long night? I think I heard Carson once or twice."

"Oh, I'm sorry, Erin. I hope he didn't wake you up." And I hope you didn't hear Eliza scaling the side of your house.

"No, it's fine." Erin bounced Carson and he squealed, waving his chubby fists in the air.

"Have you started him on cereal yet?" she asked, smiling in delight as he continued his cooing.

"No, not yet."

"Oh!" She shook her head in surprise. "We used to give them cereal almost right away, sometimes even in their bottles."

"Yes, that's what my mom said, too."

Our chatter turned to the topic of my parents, with Erin asking how they felt about being grandparents, if they saw Carson often, what they did, etc. Me, I wanted to know which of my parents was part Werewolf, but I didn't have the answer to that question. I poured another mug of coffee, finally beginning to feel almost human—a phrase that took on new meaning these days. Liam came in from outside, where he'd apparently been doing some sort of Wyoming-like outdoor chore. While I drank my third cup of morning glory, Ian and his friend Dave finally slouched downstairs and joined us.

They each poured what looked like half a box of cereal into their bowls, added a gallon or so of milk, and buried themselves in eating. I marveled a bit, wondering if this was normal adolescent-boy-hollow-leg appetite or if my grocery bill was in for an even bigger shock once I was supporting a teenaged Werewolf. Perhaps I should stock up on kibble, I thought, my mouth quirking slightly. Dave looked up at me sharply, as if aware of my focused attention, and I spoke to hide my amusement.

"So, did you guys sleep well?"

Ian shrugged. Dave elbowed him, causing a spoonful of cereal to slop onto the floor, and said, "Hard to sleep with this one snoring."

"I do not snore." Ian shouldered his friend.

"Yeah, maybe you weren't snoring," Dave said, "maybe you snuffle in your sleep, dreaming about chasing rabbits."

With a yelp, Ian pounced on his friend, knocking his chair sprawling. They jostled a bit, ignoring Erin until she raised her voice sharply.

"I said that's enough, boys! Take it outside if you're going to horse around."

As the boys settled into a truce and started back into their cereal, a knock sounded on the kitchen door and Eliza poked her head inside.

"Morning, everyone. I thought I'd check in and see how everyone's doing. Especially you, Julie, after all the commotion and revelations of last night."

"Well," I started, after the general good mornings had been exchanged and Eliza settled in at the table with her own cup of coffee. "I'm kind of glad you're here, actually, because I've been thinking."

Ian continued to shovel cereal into his mouth, but Dave paused, spoon raised, looking at me intently.

"That is...Liam, did the garage say when my car would be ready?" I didn't have to feign awkwardness.

"Tomorrow." His voice held a note of query.

"When the car is ready to go, I think Carson and I should head back to Jacksonville." I continued in a rush to stave off objection. "I know I still have a lot to learn about parenting a Werewolf, but I also think it's just too dangerous here for Carson. I don't want to put him at risk. So, until we know what's going on, I think my first course of action needs to be protecting him and the best way to do that is for us to just go home. We'll visit again, definitely, and maybe longer next time. You're always welcome to visit us in Oregon. But what Erin said yesterday—this isn't my fight, so I shouldn't be involved—well, I couldn't sleep last night. I was so worried about Carson and about everything. I thought a lot about it and returning to Oregon seems best."

Erin's face creased in understanding and she reached out to squeeze my hand. Ian looked disinterested, feigned or real. Liam's mouth was set grimly and, after a moment, he nodded in agreement with my speech.

"Julie?" Eliza said. "Maybe I should come with you?"

The MacGregors looked at her, startled by the suggestion.

Sounding slightly hesitant, she continued, "If you'd have me for a while, I think I could be really helpful. I'm a full, Carson's a full, and I could teach you a lot about what that means. Plus, I'd be there for protection, just in case."

"Wow." I pretended to think for a minute and then injected warmth into my voice. "Eliza, that would be great. I'd be happy to have the company and, I admit, I feel a little jittery right now. Having you around would ease my mind." We smiled at each other across the table.

"I think that's a wonderful idea," said Erin. "Why don't you call the Full, Eliza, and see if she agrees?"

Ten minutes later, we'd made all the arrangements. Lily happily gave permission for Eliza to accompany me to Oregon, to protect me, and to brief me on Pack

Rules and Werewolf Life 101. Liam called the garage and confirmed they still anticipated my poor old car would be shipshape—well, carshape—by the next afternoon. Erin soaked up grandma time with Carson and, although I knew she would be sad to see us go, I also sensed her relief we'd be out of danger. Me, I pushed aside guilt over this ruse, eager to get to Las Vegas and dig up any further information on who had killed Mac and who threatened these people—these Weres—who had so quickly grown important to me. We'd be very careful, I reassured myself whenever I felt a chill of fear snake through my mind. Ian acted as if none of this had much to do with him and Dave made his exit, presumably returning to his own house where the cereal box might not be empty.

Or maybe it was. I wondered what life was like at Dave's house.

****

I wanted to do—needed to do—one more thing before I left Greybull. After a quiet morning at the MacGregor's house, a morning when Carson actually settled nicely for an hour-and-a-half long nap, just like the baby books said he should, I broached the subject.

"Erin?" I took a deep breath for fortitude. "Could you take me to see Mac's—Roger's—grave before I leave?" I forced myself to raise my gaze from the floor and look at her. The action was nearly my undoing: her face worked for a moment and water glimmered in her eyes. Her tears echoed the ones I blinked back furiously.

"Of course, dear. Of course." She nodded, then nodded again, and reached out to pat me on the shoulder.

So after lunch, Erin took me and Carson to the cemetery. Greybull Cemetery was a heavily-irrigated patch of green amidst the varicolored Wyoming soils. The manicured lawn sprouted shade trees at regular intervals. Behind the trees, plains stretched out to rocky hills where gentle layers of color clearly traced geologic ages in grayish black, white, red, and purplish gray. Tombstones rose from the lush grass, echoing the exposed hills standing out from brush in the distance. Most of the stones were pale gray, like bones, like sand, with a few hewn out of sparkling black or red granite.

Erin parked the car near the main entrance. I settled Carson in his sling and followed her silently through the stones. I looked at them in passing. Names, dates, phrases of love and blessing.

We crossed a path into a different section of the graveyard.

Erin said, "This is where we bury pack."

I looked at her, but didn't say anything.

Moments later, I halted at the sight of BLYTHE on a stone one row over. At my involuntary noise, Erin followed my gaze and said, "Yes, that's Dave's parents." She nodded and we stepped through the graves together.

We paused in front of the graves for a few moments. I wondered who had chosen the inscription: "May Death Be Gentle, May Love Be Strong, May Time Heal All." Carson squawked, protesting my lack of movement and startling me out of my thoughts.

"Okay. I'm ready," I said. Erin nodded, and we set out again.

"Dotty, that's Dorothy, Dave's mom; she was one of my best friends since grade school. Roger and

Tony—her oldest, Dave's brother—played together since Roger was born; Tony was three years older. They were friends—well, as friendly as two boys can be when they are so competitive, especially after Roger manifested first and so young. Tony didn't change until he was twelve, though he is a full moon. Was. Is. I wonder if we'll ever know. Some who go wolf manage to find their way back."

"Did you...did you know about the affair?" I asked.

"What? No. No. That was one secret she kept from me," Erin said. After a moment, she continued. "Dave and Ian have always been close. Dave was so bitter after...well, after everything. He blamed it all on his mom's lover, the human. Easier than blaming his parents, I suppose."

"Here." Erin gestured ahead to a tombstone standing in the shade of a juniper tree.

I stopped cold, as if caught in a trap. Carson chortled and started to suck on one chubby fist while he waved the other one wildly at the dancing branches. I took a deep breath to steady myself, then another. Erin stood silently and allowed me to approach the grave alone.

Roger Marcus MacGregor. Other than the dates, no other inscription marred the surface, although the gray stone had room. Perhaps, they didn't know what to say. I certainly didn't. I hoped seeing his tombstone, being here, seeing it carved into stone, would somehow make it real to me. I missed Mac and I kept having horrid visions of him, beheaded, his eyes glazed and fixed on me, and yet...and yet, it still didn't seem real.

Somehow, I thought I should feel something, some release of emotion, but I just felt empty.

I'd thought here, here if anywhere, I would find a sense of communion, of closure.

But the words on the tombstone seemed meaningless. Foreign.

I sank down on the grass, the blades both sharp and soft as my fingers dug into the ground. Mac? My mouth moved without sound.

Carson screamed. I jumped up and whirled around, heart pounding. Erin was right there; she smiled gently at my reaction. Carson started crying in earnest and I realized, no, there wasn't any danger, just my fussy baby throwing a fit. He cried in that angry way, no tears yet, just scrunched up beet red face and wide-open mouth. Dammit.

I jiggled him and swayed from side to side, trying to recapture—or capture—some connection with Mac. Carson redoubled his vocal efforts. Tears sprang out of his clenched eyes. I loosened him from the sling, attempted various holds, and tried to lay him down on the ground and tempt him with interesting things like grass. No good. He was his most recalcitrant self, and any hope for a moment of healing faded.

I gave up and Erin took us home.

Chapter Nine

Erin and I played with Carson in the living room when the phone rang. Carson was in the midst of tummy time and kept doing that airplane thing where he tensed his strong-man neck and lifted his head, arms, and legs off the floor while balancing on his taut belly. He really concentrated: breath held, eyebrows raised until his forehead looked like a Shar-Pei, arms rigid like a skydiver. After ten seconds or so, he collapsed limply and rested before trying again. He wanted to roll over, but each time got stuck on his own arm and wasn't able to manage it. Simple, developmental stuff, but Erin and I were wholeheartedly amused by his antics.

Erin left to answer the phone and I heard the nondescript rise and fall of her voice, the homey sound of the oven door as she checked on the cornbread, the clatter of the pot lid as she stirred the chili. After a few minutes, she came back in the room and held the phone toward me.

"It's Eliza, for you."

"Thanks," I said, taking the phone. "Hello?"

"Hi, Julie. Listen, if you're up for it, I'd like to take you to meet a couple of my pack friends. I cleared it with Erin and she's happy to watch Carson for a while after dinner. I thought you could leave him for two or three hours? If he eats first and maybe even goes to sleep?"

I glanced at Erin, and she nodded in confirmation.

"Okay," I said after a moment. Erin was his grandmother, after all. I wasn't used to leaving Carson with anyone, but I suppose I couldn't ask for a better babysitter.

"Do you think he'll be safe here?" I directed my question to Erin and, over the phone, to Eliza.

Eliza was decisive. "Yes. Erin and Liam will be there, as well as Ian. Ian's strong—waxing moon, you know—even though he's a pup. I doubt our prowler will return, with everyone home, but even if he does, I'm sure Carson will be safe without you."

Her voice revealed no irony, so I tried to mask my sudden reaction—the bitter knowledge *I* was unlikely to help in an emergency anyway, as a mere human. Vulnerable, weak, and sans super-senses. Of course, she was right: Carson would be just fine without me.

****

Eliza picked me up in her car, nearly as dented as my poor vehicle after yesterday's accident. Well, it hadn't been an accident, but I didn't really know what else to call it. I dithered a bit on what to wear and, after changing several times, ended up in a jean skirt and a black top with lace at the hems. I'd even brushed on some mascara and lip gloss, as if a bit of makeup would somehow impress the Werewolves I was about to meet. I felt like this was a job interview.

As we pulled out of the long driveway, Eliza shot me an assessing look. "Ready to meet some Weres?"

"I suppose so. I need to be back within three hours, okay?"

"Sure. I thought it would be good for you to talk to learn more about Weres and pack life, since I know you're thinking through some decisions."

I shot her a glance, wondering if my bitterness about being human was so visible. Instead of addressing that issue, I tried to lighten the mood. "Decisions? Eliza, no way am I moving to Greybull. I know Liam thinks I should, but I can't imagine living here."

"That's not what I meant and you know it."

I waited a beat to see if she would push. She didn't add anything, so I pretended I didn't know what she meant and changed the subject.

"Hey, speaking of learning more about Weres. I wondered what happens to your clothes when you change form? How come they don't rip apart, like in the movies?"

Eliza laughed. "I don't know. They just don't."

"But how does it work? Surely someone knows."

"Julie, it's not rocket science. It's magic. It just works—I don't have an explanation."

"Huh. Magic, but somehow genetic." I thought for a moment and followed up on her unsatisfying answer. "Okay, so if you change into a wolf and then go swimming, when you change back, are your clothes wet?"

"Yes."

"If you have things in your pockets? Or jewelry?"

Eliza started to sound exasperated. "You've seen me change with jewelry. It's just like anything else we wear. And anything inside the clothes stays right where it was."

"That's so…weird."

"You discover the existence of Werewolves and the weird part is what happens to our clothes?"

"Well. Yes."

We drove down the same two-lane highway where my car had been forced off the road yesterday and I scrutinized the brush closely, trying to find the exact spot. It all looked the same, though, especially in the evening's dim light.

"We already passed it," Eliza said. "The spot where you were, about a mile and a half back."

I glanced backward, then shook myself slightly and settled back into the seat. I thought about asking if she smelled or saw the traces of the accident, but then didn't bother. Probably both.

"So, where are we going?" I asked.

"The Snakebite. It's a bar in town."

We neared Greybull—such as it was—and Eliza dutifully slowed to obey the speed limit. At the second stoplight, she turned left off the main drag, drove two blocks, and then parked. The Snakebite must be a popular place because the otherwise deserted street was lined for a block and a half; there was also a small parking lot full of assorted cars and pickup trucks.

"These aren't all—" I stopped momentarily, letting two guys in cowboy hats pass us on the sidewalk. I lowered my voice and started again. "These aren't all pack, are they?" I gestured to the parked cars, the two cowboys now entering the Snakebite, and the whole area.

"No."

"Okay." Then how could we talk about anything important without being overheard? I pushed my curls behind my ears, brushed imaginary dust off my skirt, and followed Eliza into the bar.

The inside of the Snakebite looked like one of those surreal drawings where the stairs went every direction at once. Really, it did. I stood in the door for a moment, blinking and trying to gain perspective on the place. The building was open to the top of its three stories without one main space; instead, tables and chairs ranged on many-leveled terraces interconnected by flights of stairs and catwalks. My first thought was the layout must be hellacious for the waitstaff, but then I noticed the higher platforms had pulley-systems to raise and lower buckets. As I watched, a barmaid loaded a bucket with five bottles of beer and a cocktail: she slotted the bottles and glass into some sort of insert, then tilted her head back and called, "Order up" as she jiggled the rope. Above the general din, I heard a bell ring as it jangled near the platform's edge. A customer at the top gave a wave, pulled on the rope, delivered the drinks safely, and resumed his conversation.

Thank goodness safety rails lined the walks and platforms, my second thought. Otherwise, I foresaw the need for lots and lots of liability insurance to cover all the drunken pratfalls. Emphasis on falls.

Only after I comprehended the general layout and system of the Snakebite did I turn my attention to its décor. If it's possible to consider massive, dead, stuffed animals décor. Which it might be, in Wyoming. Somehow affixed to the railing of the highest platform was an entire bighorn sheep, its white body a bit worse for wear due to the pall of smoke in the air. Elk, moose, pronghorn antelope, and mountain lions: their fixed eyes glinted from around the room, a litany of

Wyoming wildlife. Driving across the state, I'd been shocked at the herds of pronghorn jumping through brush and leaping across the highway—well, it seemed like most of them had ended up here. The main bar of the Snakebite occupied a front and center position twenty paces from the door, predictably covered in dead rattlesnake skins. The snakes were tacked up so their rattles hung down like some kind of fringe, right above the bartender's head.

Eliza watched me absorb the surroundings with amusement. "Some bar, huh?"

"That's for sure." I shook my head. "If it weren't for all the dead animals, this could be a trendy bar in a big city; one with bouncers and a roped off VIP entrance. I didn't expect to find something like this here in Greybull."

"But the taxidermy makes it all Wyoming," Eliza said.

"I guess so." I made another mental note *never* to move to Wyoming. In case I was likely to forget and need an extra reminder. Dead, eviscerated, and re-stuffed animals with creepy glass eyes? Definitely not my style.

"This way." Eliza gestured to a middle-level platform on the left side of the bar. I followed her gaze and saw a four-top table with two people watching us. As we threaded our way through the bar, I tried to act nonchalant and observe the two Weres without seeming to. The woman had shoulder-length light brown hair and long bangs pushed off to one side. She wore a navy tank top layered over a gray tank; the cut of the tanks emphasized her broad shoulders, even though I didn't think she'd be that tall when she stood. Her fellow

Were was very handsome with short hair slightly spiked with gel and wide-set eyes, both nearly black. As we approached, he smiled to reveal startling white teeth, especially next to his olive complexion. He looked like he should star on a soap opera or a toothpaste commercial.

After preceding me up the stairs, Eliza skirted the table to the side and put her hand on my arm.

"Julie, this is Alyssa and Brian. Guys, this is Julie," she said.

"Hi," I said and forced my hands to stop fidgeting with the lace at the bottom of my shirt.

"Hi, Julie, Eliza. Have a seat." Alyssa pulled out the chair next to her. This close, I saw her hair still bore dual impressions of a hat brim and a ponytail holder. She was very tan—her skin sun-kissed and rosy on her shoulders—and her eyes crinkled up as she smiled.

Eliza sat next to Alyssa, and I took my place on the other side with Brian.

"So." Brian turned to me and I saw his dark red t-shirt had a space ship printed on it. "You're the mother of this extremely strong four-month-old full moon wolf we've heard about."

"Yes. You can't be more surprised than I am," I said.

Alyssa cut Brian off. "What do you want to drink, Julie? Eliza?"

Noting the two Weres already had bottles of beer in front of them, I said, "Beer is fine," and Eliza agreed.

Brian grabbed a little notepad and pen chained to the table, just like those pens in banks. He jotted something down, ripped off a piece of paper, folded it, dropped it in our bucket, and lowered it. When it reached the ground, he rang our bell and a waitress hurried over. Eliza and Alyssa made small talk while we waited for the beers. Brian pulled them up a minute later, used the bottle opener hooked to the bucket, and handed them around.

I took a long, cold swallow. Then I remembered I was still on a pretty heavy-duty dose of ibuprofen, legacy of the car accident. Whoops. Sorry, liver. But one beer would be okay, right? Right.

"So, you are both pack, both from Greybull?" I asked. I had a zillion and one questions about being a Were, but somehow none of them sprang to mind.

"I'm a half moon," said Brian, "and Alyssa's a crescent."

Crescent. I mentally recited the classifications: full, waxing, half, waning, crescent. Alyssa was one of the weakest werewolves and Brian average. Okay, this gave me a different perspective than hanging out with the uber-powerful Eliza.

"How old were you when you manifested?" I asked Brian.

"Fourteen," said Brian, "not early, not late. I'm five years older than Mac, so he had already turned and it drove us older boys crazy. I was *very* ready."

"Julie, you had no idea you had any Were heritage?" Alyssa asked.

"No. Lily, uh, the Full said my Were blood might come from my mother's side of the family. She was from Ohio, near Cleveland, and apparently there's a pack in the area."

"I was a dark moon, too."

I was in the middle of another sip of beer when Alyssa spoke and nearly caused me to spit cheap

American brew all over the table. Instead, I managed to confine myself to choking, getting beer up my nose, and dripping it down my front.

When I stopped coughing, I swallowed several times and wiped my watering eyes.

"You were a dark moon wolf?" I asked, needing absolute clarity. "You changed? You were bitten?"

"Yes."

I became uncomfortably aware of both Eliza and Brian watching me.

"On purpose? Did you have someone—some Were—bite you on purpose?"

"Yes."

"And now you're a Werewolf?" I asked.

"Yes." Alyssa's face was perfectly still. "I'm one of the weakest Weres in our pack. After all the risk and...pain...I can barely call the moon. Although, I do have the other...benefits." Her voice cast doubt on the last word.

"Pain?"

Alyssa glanced at Eliza and all of a sudden, I realized this was the true purpose of our evening's jaunt: to make sure I knew what it meant to be a dark moon. What it would mean, to be bitten. I sat up a bit straighter, from either irritation or interest. I wasn't sure which.

"Go ahead, tell her the whole story." Eliza leaned back in her chair and sipped slowly from the bottle. I knew her posture was a lie and her attention focused on the conversation; her relaxed stance and casual glances around the bar belied the tension I sensed radiating from her.

Alyssa nodded slowly and took a moment to muster her thoughts. I had the feeling it wasn't a story she told often, probably because the other Weres had lived through it with her.

"My father is a Were, but my mom's human. They've been married for a long time, since right out of high school, and they've always been very much in love—I was always embarrassed the way they carried on, kissing, pet names, and the whole nine yards. My dad didn't mind his kids wouldn't be full Weres. He just wanted to be with my mom, no matter what."

I couldn't help thinking about Mac, wondering if he ever would have felt that way. Loss and bitterness warred within me. To Mac, being Were was more important than anything. Than love. Than me. I wrenched my attention back to Alyssa as she continued.

"We weren't supposed to know he was a Were, of course—my sister and I. But I saw him change one night during a full moon, in the middle of the night. He had no way of knowing I was still up and happened to look out my window. I thought I was going crazy, so I woke my sister and we stayed up all night, waiting for him to get home. Waiting for an explanation." Alyssa took a large swig of beer. "My sister Ashley was thirteen months younger than me; we were practically twins and just as close."

Oh crap. I took another drink and stared at the bottle, in lieu of Alyssa.

"The minute Ashley heard about Weres and learned she was a dark moon, she started begging my dad to bite her. He wouldn't, of course. Ashley was in tenth grade and it was an awkward time for her, socially. She was convinced becoming a Were was the solution."

The other three at the table looked at me for a long moment.

I broke the silence after I couldn't stand it any longer. "What did you think?"

"Me? I didn't want to risk it. Not until...not until several years later."

Brian reached across the table and took Alyssa's hand; she turned up her palm and curled her fingers around his tightly.

Ah.

"So..." I wasn't sure how to ask.

"No. No. It wasn't Brian."

"I wouldn't bite her. It didn't matter if she was a Were or not. I didn't care." Brian cleared his throat after his voice cracked.

"Maybe you didn't, then. But you would have." At Brian's glance, Alyssa rephrased. "You might have."

"It doesn't matter now," Eliza said and they turned to her, then Alyssa nodded and began again.

"Right. Well, Brian wouldn't bite me, but my sister's boyfriend did. He bit both of us, at the same time, at our request. So here I am, a Were. Ashley died."

I knew it was coming, of course. I was pretty sensitive to verb tenses these days, and everyone had cautioned me death was a likely result of a dark moon getting bitten. Nonetheless, I winced at the raw statement, somehow made even stronger by the utter lack of emotion in Alyssa's voice.

After a moment, I said, "I'm sorry."

Alyssa's mouth twisted. "Me too. I wouldn't do it again, knowing what I know. It wasn't worth it. My sister meant everything to me." Brian tightened his hand on hers as she repeated, "Everything."

"Uh… How common is it, for a dark moon to die after being bitten?" I asked.

"Nearly half the time," Eliza said. I turned to her in shock, and she nodded confirmation. "In the past, only one in five survived, but modern medicine has helped. If a Were-trained doctor is around, the dark moon can be stabilized during the transformation—to some extent, anyway."

"And…" I wasn't sure how much to press Alyssa, but I had to know. "And it was painful?"

"Like my body was torn apart, molecule by molecule. Like melting in a crucible."

I looked down at the table, only to notice I'd been tearing the label off my beer bottle into teeny, tiny bits and rolling them into balls. I'd accumulated a little pile of them, right next to my now empty drink. I had the sudden urge to call Sheila, to call my mom, to talk to anyone who wasn't involved in all of this Were drama and madness. Eliza must have sensed it, because she lightened her tone and asked if I wanted another beer. When I declined, talk around the table turned to lighter topics by unspoken common accord. I asked about all the rattlesnake skins, Brian revealed he was a mechanic by day and inquired about the damage to my car, Alyssa and Eliza talked about some recent mining activity in the area. I heard "mining" and assumed gold, silver, or something valuable like that, but it turns out Greybull's mining claim to fame is bentonite, an expanding clay like the kind used in clumping cat litter.

Who knew that stuff had to be mined? I definitely needed to remember to tell Sheila. Discussing the ignominy of basically mining cat litter broke the remainder of the tension and the rest of our time passed quickly. As soon as Eliza realized I was restless to rejoin Carson, we said goodnight, climbed down to the main floor, and headed out.

I couldn't stop thinking about Alyssa's story. I remained quiet all the way back to the MacGregors' house.

Chapter Ten

Eliza, Carson, and I left Greybull the next day, determined to get a few hours of driving under our belts while the baby took a nice afternoon nap. Since the car hadn't been ready until after lunch, Erin urged us to stay one more night and start fresh the next morning, but I felt way too antsy to oblige. I found myself continually looking over my shoulder, startling at random noises, convinced our mysterious enemies somehow knew we were on the way and would take steps to deter us. But instead of more prowlers or blue sedans, we had a string of well-wishers dropping in to say goodbye to me and Carson. Don Reid the pharmacist, at whom I now smiled in shared knowledge, Ian's friend Dave, the Sanchezes, and Lily Rose all stopped by to see us off. Strange, how quickly I'd been adopted into this little community and I wondered how much of the warm feeling was small town America and how much was pack, the real meaning of pack. Certainly Carson was much more relaxed and stranger-friendly than customary. Perhaps his little Were senses smelled the affinity he held with these otherwise unknown folks.

I found myself hugging Erin fiercely, teary-eyed at saying goodbye to this generous woman who'd opened her heart and home to me and Carson. I vowed I'd be back soon and I'd make a serious effort to visit these new relatives.

All partings uttered and good wishes given, Eliza and I sped down the highway, grimly intent on our covert mission.

Five hours into our trip, my cell phone rang and I knew without looking it was Sheila. She'd texted me several times in the last few days, asking if I were okay, and she'd called me the night before. I hadn't answered. I just didn't know what to say. Strangely enough, it was easier with my parents: I'd spoken briefly to my mom and told her I discovered Mac had been murdered while investigating a case and I visited with his family for a while. She was worried about me, of course, but also glad I made an effort to reach out to Mac's family since they were, after all, Carson's relatives. My mom was definitely of her own generation and couldn't claim to understand my decision to raise Carson by myself, but she was also unconditional in her love and support for me. I basked in that for the duration of our phone conversation and the unspoken—Werewolves, murder, me playing Librarian Detective—didn't present a big obstacle. I guess in some ways, it seemed natural for kids to hide certain things from their parents. With Sheila, however, the truth loomed so large and insurmountable before me I didn't know how our friendship could survive it. Or survive without it.

Eliza must have read my grim thoughts. "Is that your friend Sheila again?"

"Yeah."

"Are you going to tell her?"

I glanced over at Eliza, sharply, but she kept her gaze on the road. "Am I allowed to tell her? What about pack law?"

"Well."

"Um, 'well' what?"

"Well, yes, there's pack law. But you're not exactly pack, are you? Conceivably, you could have told Sheila about Carson's transformation before you even knew what it meant—before you'd even heard of pack or pack law, right?" Eliza glanced over at me. "If you'd told her before you even came to Wyoming, then she'd already know. How could you get in trouble for that?"

"Actually, I imagine all too well how I could get in trouble for that. Isn't it possible I would still be blamed for telling a human about the existence of Werewolves?"

Eliza's brow creased in delicate lines. "I've been thinking about it for the last couple of days and I'm just not sure. There might be a loophole. After all, you're human—dark moon wolf, yes, but human. And you're the mother of a very strong full moon. I don't think they'd take drastic action against you or Sheila. They need to keep you as an ally and they need to preserve access to Carson. At most, they might pledge Sheila to secrecy or...something."

I considered Eliza's logic for a few minutes, before slowly shaking my head.

"I don't know. Earlier you explained if Mac had told me about Were life, the council might have had us both killed. I'm not sure I'm willing to gamble Sheila's life on a loophole."

And so I didn't call her back.

****

Three and a half days later, we arrived in Las Vegas. I'd reaffirmed that car travel with a four month old was the ninth level of Hell. Eliza took it in stride, even the car seat diaper changes and the seven-umpty-million stops for feeding, pacifier retrieving, and other things designed to save our eardrums. So much for my pipe dream Carson would love his new car seat and spend his time happily cooing or napping.

"So what's our plan?" I asked, as we exited the highway and rolled into central Las Vegas.

"Most recent scene first, don't you think? Let's go to the park where Carlos was murdered."

"Hey, Eliza?"

"Yeah?"

"Your sense of smell is a lot better in wolf form, right?" I asked.

Eliza turned, regarding me with narrow eyes. "Yes. Why?"

I didn't answer, but just grinned at her and pulled into a conveniently located grocery store. Carson sat snoozing, for once, so I idled the car in the shade.

"Be right back," I said and quickly opened the door.

"Julie Hall."

"What? I'll be right back. Stay with Carson." I dashed into the store.

When I came back to the car holding a street map and ostentatiously dangling a brand new red dog collar and leash, Eliza collapsed back in the seat and groaned theatrically.

Smiling widely, I used my breeziest voice. "Well, you can't just walk around the park without a leash, can you? I wouldn't want to get in trouble with the law."

"No one is going to believe I'm your…pet dog."

"Sure they will. You'll be, what, some sort of wolf hybrid? A husky-wolf cross. Or that big dog—a Great Pyrenees-wolf cross. Or something. I know you'll be very, very well behaved, won't you, Fluffy?" I patted Eliza on the top of the head, enjoying the moment immensely.

Eliza closed her eyes and groaned again.

"Only for you, Julie. And for Mac."

My zany mood evaporated like a bubble hitting the sidewalk.

"For Mac," I said and cleared my throat. "Where's this park?"

****

We stopped and asked for directions only twice, which I considered a minor miracle. When we were close to the park, Eliza told me to pull over. She unbuckled her seatbelt, pulled the flickering shade around herself, and lay there on my passenger seat, a large buff-colored wolf.

I leaned over and fastened the collar around her throat. Good thing I'd bought the largest size they had.

"Act like a dog now, Fluffy. Don't forget," I said, gaining back some sense of humor. "And don't shed in my car."

Eliza's mouth lolled open in laughter and she scratched one ear vigorously, causing my poor small car to bounce about.

"Bad dog," I muttered. I drove the last few blocks and tried to no avail to find a shady parking spot—Las

Vegas in June is HOT. As I cut the motor, Carson woke with a squeal. Good timing, for once.

When I unhooked Carson from his car seat and picked him up, he spotted Eliza—or Fluffy, I reminded myself—and squealed again. He made little "uh, uh, uh" sounds and waved both his hands in her direction. I opened the passenger door and Eliza hopped out, staying right by my feet as I awkwardly used my free hand to snap on the leash. She sat back on her haunches.

"Come on, uh, Fluffy," I said. With a gentle tug, I led her in the direction of a lone tree, where I could sit and tend to Carson. My baby liked being out of the car. He stretched and curled his little body like a caterpillar, then lifted his toes up to the breeze. He took turns staring at his feet, the leaves, and the big furry wolf lying next to us. I wondered if he could tell she was a Werewolf. I wondered if she seemed like kin to him.

The park wasn't crowded, which made sense since it approached noon in the middle of June. Like I said, Las Vegas was hot. Anyone with any sense was probably inside or at the pool, so only a few brave souls roamed the park. One little girl pulled her mother's hand in our direction.

"Mama, mama! Doggie!" she cried.

The woman smiled at me. "Is your dog friendly? Can my daughter pet it?"

"Yes, she's very friendly," I said, wondering how Eliza liked being referred to as an "it."

The two came over and the little girl eagerly plunged her hands into Eliza's fur. She patted her—mostly gently—and said, "Good doggie, good doggie" over and over. Eliza reached up and licked her cheek, which caused a paroxysm of giggles.

When the two left, I stood up, stretched, and said, "Okay, Fluffy. Let's get down to business. You lead."

Under the guise of a slow walk, Eliza led me around the park. We passed a play structure tenanted by a few hardy preschoolers, then followed a trail toward empty basketball courts. As we neared a stretch of sand laid out for volleyball, Eliza's fur stood up. She growled, deep in her throat. The rumble made my own pulse quicken.

"Shh, Fluffy," I said with a gentle tug on the leash. Her growl subsided, but her massive ears swiveled this way and that. Her head dropped to the ground and I let the leash hang slack, following as she crisscrossed a ten-foot patch of ground. She moved slowly, nose pushing into the scrubby grass. I scoured the area with my own gaze, looking for some trace of struggle, some sign of events, but found nothing my human senses could perceive. Dammit. I kept looking for something. Like a footprint from some weird-soled shoe we could trace back to a custom designer who only sold to one person in Las Vegas. A cell phone carelessly dropped out of someone's pocket. A key that opened a safety deposit box with all the answers. Something of that nature. An actual clue.

After Eliza finished that area, she swung her muzzle to follow a winding path back through the park. She stopped to snuffle once or twice, cleared her nose with a whuff and continued head-down to a parking area on the opposite side of the park. She crossed back and forth across the pavement, sneezed, and sat up to look at me.

"All done, girl?" I said.

She pushed her wet nose into my hand and I reflexively petted her, scratching her ears and running them through my hands. Her fur really was soft. She closed her eyes in pleasure, then turned and gave me a huge sloppy lick on the hand.

"Gross, Eliza," I said, wiping my hand on my cropped pants. "I mean, Fluffy." She grinned at me, white teeth gleaming in the desert sun.

"Ready to go back to the car?" I asked. She stood and wagged her tail, so I took that as a yes.

When we got back to my car, Carson squawked in disapproval and tried to squirm out of my arms. Muttering apologies, I snapped him back into his seat, took off Eliza's leash and collar, opened the front door for her to bound in, and went around to my side.

As I slid into the driver's seat, Eliza said, "I can't believe those people really believed I was a dog."

I jumped, hand flying to my throat, then turned to face her. She lounged in the passenger seat, not a hair out of place.

"Jesus, Eliza. You changed right there, where anyone could see you?"

"Who's going to see me?" Eliza gestured to the empty park.

"Well...okay. You startled me."

"Serves you right. 'Fluffy.' "

I started the car, desperate for air conditioning. "So?"

Eliza sat silent for a moment. "Well, Carlos was killed there, no doubt. I could still smell the blood." She grimaced. "Two Weres have been to the scene. I think one of them was there more recently than the other.

122

Scent from at least five humans, some of whom may have been police. I also smelled a German shepherd, probably with the officers."

She let out a breath and shrugged. "Hard to tell the sequence of everything. It happened, what, five or six days ago? And the damn park has sprinklers, which doesn't help the scent trail."

"Did you track the Weres back to the parking lot? That other lot?"

"Yes. Both of them. One may have been following the other—one of them definitely walked around the parking lot for a while. I think the other went straight to a car."

"Okay. So what does that tell us?"

"Nothing."

I glanced at Eliza, surprised by her bitterness.

"Nothing?"

"Nothing. So what? There were two Weres. We knew there were Weres. Who are they? Who were the people? Why did they kill Carlos? Why was his body discovered right away when Mac was missing for days?"

Eliza shook her head. "Maybe we'll find something where Mac was killed."

My throat tightened. "Okay."

****

We visited the site where Mac's body had been found, in an alley that looked like any other alley. With no clues and no scent trails, this long after his murder.

Feeling less than hopeful, we moved on to the motel parking lot where Mac's head had been found. The motel didn't look like the site of a murder. It looked like the kind of place that boasted weekly rates and, one imagined, had long-time residents setting up meth labs in their dingy bathrooms. Even standing at the site, somehow Mac's death still didn't seem real to me. This place was unmarked by the event, no signs or new bits of knowledge.

Eliza prowled the perimeter of the parking lot, presumably preserving the hope of finding some helpful information, but after fifteen minutes, even she conceded defeat.

"I can't find anything. I can't even tell where his head was," she said, with a twist of the mouth as she heard her own words.

"Okay." I leaned over and sank my nose into Carson's hair, trying to clear my mind and muster productive thought. "So now what?"

"I'm not sure." Eliza wiped her forehead and reached back to lift her hair off her neck. She twisted it into a knot and deftly tucked it in so it stayed up—a feat I could never have managed. "Well," she said after a minute, "I guess we should get a late lunch and figure out the next step. I'm starving."

****

We didn't really expect to sweep into Las Vegas, discover some crucial and overlooked piece of information, and single-handedly capture the bad guys. At least, that wasn't a conscious expectation. But now that we'd come up empty, I realized for the first time we didn't know what the hell we were doing. We'd found no clues. Nothing. We didn't even know what to do next. For Eliza and me, it started out as a silent and somber lunch, but then Carson in his sometimes-contrary way decided to be the world's happiest baby. Devouring my club sandwich and fries, I bounced him on my knee and he chortled and drooled and held onto a shiny spoon for dear life.

Catching me in that weird moment of uncertainty and delight, my phone rang, Sheila's picture flashed, and I answered the phone without thought.

"Hey," I said, feeling mostly relief to talk to her, regardless of my confusion about what to say.

"Hi, Julie. How are you? What's going on? I've been really worried."

"I'm okay," I said, then paused.

"Are you?" Sheila waited for a second and then rushed on. "I didn't want to pester you, truly, but I've been really concerned. I haven't heard from you in days. Almost a week. I know you're spending time with Mac's family—"

"No, I'm not there anymore."

Shit. I froze, not knowing what to say. Then Carson managed to somehow throw his spoon halfway across the room and I laughed.

"Oh geez, Carson. Sorry," I called to the woman who'd been hit in the foot by the flying spoon. Thank goodness she wasn't annoyed her lunch had been so unexpectedly interrupted. "Sorry, hold on…Carson just threw his spoon across the restaurant."

"Oh." Sheila sounded confused. "Where are you?"

"Las Vegas."

"Las Vegas?"

"Yeah." I glanced over at Eliza and decided to stick as close to the truth as possible. "I decided to come to Las Vegas, to see where Mac was killed. I thought it might bring some type of closure."

Sheila still sounded confused, though a bit warmer. "Has it?"

"No, not really. You know how morbid I can get, imagining things over and over, replaying them in my mind? Well, somehow I thought being here would snap me out of it, but we visited the murder site and it still doesn't seem real."

"'We' meaning you and Carson?"

"Yes and Eliza Minuet. She grew up with Mac and wanted to come, too."

Carson chose that moment to morph into Ragingly Hungry Baby Who Needs to Feed Right Away. He started pulling on my shirt, making little crying gulps. I juggled the phone for a minute, then said, not without a feeling of gratitude, "Hey, Sheila, Carson's hungry. I'll call you back, okay?"

"Okay…" Sheila hesitated. "Take care of yourself, Jules."

The rest of our meal passed in relative quiet, as Eliza and I were deep in thought. We discussed our options. Should we just call it quits and go home? No, we decided. Should we parade around town, hoping the people killing werewolves would notice Eliza and reveal themselves by attacking her? That was Eliza's idea, quickly vetoed by me. Should we call Lily, admit we were in Vegas, and ask if she or the council had any ideas? That one was pretty much a rhetorical question, since neither one of us wanted to involve the council at this point. I still felt it highly probable someone from the council was involved. Should we track down the council investigators Tim Rogers and Kayleigh Anderson, in the hopes they would allow us to help with the investigation but not reveal our involvement to anyone else?

We sat musing over the last idea, while we each nursed yet another glass of iced tea. Eliza hadn't met either Were investigator personally, so it was impossible to predict what their reaction might be to a pair of amateur intruders. Under usual circumstances, the investigators would be unlikely keep our involvement secret from the council. Yet, in this instance, I wondered if self-preservation might work in our favor: Tim and Kayleigh must be alarmed by the fact two of their fellow Weres had been murdered while working on this case. Surely, it crossed their mind an internal traitor might be responsible and they could be the next victims. Unless, of course, one of them *was* the traitor. This latter thought gave us the most pause.

After we couldn't drink another sip of iced tea, we finally pushed back from the table. Carson had fallen asleep and lay like a ragdoll over my shoulder, breathing sweetly.

"All right. Let's go see Tim and Kayleigh. It's our best option right now." Eliza waited for me to nod in concurrence, before reaching for her phone. "Now, I'm not sure where they're staying, but I bet I can weasel it out of Lily."

"Without making her suspicious?"

"Just watch me." Eliza flashed a confident grin at me and hit speed dial.

"Hi, Full, it's Eliza. No, not yet, we're still en route. Travel is sure a lot slower with a baby. Yes, true. Well, we wanted to check in on things with the pack. Any developments?"

Eliza sat up straight, radiating sudden intensity that raised the hair on my arms. Her eyes narrowed.

"When? And what's the council doing about it? What about Tim Rogers, is he still in Las Vegas? Has he changed hotels? What precautions is he taking?"

I heard Lily's voice raise on the other end of the phone.

"Yes. I know. I *know*, Full. Yes. It's my job to take care of Julie and Carson. It's the council's job to solve the crimes." Eliza sounded as if she repeated instructions and I heard slight anger burning under the docile language. She crossed her fingers and scowled across the table. "Yes, I promise. Okay, I won't tell her. Yes, we'll drive carefully and I'll call you in a couple of days."

Eliza hung up the phone.

"Dammit!"

"What happened?" I demanded, "Was someone else murdered?" Conscious of my sleeping baby, I tried to keep my voice down, but injected urgency into the words.

"No. Well, maybe. Kayleigh Anderson is missing."

"Missing?"

"She and Tim were tracking some rumors about a feral dog sighting. Tim scouted on the ground and Kayleigh did some background work, posing as the owner of a lost dog, talking to the police, and the local pounds. She never arrived back at the hotel. No trace of her since yesterday."

I closed my eyes and sent fervent wishes into the universe for Kayleigh. My jealousy of her vanished, even if she was a hot, blonde Californian Werewolf friend of Mac's.

"Lily says Tim reported to the council immediately and changed hotels. Actually, she said, 'He's not staying at the Silver Token any longer.' So, I guess we know where he *stayed*, if not where he is now. I wanted to know what else the council planned to do about this—if they sent more investigators or what—but, well, you heard the rest. Full was fairly adamant I needed to remember I wasn't involved. Oh, she didn't want me to tell you any of this, either."

I digested the story for a moment, in silence, before a thought occurred to me. "Are you going to be punished for going against your Full?"

Eliza shrugged gracefully and flashed me a smile. "Perhaps. We can't afford to worry about that right now; there are more important things at stake. Either there's been another murder or Kayleigh's in grave danger."

I glanced down at Carson and stroked his back gently. "Okay. So do we start at the Silver Token Motel?"

Eliza's voice held a grim note when she said, "Actually, I'd like to meet Suzy Zhang, the registered lone wolf in Las Vegas. I know Mac questioned her once, but I have a hard time believing all this activity happened in her own city without her knowing something about it."

"All right, then. Suzy Zhang it is. Right after we check into a hotel, okay?"

Although I tried to hide it from Eliza, I felt a sense of relief, because chatting with a lone wolf seemed a lot safer than our other option. I would not give up this quest and retreat to Oregon, but I felt a twinge of panic about the whole situation. I was mostly worried about keeping Carson safe. His limp, sweaty weight on my shoulder, sleeping with such trusting abandon...well, I felt pretty mama-bear with some second thoughts about exposing him to danger.

****

After a cursory motel check-in, a quick internet search revealed the address of our lone wolf and we were on our way. We used our time in the car to coordinate our story and set clear objectives for the encounter, so when we reached Suzy's house, we were ready. Carson snoozed away, so I transferred him from the car seat into the sling and followed Eliza to the front door.

A minute after the doorbell rang, we sensed movement behind the rippled glass windows beside the door. After a pause, we rang again and a woman's voice called out, "Who is it?"

I shot a glance at Eliza wondering if Suzy Zhang was always so cautious, if she sensed a fellow Were had come to visit, or if she was nervous because of the recent incidents.

As per our agreed-upon story, Eliza spoke clearly, "We've been sent by the council and we need to speak with you."

After a slight hesitation, the door opened a crack and a middle-aged woman looked out at us. She had thick black hair that might have been beautiful, had it not been for what I might unkindly call a poodle-perm, making her appear about twenty years older than her actual age. Her outfit didn't help: pleated jean shorts and a t-shirt with appliqués of flowers and butterflies. The t-shirt was tucked in, and she wore a braided leather belt. So, in sum, she looked exactly like what we discovered she was: a fairly dowdy elementary school teacher who lived alone and had a bunch of cats.

Both Eliza and I were surprised by the cats, considering Suzy *was* a Were, albeit a crescent moon. I quickly understood why she'd decided pack life wasn't for her. In fact, I could hardly imagine a less likely Werewolf.

"I've already spoken to several investigators sent by the council," Suzy said softly. "I don't think I have anything else to say that could possibly be helpful."

"Nevertheless," said Eliza and, as if that was somehow an explanation, she pushed the door open and stepped into the house. Suzy shrank backward, and I honestly wouldn't have been surprised to see her lie belly-up on the carpet to placate Eliza's wolf.

Suzy smiled uncertainly and said, "Of course, of course, come in, please," after the fact. She gestured to the couch in the front room.

Eliza stalked across the carpet, spine straight, and settled onto the edge of the couch in one easy motion. Three or four cats sprang out of room as soon as she entered. I followed her, feeling kind of sorry for Suzy Zhang, who probably became a lone wolf so she didn't have to deal with Weres traipsing through her living room. Suzy looked slightly puzzled by me, then actually shrank back into herself even further as she scented Carson. Yes, Carson, my oh-so-intimidating just-turned-four-and-a-half-months-old baby. Yes, a full moon wolf, but come on.

"Start by telling us exactly what you told the other council investigators," Eliza commanded.

Suzy took a seat on the edge of a rocking chair, smoothing her shorts over and over again in nervous action.

"Um, I told them I don't know anything about all of this." She glanced at Eliza and hurried on, "I mean,

the first investigator? He told me there'd been, um, a
Were who killed two people when in wolf form? But I
didn't know anything about it and I still don't. My life
right now revolves around my school, my home, my
friends—I lead a quiet life—I haven't come across
anything or sensed anyone—any other, uh, you know,
Weres. I mean, every once in a while, there will be
some scent of, uh, one who's probably here on
vacation. But never any pattern, any repeated particular
Were or anything. Never anything near my house. Or,
at least, not until you council Weres started coming."
Suzy's eyes widened and she hastily added, "Not that I
mind, of course. I'm happy to help the council, it's the
least I can do, really."

"Hmm." Eliza leaned back. After shifting weight
for a minute or two, Suzy glanced at me as if looking
for aid. When Eliza spoke again, she jumped.

"What specific questions did the other investigators
ask you?" Eliza asked.

"Oh. Well, the first one asked me about certain
dates and what I was doing and if I'd sensed anything
out of the ordinary. The second group, well, they were
mostly interested in the time surrounding the murder of
that first Were investigator. They asked me a lot of
questions. I don't think I was very helpful, though…"

Somehow, none of that surprised me, especially the
fact she hadn't been helpful. I raised my eyebrows at
Eliza as our gazes met. Surely there wasn't much
reason to continue with this poor, nervous Were?

"The third investigator," Suzy continued in her
small voice.

"What?" I interrupted her.

"The third investigator? He focused on the other three, because he was checking up on their performance for the council." Suzy's voice became even more hesitant.

"Ah, yes." Eliza continued to lounge on the sofa. "And what did you report to him?"

"Um. I told him they'd been very thorough, asked a number of questions, it wasn't their fault I wasn't more helpful—I just don't have any information. He made sure they'd given me a way to contact them if I thought of anything else, so I said, sure, they left their cards and the number for the Silver Token motel."

"Do you still have their cards?"

"Yes, of course."

"Did this third inspector leave his card?" Eliza asked with studied nonchalance.

"Uh, no. But I'm sure he meant to." Suzy smiled at us.

Eliza gave a dubious hmmm. "Rose, who did the council say they'd sent? It's slipped my mind. Was it Ben or Dave?"

With a start, I realized Eliza meant me. We'd agreed not to use our real names for this bit of sleuthing.

"I can't remember. It'll come to me in a minute. Wasn't it Ben?"

"His name was Taylor, Taylor Dunn," Suzy said helpfully.

"Of course. Taylor. Well, we'll have to check with him next." Eliza's grim gaze met mine.

"Taylor…is he the tall one, dark hair?" I addressed my question to Eliza.

Suzy said, "Oh, no, he's blond, with a beard, only average height."

"I think you met him in Boston last year, remember?" Eliza said and I nodded.

Eliza stood. "Now, Suzy. This is important and I need to make sure you understand me clearly. The council is worried we have a traitor within our midst, someone in league with these murderers. We've been sent to keep tabs on the situation and the other investigators do not know we're involved. We need to keep it that way. If anyone else comes here to talk to you, do not mention Rose and I were here. Do you understand me?"

"Yes, of course, I won't mention you were here... I didn't even catch your name and I won't mention Rose's name. A traitor in the council?" If possible, Suzy looked even more nervous.

"Don't worry. You've been safe so far; there's little reason for concern." Eliza nodded briskly and headed for the door, trailing me in her wake.

Carson woke as we reached the car, and his mood seemed much better than ours. I strapped him into his cow-print car seat and wrapped his fingers around a teething toy he'd probably drop in two minutes, but his random attempts to stick it in his mouth might amuse him for that short time. Eliza slid into the passenger seat and shushed me when I got into the car.

"Wait until we're out of here," she said.

"Okay. But where are we going?"

"Let's head back to the hotel and regroup."

A few blocks away from the house of Ms. Suzy I-did-have-something-interesting-to-say Zhang, I asked the most obvious question. "Do you think Taylor Dunn was really sent by the council to check up on the other investigators?"

"No. Good job getting a description, by the way." Eliza flashed me a smile.

"Thanks, I had given her up for useless when she mentioned the third investigator. Do you think he's the same Were Tim and Kayleigh were tracking, the one who kidnapped Kayleigh?"

Eliza shrugged. "I hope so. May the moon guard us if we're dealing with too many rogue Weres here—especially since a number of human accomplices are involved."

"I wonder if they had the Silver Token staked out. It may have only been a matter of time before Tim or Kayleigh—or both—were abducted."

Neither of us had any more to say. And Eliza didn't comment on the long and circuitous route I took back to our hotel.

Chapter Eleven

When we drove into the parking lot of the motel, I felt jumpy and Eliza cased the vicinity with narrowed eyes. I'm sure Eliza's super Were senses worked in overdrive. Me, I found myself glancing around with my humble human eyes, seeking shadowy figures skulking about. I was so focused on these imagined stalkers, I almost missed her.

Sheila stood arms akimbo in the middle of the walk, right in front of the row of room doors. Her blonde hair streamed loose halfway down her back and her white tank top made her look even more tanned and toned than usual. She wore jeans and red lizard-skin wedge sandals—the ones I knew she wore when she needed an extra jolt of Sheila-ness—and she looked both pissed and worried.

"Sheila!"

Eliza glanced at me, then followed my gaze. Her forehead wrinkled. "That's Sheila? Your friend Sheila?"

I pulled the car in and opened the door. As I stepped out, Sheila strode forward, lifting her hands up to the sky.

"So here you are," she proclaimed loudly. "My best friend who drops off the face of the earth and leaves me no choice but to follow her to some cheap motel off the Strip and demand answers."

Then she gave me an equally dramatic though no less sincere hug that ended in a little shake. "Are you okay, Jules?" Her blue eyes searched my face.

I nodded, dumb with surprise and relief. "I am okay. I think. Unless I'm going crazy or something."

"Going crazy? Jules, you've always been crazy." Sheila turned toward Eliza, who'd released Carson from his car seat and watched us with a bemused look.

"You must be Eliza Minuet, Mac's friend?" Sheila stepped toward Eliza, who juggled Carson to shake hands.

Eliza turned to me and said, "Julie, why didn't you tell me Sheila was a Witch?"

A moment of silence hung between us, during which I stared at Eliza. Then I turned to Sheila, expecting to share a laugh. But Sheila didn't laugh. Instead, her blue eyes narrowed and fixed on Eliza. Her usually dramatic stance tightened into something coiled and contained.

"Julie, step away from her," Sheila said, a note of urgency in her voice.

I didn't move.

"You're a *Witch*?"

Eliza held up her free hand. "Calm down, Sheila."

"Don't tell me what to do," Sheila snapped. "Who are you? *What* are you?"

I took Carson from Eliza, stepped between the two of them, and spoke in a light tone. "Sheila, this is Eliza. She's a Werewolf. Eliza, this is Sheila, my best friend. Who may or may not be a Witch and has some serious explaining to do."

I looked from one to the other. Eliza remained at ease, seemingly amused by this turn of events. Sheila's spine was utterly straight, her hands clenched by her sides.

I said, "I suggest we continue this inside, unless you both *want* to create a scene?"

With those words, the tableau broke. Sheila continued to watch Eliza, I grabbed the diaper bag from the car, and we filed into the motel.

Sheila perched on one of the two queen beds in the air-conditioned room. Eliza dropped lithely onto the opposite bed and lounged on one side, sporting a small grin. I laid a blanket on the floor between the beds and put Carson down where, oblivious to the mood around him, my baby proceeded to kick and coo at the ceiling. I joined Sheila on the bed closest to the door.

"Sheila, how did you get here? How did you find us? What the hell does Eliza mean, you're a Witch? A *Witch*?" I said.

Sheila held up her hands, fingers spread wide. "Since when do you run with Werewolves?"

"Uh, since my *baby* turned *into* a Werewolf, since I found out Mac was a Werewolf, since I learned he was murdered by someone who knew he was a Werewolf, and since that same someone's been trying to kill me— or Carson." I jabbed her shoulder with my finger. "Don't avoid the question. You're a Witch? A *Witch*?"

"Jules, are you sure she's a Werewolf? And not...something else?"

Sheila looked askance at Eliza, who held up one finger, pulled wispy shadows across to cover her body, then almost instantly lay in wolf form on the bed, her mouth open in what definitely looked like a grin. Sheila bolted upright, scrabbling off the back of the bed toward the door, but halted mid-step. Almost as suddenly, Eliza's buff-colored body wreathed in darkness again and she sat upright, crossed her legs, and held out her hands in a placating gesture.

"I'm sorry," she said. "Truly. I should have warned you. I just thought hours of talk could be quite easily replaced by a demonstration. You know, a picture's worth a thousand words and all."

I rubbed the prickles from my forearms. "It's okay, Sheila, really. She's not going to hurt you or anything. But she really is a Were and quite a powerful one, at that. What else would she be?"

They both ignored my question.

"What I want to know," said Eliza, "is how did you find us?"

Sheila shot another narrow look at Eliza, gave a theatrical sigh, and shrugged her shoulders to indicate the Werewolf had passed some sort of test. Sheila addressed her answer to me.

"You said you were in Las Vegas. I hopped a direct flight from Medford—cost me a fortune, by the way, walking up to the counter and getting a seat on the next flight, but I suppose, dear Jules, you're worth it. And worth the favors I called in to have my classes covered." She winked at me. "You always stay at the same motel chain. I've sadly failed to improve your taste in that regard. But, in this case, your habits came in handy, because it only took me a few phone calls to figure out where you were staying. Elementary, dear Watsons." She gave the two of us a small bow.

Eliza snorted softly at her posturing. "And you're a Witch."

Sheila opened her mouth and closed it again. She looked at Eliza, looked at me, and made a little moue.

"Speechless? Sheila?" I punched her lightly on the arm. "What the hell is Eliza talking about?"

Sheila swiped her long bangs away from her face, took a deep breath, and turned to face me. "Yes, I'm a Witch."

Funny. As soon as Eliza had said the words they rang true. Yet hearing them from Sheila's mouth jarred me into numbness. Two worlds I thought were separate—my "real" life in Oregon and this new life that included Carson-the-Were-pup—crashed together. This time, I was the only one living in an illusion. I looked at Sheila, my best friend, the person I trusted with all my secrets, the one who often knew my mind before I did.

Apparently, I didn't know her at all.

"You're a Witch. You're a Witch and you never told me? Did you know Mac was a Were? Did you know that was the reason things weren't working between us? Why didn't you tell me? Who *are* you?" The words tumbled out almost before they entered my mind. Carson reacted to the tone of my voice and paused in his kicking.

"Jules! Julie. What do you think I should have done? 'Hi, I'm Sheila. Would you like to get coffee? By the way, I'm a Witch?' " Sheila shook her head and a note of bitterness crept into her voice—bitterness I didn't expect from my exuberant, confidant friend. "Oh, believe me. I've tried that. I've spent my life trying to draw these boundaries."

She twisted her mouth, paused to regroup, and then continued in a normal tone. "I didn't know Mac was a Werewolf. Actually, until now, I'd never met—never knowingly met—a Were."

Eliza cocked her head. "You can't tell I'm a Were?"

Sheila spread her hands wide. "I'm sure there are ways to tell, probably certain spells I could use to scry. I could research it. But, no, just meeting you like this, I would have no idea."

"Interesting. Well, you clearly smell like a Witch," said Eliza.

Sheila let loose a peal of laughter. "Whatever that means. I'm not sure if I should be offended or not."

I looked between the two of them, as they shared a small smile.

I closed my eyes and rubbed my forehead. "Sheila?" My voice came out thicker than usual, and I swallowed hard.

Instantly, Sheila stopped laughing and placed a hand on my arm. She spoke quietly.

"Jules, I'm a Witch, but it's still me. Growing up, I was always a little—different. A little fey. The other kids knew it, I think. They—well, never mind that. When I was twelve, Granny Emma told me I was a Witch, as was she, and her grandmother before her. The gift often skips a generation."

I kept my gaze on Carson. I sensed, rather than saw, Eliza nod.

"My grandmother taught me. It was…miraculous. Marvelous. I spent summers with her in Maine and those were the best months, the best times of my childhood. Finally, I understood what was going on, why I was different. I found peace with myself."

I looked up to find the full force of Sheila's gaze turned on me. Her blue eyes held mine and I saw something in them, something that maybe mattered more than her being a Witch, a vulnerability my friend had never shared. Maybe not with anyone.

After a moment, she pulled back and made a finis gesture with her hands. With a lighter tone, she said, "So, yes, I'm a Witch and I'm glad you know. I should have known you could handle the news, Jules."

I nodded slowly. "Okay. So, what does it really mean to be a Witch?" The word still felt weird on my tongue, but as I uttered it, Sheila flashed me a huge smile. I smiled back, and tried for a lighter tone. "Hey, I didn't even know there were real Witches, but I suppose if Werewolves actually exist, then the field's wide open. Who knows what we'll meet next: Zombies, Goblins, Fairies, Vampires, Unicorns?"

I glanced at Eliza, who rolled her eyes.

"Most of the magic I do is minor: enchanting small objects, scrying, working with dreams, things of that nature. I could manage more complicated spells, but I'd have to look them up and study for a while," Sheila explained.

Eliza started to speak, but I interrupted her.

"Look them up? Look them up where?" I asked, ever the librarian.

"My granny left me her spellbooks and journals. They're not very well organized, so it takes me a bit of browsing. They go back generations in my family."

"My grandmother left me her collection of ceramic chickens," I said, then realized how inane I sounded when both Sheila and Eliza turned to look at me.

"What?" asked Eliza.

"Never mind. So, do Witches have a central archive? Or, uh, covens that keep records? Have you—"

"Julie, can we talk about the books later?" Eliza broke in. "I'm worried Kayleigh might not have much more time."

Sheila said, "Who's Kayleigh?"

****

By the time we brought Sheila up to date on the situation, it seemed like days later, though only a half an hour had passed. Sheila handled the whole scene with remarkable aplomb, considering the worst thing she had imagined dealing with was a depressed and desperate me. But here she was, learning about rogue Weres and murders and human enemies and kidnappings. And she'd shared her secret. I was a bit worried she'd pull a maternal role and start to chastise me about returning to Oregon and letting the experts solve this crime. Instead, she gamely took in the situation and signed up for the fight.

Even though we were in a hurry, Sheila gave a brief explanation of her magic. She said witchcraft consisted of calling on the four elements and using one's will to manipulate their energy toward the desired effect. Each spell needed specific manifestations of the elements in order to have the best rate of success. For instance, a scrying spell worked best with a smooth pebble representing earth, though spells related to dreaming worked best with plants serving as the earth-totem. It all sounded pretty complicated to me—no wonder her granny left her multiple volumes of material.

"Talk to me about the scrying spell," said Eliza, sounding just a hair short of commandeering. "What do you need and what would you see?"

"I focus the spell on a particular person and see them at that moment. I need...Let's see. It needs to be someone I'm familiar with or I need a personal item from that person. I need a smooth pebble, preferably a black pebble, about so big." She held up her finger and thumb an inch and a half apart. "Spring water in a metal, silver-colored bowl—doesn't have to be actual silver, any silvery metal works. A candle, lilac-colored, but unscented."

"What about wind?" I asked.

"My breath. That's one of the most commonly used forms of wind, luckily."

"Yeah, especially since the other stuff is so specific. A lilac candle? Can't you just say light purple?"

Sheila arched her brows. "Certainly one could say light purple. But holding the idea of lilacs in one's mind aids the spell."

"Uh-huh." I loved the lofty tone from someone suddenly very comfortable being the resident expert Witch.

I wasn't a hundred percent sure why I felt snotty all of a sudden. From the looks Eliza and Sheila gave me, I acted a bit rude, too. Sheila—exuberant Sheila, who actually had men stop in their tracks to watch her as she passed by, who was smart *and* savvy—was also a Witch. Sitting in a room flanked by Eliza and Sheila, I felt powerless and all too human.

Carson, being held by Eliza, started to cry and twisted his little head, looking for me. I took him into my arms, glad someone needed me, anyway, and he immediately rooted against my shirt. Great. Here we were, the Three Musketeers: Were woman, witchy woman, and warm-milk-on-demand woman. If we found the bad guys, maybe I could just squirt them to death.

While I sulked and nursed Carson, Eliza and Sheila continued to discuss our next steps. Eliza wanted Sheila to try scrying for Kayleigh, but Sheila said she needed more than just a name and a description for the spell to work. So we had only one option, head to the Silver Token and see if we could find Kayleigh's possessions.

Chapter Twelve

The Silver Token motel ended up being as cheesy as its name and announced itself with a huge neon sign showing a blinking silver coin dropping into a slot machine. A smaller sign announced "Vacancy." As I slowed to pull in the parking lot, Eliza said, "Wait, drive past." Since I didn't have my turn signal on anyway—whoops—I continued down the road.

"What's up?" I asked.

Eliza cracked the window a teensy, weensy bit and tilted her head back.

"There's a Were nearby. Did you see anyone hanging around outside the motel or on the street?"

Sheila and I shook our heads. My heart beat hard, but I fought to drive normally.

"Hopefully, he couldn't scent me, since I'm in the car," Eliza continued.

"Do you recognize the Were?" I asked, then answered myself. "I guess not, or you wouldn't be worried about it."

"It's one of the Weres from the park where Carlos was murdered," Eliza said, with a grim set to her mouth.

Damn. I'd hoped it might be some random werewolf gambling away his savings.

"What do we do now?" Sheila asked.

Eliza answered slowly, "Well, this is what we wanted, right? To find one of them? I think we head back to the motel, with the car windows shut tightly. You park the car and we look around. Even if it's a hostile Were—which we don't know for sure—there are three of us, which they can't expect. I'm a full moon wolf. A very strong full moon wolf. And I'm already on my guard."

Sheila and I looked at each other through the rear-view mirror. After a long moment, I said, "Mac was a full, too. And now he's dead."

Eliza set her jaw. "Fine. Then let's just go home, is that what you're suggesting?"

I turned the car back toward the Silver Token.

"Don't worry," said Eliza, "we might not even get out of the car."

My palms sweated against the steering wheel as we turned into the parking lot. Through the windows, I saw a couple in the office, probably checking in. A man walked toward one of the room doors. Several people piled into a cab, looking pretty drunk already at seven in the evening. A woman paced back and forth along the walk, talking into her cell phone and gesturing as if the other side of her conversation could see her. I glanced into the backseat and saw Carson had fallen asleep—which was good, at least he wouldn't call attention to us. With a nod from Eliza, I pulled the car into an empty spot near the office.

The motel room doors opened onto the cement walkways on either side of the parking lot, with exterior metal staircases leading to a second floor. The staircases, like the room doors, were coated in peeling green paint that had seen better days. The motel's once-white siding had aged to an unfortunate gray, and most of the rooms had curtains drawn tight to the outside world.

"What now?" asked Sheila, leaning over the seat. "Can you scent the other Were?"

"Mmm, maybe," said Eliza. Suddenly, shadows slid over her, hiding her completely from sight even though we sat mere inches from her in the same car. We heard, "stay here," then the door opening and closing.

"Shit, Eliza," I hissed, peering through the window.

I couldn't see her. I knew she was there and it seemed as if she ought to be visible, if I could just force my eyes to focus. Alternately, I felt I should see some sort of cloud of darkness, if not Eliza's actual form. Instead, my eyes continued to slide from the very spots I wanted to watch, as if the entire evening darkened with a subtle haze that lacked direction or focus.

"What the hell?" Sheila exclaimed.

"She called the moon, called on it to shift light and darkness. She's out there somewhere, and I'm going to *kill* her when she gets back here."

"Can the other Were sense her through that?"

"I have no idea. I imagine she can't hide her scent."

We waited for a few minutes. I noticed Sheila—like me—glanced in all directions as if we should see something.

"Should I...should I lock the doors?" My hand hovered over the button.

"What if she needs to get back into the car in a hurry?"

"Damn you, Eliza. What happened to looking around?" I studiously unclenched my hands. "Is Carson doing okay?"

"Yeah, he's still fast asleep."

"I hope no one can scent *him* in the car."

A sudden cackling laugh broke through the ambient noise of the night and caused both of us to bolt upright. I grabbed the steering wheel reflexively, heart pounding. The shrieking laughter continued, coming from the staircase at the far side of the motel. A man stumbled down the last few green steps, seemingly drunk, and weaved down the walk. He stopped mid-stride, one foot in the air, and extended his hands to the sky. Dropping to one knee on the pavement, he declaimed in a loud voice, "Oh blessed night, oh angel darkness, oh silver mother moon, watching all your children!"

I relaxed incrementally. "Only in Vegas," I said to Sheila, as the drunk man continued to bellow poetry at the top of his lungs.

The next moment, Eliza stood at the man's side. She grabbed him around the shoulders and walked him toward our car. He turned to her in mixed confusion and pleasure, stumbling slightly.

"Do I know you?" he slurred in a loud voice. "You smell like cats."

Eliza appeared nothing more than solicitous as she collared him the last few feet to the car. Keeping one hand on him, she wrenched open Sheila's door and said, "Front seat." Eliza's face was coated in a film of sweat, and she breathed hard through her fixed smile. Sheila quickly scrambled out of the car and into the front seat, upon which Eliza got into the backseat, in the middle, next to Carson, and pulled the man in after her. She reached over to close the door, hitting the door lock firmly.

"Okay, go," she said, one hand gripping the man's arm.

He wasn't much to look at: a little shorter than six feet, skin the color of black coffee, hair about a week past needing a trim, a bit of a baby face and a genial demeanor. Muddy brown eyes surrounded his widened pupils. I would pass him on the street without a second glance—unless he acted like a crazy drunk. He peered over Eliza into Carson's car seat. I made a mental note to thank her for not sitting this crazy guy next to the baby.

Then he said, "Coochie coo, little puppy," and broke into laughter again as chills shot up my spine.

"Go! Julie, get us out of here. I don't know how long I can hold him, and we need to get away from people," Eliza said urgently.

Shit! This drunk was our Were?

The engine roared before I realized I turned the ignition. Taking a deep breath, I steadied myself before switching into reverse and driving out of the parking lot. It seemed kind of risky to bring him back to our hotel, but I couldn't think of anywhere else to go, so I headed in that direction. My mind swirled.

Eliza growled in the backseat, and I looked into the mirror to see her lunge and hold the man down with both hands. Sweat poured down her face—and mine, as I started freaking out about the two of them having a violent confrontation right next to my baby. Of course, Eliza looked kind of sexy and tough. Me, I just looked sweaty and wild-eyed.

My incongruous thoughts were broken by the man dissolving into a fit of giggles. Eliza loosened her hold, though once again she made sure to maintain physical contact with our mystery guest.

Sheila turned around in her seat staring at the two of them. I saw the tension radiating from her clenched muscles. We two humans were definitely in the midst of some fight-or-flight thing, but we weren't sure what to do with the adrenaline rush.

"Sheila," I said in a low voice, not wanting to distract Eliza from her task. "Where the hell should I go? Back to the hotel? Do we bring him back to the hotel?"

"Where else? I don't know—we didn't exactly plan where to take a hostage." Sheila glanced at me. "Worst case, we ditch him there and find a new hotel."

By the time we pulled into the motel, my neck muscles were knotted and I was sure I had lovely pit stains to attest to my not-so-attractive nervous sweating. When I stopped the car, Sheila jumped out and ran to the back door, presumably to make sure the Were didn't run away. Me, I ran to the other door, opened it, and unsnapped Carson's buckles with shaking fingers. I snatched him from the car seat and backed away from the car. My baby, of course, woke up and started to scream. Great. Nothing like keeping a low profile while moving a hostage Were into our hotel room, right?

Several anxious minutes later, we made it into the room without overly alarming any of the general populace. Eliza hadn't let go of our mystery Were for a moment, Carson settled down in the sling and looked around with bleary eyes, Sheila paced next to the door. Our Were placidly spoke to the lamp on the bedside table. With the four of us jammed into the small room, already crowded just with the two beds, the luggage, and the baby paraphernalia, I wished I'd followed Sheila's advice and looked into a more upscale hotel. Although in that case, she never would have found us.

"Sheila," Eliza's voice sounded strained, "check his pockets for a wallet or anything else."

Sheila sidled up to the Were and gingerly reached into his back pocket to extract a fat black wallet. Backing away several steps, she flipped it open and pulled out a driver's license.

"Tim Rogers," she read. "A New York driver's license."

"Oh," Eliza and I said in chorus. Eliza didn't relinquish her hold on the Were—on Tim—but the set of her shoulders loosened.

"Isn't that the other council investigator?" Sheila asked.

"Yes. What do you think, Eliza, does that mean he's okay? Now what?"

Eliza quirked her mouth to the side. "I guess now I let him go, and we have a talk."

"What are you doing, exactly, anyway?" I took a few steps closer to Tim, staring intently at the wall and giggling.

"I, uh, I called the moon and kind of made him insane. Temporarily."

"Oh. Is that all," I said. Sheila turned to stare at Eliza.

"Hey, it worked, didn't it?"

"Whatever happened to staying in the car and just checking things out?" I demanded.

Sheila jumped in. "Jules, Eliza, can we talk about this when we don't have a currently-insane potential-ally Werewolf giggling in our hotel room?"

Right. Yes. Of course. I gestured Eliza to proceed.

Eliza drew in a deep breath, then released Tim's arm. All three of us tensed as we watched him. For a few seconds, nothing seemed to change. Then he stopped giggling, but remained staring at the wall. In the next instant, he whirled around to face us. He dropped into a crouch, arms raised. His eyes widened in alarm, pupils no longer dilated. My skin felt tight from the energy spilling into the room, and I noticed Sheila hugging her arms as if to ward off a chill. Tim and Eliza remained still, both ready for sudden movement, their gazes locked as if they were the only two in the room. One of them growled softly; I couldn't tell which.

I cleared my throat and tried to speak once or twice before sound emerged. "We're here to help you, Tim. We're sorry—Eliza's sorry—she called the moon on you. She thought you were one of the enemies."

Tim didn't respond, so I continued my halting explanation. "We're on the side of the council, trying to figure out who murdered the Weres and kidnapped Kayleigh."

I saw the effort Eliza extended as she forced herself to drop her hands, stand in a relaxed pose, and take a step backward. She took a deep breath.

"It's true. I'm Eliza Minuet, from Roger MacGregor's pack in Wyoming. This is his son, Carson."

Tim's gaze moved between the three of us—four of us, actually, since he definitely noted Carson. He gradually straightened, though I had the feeling he might still pounce at a moment's notice.

"Well, I must say this was a bizarre way to introduce yourselves, if indeed you mean me no harm." His mild voice was utterly at odds with the sense of deadly energy that still radiated from his figure.

"I apologize. I thought you might be one of the Weres responsible for all of this," Eliza explained again, hands open and spread wide.

"We don't know anything about the Weres involved," Tim said.

"Actually," I said, "we do. Suzy Zhang reported a strange Were visited her—called himself Taylor Dunn—and asked a lot of questions about you and Kayleigh. He's not too tall, blond, and has a beard. In the course of their conversation, she told him which hotel you were at."

Tim looked at me for a moment, before he nodded and his shoulders relaxed.

"All right," he said, "If we're going to work on this together, I need to know everything you know. And I want to know how a full moon," he gestured to Eliza, "a Witch," he tilted his head to Sheila, who had been silent through this whole exchange, "and, apparently, a dark moon with a full moon pup ended up as part of this investigation."

Sheila extended a hand in a grand gesture. "It's a long, long story, Tim Rogers. I, for one, need some sustenance before this exchange. And perhaps a glass of wine. It's been a very trying day."

Eliza laughed, I rolled my eyes, and Tim just looked puzzled. Leave it to Sheila.

Chapter Thirteen

Even though we were all conscious of the grave danger Kayleigh might be in, we decided Sheila's point had merit. Funny how relief from fear made us all hungry. After taking care of mundane details—changing Carson's diaper, returning Tim's wallet, introducing ourselves fully, etc.—we piled back into my car and headed to a nearby brew pub. We ordered food and drinks and started from the beginning.

Now that we weren't trying to abduct him or make him insane, Tim turned out as genial as he appeared. I wondered how strong a Were he was—after all, he'd been overcome by Eliza pretty easily—but I reminded myself of the incongruous Lily Rose and tried not to jump to conclusions. I almost asked him outright, but realized at the last minute it might be a rude question. I'd find out from Eliza later.

Tim listened intently to Eliza recount our meeting with Suzy, raised his eyebrows at our brief explanation of Sheila's witchcraft, and nodded as my history with Mac apparently explained both Carson's existence and our vested interest in the investigation. Tim didn't seem surprised our presence in Vegas wasn't sanctioned by the council; apparently, he had gathered as much from our unorthodox grouping and behavior. He listened with a neutral expression to our speculations about a traitor within the council, nodding in agreement with some of our points. In trade for our stories, he told us about the last few days and Kayleigh's disappearance.

"So," he concluded, "she's been missing for just over a day. Mac was missing for four days before his murder, so hopefully she's still alive. It's actually a good sign she was kidnapped, I think, since Carlos was murdered right away. Carlos must have been onto something forcing them to kill him immediately. But we don't have time to waste." He ran a hand over his head, leaving several of the tight dark curls standing straight up. He explained he'd already retraced Kayleigh's steps through the city, confirming her presence at two police stations and an animal control office before losing her scent. He hadn't sensed any other Weres at those locations. He'd returned to the Silver Token to see if traces of anyone staking out those rooms remained.

I stared down at my nearly untouched pint of stout. No, I didn't like stout, I hadn't forgotten, but somehow ordering it made me feel closer to Mac. In a weird and kind of painful way. A silly notion and right then, I really wished I'd ordered a pale ale after all.

Eliza leaned forward, articulating clearly, "Tim, do you have access to Kayleigh's things? Her personal possessions?"

He nodded, gaze moving to Sheila's face.

"All right then," said our Witch as she lifted her glass, "bottoms up and let's get to work."

****

Of course, it wasn't quite that easy. They dropped me back at our hotel first, so I could put Carson to bed before he lost it completely. Sheila took a moment to nick into the office and pay for another room; she was lucky enough to get one next door to Eliza and me. While Sheila made arrangements and Tim was in the bathroom, Eliza checked in with me.

"Will you be all right alone here for a while?" she asked quietly, searching my face. "We need to get Sheila's supplies and I'm not sure I trust Tim enough to send Sheila alone with him."

"Do you think he's a traitor?" I kept my voice equally low and my eyes trained on the bathroom door.

"I don't know. I haven't found anything suspicious, but..." She shrugged.

"I'll be fine," I said. I'm pretty sure she knew I lied, but she let my words stand.

"You *will* be fine. If I could be in two places at once..."

Tim came out of the bathroom and Eliza smiled at me, squeezed my arm tightly, and turned to include him in the conversation.

"So, Tim," she said lightly, "you know this area better than we do. We need to find a silver metal bowl, a smooth black pebble, and a lilac-colored candle. Any ideas?"

****

After the three of them left, I locked the door. Actually, I locked three locks on the door and closed that little weird metal bar thing they have in hotel rooms. I checked the lock on the window. Then I made sure the room phone worked, just in case I needed to call 911 or something. And I confirmed I had cell coverage. Just in case. Because I would be fine.

Carson definitely picked up my tension, because it took almost forty-five minutes for me to get him to sleep. Finally, he conked out on one side of the hotel bed, and I slid from his side to sit with my back against the headboard, knees up and hugged to my chest. The room was almost totally dark, just enough light for me to watch my sweet little boy breathe. I told myself to stop looking at the clock; they'd be back soon and the shopping just took longer than they'd expected. I tried to slow my breathing to Carson's and mimic the relaxed abandon with which he sprawled on the bed.

No good.

I got to my feet, paced around the room and, against my better judgment, went to look out the window. I knelt down, eyes level with the sill—I'd read in some mystery novel you were less of a target if you didn't put your body where expected—and carefully prepared to twitch aside the curtains to peek out.

I practically jumped through the roof when someone tapped on the door. *Dammit!* My heart imitated a jackhammer for a moment and I sank back, hand to chest, catching my breath. The tap came again, this time in a shave-and-a-haircut pattern, probably Sheila. To be on the safe side, I checked through the curtain and confirmed Sheila, Eliza, and Tim. I checked once again through the peephole, just for surety, unlocked my gazillion locks and that metal bar, and opened the door.

"Carson's sleeping," I said. "What the hell took you so long? I've been freaking out."

Sheila winked. "Can't rush perfection, Jules."

Eliza raised her eyebrows and elaborated. "Our friend Sheila wasn't happy with the seven million shades of light purple candles we found at the first store, so we had to go to a different store to find the perfect lilac candle. Then we had to stop at Tim's hotel so he could retrieve something of Kayleigh's."

"Oh."

Standing behind Eliza and Sheila, Tim held the shopping bags. So now we knew where he stayed. He looked less and less like a traitor.

I asked, "Are we doing this in Sheila's room?"

"That would make the most sense," said Sheila.

"Eliza, do you think Carson will be safe in the room, if I turn the baby monitor on and lock him in and I'm just next door?"

Eliza looked around the parking lot, considering. "I think so. We'll be right there. But if you feel safer, you can stay with Carson and we can handle the scrying."

I was torn: it felt unnatural to leave Carson right now, even to go next door. At the same time, I wanted to witness our so-called Witch at work and I wasn't sure I could handle waiting alone.

"Eliza, will you stay on high alert? With all your senses?"

When she nodded, I made my decision and told myself not to second-guess everything. I checked on Carson one more time—still sleeping peacefully—placed the monitor right next to the bed, and locked him in. Once in Sheila's room, I sat by the shared wall, somehow feeling an added closeness. Immediately, I turned on the receiver part of the monitor. I knew I was over-reacting a bit: when at home, Carson was often much farther away, but this felt like more distance. I wasn't a hundred percent sure if the hotel environment was to blame or the potential deadly danger we faced. Okay, that was a lie. I was sure the reason was the deadly danger. But even if I was in the room, what help would I be? Me, the powerless human? I let out a breath and turned my attention to Sheila's preparations.

Sheila spread out one of her scarves on the carpet and arranged the items carefully. She uncapped a bottle of expensive mineral water and poured it into the bowl. Picking up a small rock Eliza said they'd bought in the gardening section at the superstore, our Witch held it tightly for a moment, before releasing it into the bowl where it sank with a faint plop. She set the lilac candle behind the bowl, so she, sitting cross-legged, the bowl, and the candle were in a line.

"Tim?" she said, not lifting her gaze from the bowl.

"Here's Kayleigh's brush. She uses it frequently." Tim handed the brush over. It wasn't remarkable, just a tortoise shell brush with no evidence it belonged to a kidnapped Werewolf.

"Perfect." Sheila studied the brush for a moment, closed her eyes, ran her fingers along it and even brought it to her face. She untwined one long blonde hair from the tines and, with a slight hesitation, wrapped it around the candle. She then placed the brush directly in front of her, nearly touching the bowl.

Looking up at us for the first time, Sheila took a breath, released it slowly, and nodded. She leaned forward, struck a match, and lit the candle.

I found myself holding my breath, even as Sheila blew carefully on the surface of the water. Small ripples moved in the bowl as the candle flame danced. The water fell still—as still as the four of us in the room—and Sheila gazed intently into the bowl.

Several minutes passed with the baby monitor's faint white noise the only sound in the room. Suddenly, the candle flared, its flame shot up several inches, and then just as quickly guttered. A thin coil of smoke curled upward as Sheila sighed deeply and sat back. She pressed her palms against her eyes, rubbing firmly, then looked at us all.

"Give me a minute, folks," she said. She flopped back on the floor, apparently oblivious to the fact this *was* a motel and the carpet was none too clean. She closed her eyes again.

"Wow, am I going to have a headache. I guess I'm a little out of practice." She opened her eyes. "Okay. I saw her, so she's still alive. That's the good news. The not-so-good news is she's confined, locked in a room, and it looks like she hasn't been treated very well."

"Describe the room," Tim said.

"Off-white walls, beige carpet, both on the run-down side. Stains on the carpet. One door and a window with heavy dark curtains—I couldn't see anything out the window. No furniture except for a mattress, a bare mattress on the floor. Kayleigh lay there, curled on her side, wearing what almost looked like a hospital gown? She had visible bruises on her arms, on the inside elbow, almost like track marks." Sheila roused herself on one elbow. "Don't you Weres heal quickly? Does that mean the bruises are recent? How long would they take to heal?"

Eliza answered, "We do heal quickly—bruises usually fade in minutes, unless there are mitigating circumstances of some kind."

"What else?" Tim asked.

"Her hands and feet are bound with duct tape and thin chains woven around them, almost like necklaces. Silver, I'm guessing?"

Eliza nodded grimly. "That would definitely slow healing, the presence of silver."

"The room was brightly lit." Sheila thought for a minute. "I think that's all." She groaned and held her head tightly. "My head is going to explode. Does anyone have any ibuprofen?"

"I do," I said, "back in my room. Hold on a second."

Carson still slept soundly, so I closed the room door lightly and darted into the bathroom to grab my bottle of ibuprofen. On the way out of the bathroom, I registered the front door open about two inches, letting in the light from the parking lot. Then, I saw the figure leaning over the bed. I shrieked and instinctively threw what I had in my hand. Yes, I chucked a pill bottle at the intruder.

I'm sure it would have been more impressive had I been holding a ninja-star or something, but my aim was true and the pill bottle distracted the person. At least, he jerked slightly and it took that extra second or two for him to pull out his gun. I saw the dark metal barrel reflecting the parking lot lights and I froze in place; time stretching as the gun moved to point in my direction. So focused on the weapon, I didn't even notice the door swing fully open and I wasn't aware anyone else had entered the room until someone tackled the man. Apparently, he wasn't aware either, because his attention didn't waver from me. Then, in the next instant, everything turned into a blur of shadow and noise on the hotel room floor. Grunts, growls, what sounded like the man swearing and—my heart jumped—one, two noises I retroactively identified as gunshots from a silenced weapon.

My paralysis broke, and I jumped onto the bed nearest the bathroom. I actually leaped over the writhing mass between the beds, hoping like hell no one would shoot wildly toward the ceiling, and landed next to Carson whose eyes and mouth were wide in the dark, though no sound. I grabbed him to my chest, rolled over the bed, and backed away from the fight. Should I run out the door? Were there others in the parking lot?

Just as suddenly as it began, the room went quiet, except for the thudding of my own heart and panting—my own panting and someone else's. Then Carson let loose with a siren wail, which served to electrify my remaining nerves. At the same time, I felt somehow reassured. This, I could handle.

"Julie, is he okay?" Eliza knelt in the dark room. She cleared her throat and spat on the carpet. "Shit."

A shadow appeared at the front door. I jumped back in fear before the lights flicked on and I saw Sheila. She looked as wide-eyed and pale as I felt.

"Julie? Are you both okay?" Eliza asked again over Carson's cries.

"Yes," I said. "At least, I think so." I checked Carson over with quick pats, but he seemed absolutely fine.

When I looked at Eliza, I recoiled. The strong hotel lights revealed a scene of B-movie horror: she was covered in blood, surrounding her mouth, spreading down her front and all over her hands. She spat again and I felt my gorge rising as I realized why. I slumped back against the wall quickly and closed my eyes. I told myself sternly not to faint and held tight to that thought for the space of several breaths.

"We have to move quickly, folks," said Tim and I realized for the first time he was on the floor with Eliza. And the body. I couldn't see the whole body from where I stood, only one leg lying oddly and sticking out from between the beds. "First, Sheila, inside and close the door. I'm not sure how much attention we just attracted, but let's not invite gawkers."

Sheila promptly obeyed, looking relieved to have someone issuing concrete orders.

"Eliza, get one of the spare blankets from the closet," he continued. "Unless you're injured?"

"I'm fine. Just overzealous. I didn't mean to kill him." She grimaced.

"Better him than one of us." Tim gestured with his chin toward the closet and Eliza followed his direction.

From Tim's movement and the change in position of...the leg, I knew he riffled through the man's pockets. He tossed a gun on the bed and pulled out a key ring, some tissues, a pack of cigarettes with a lighter. No wallet. No pack of matches with the name of the hotel where Kayleigh might be held. That would have been nice. Miss Marple probably would have had that kind of luck.

"Julie," Tim's voice was grim. "Look at this man and make sure you don't know him."

Carson had stopped crying, though he was wide awake and looked, in fact, like he'd never sleep again. I handed him off to Sheila, steeled myself, and walked around the bed.

The man wore khakis and a striped golf shirt. At least—I swallowed hard and dug my fingernails into my palms—it looked as if it had been striped, underneath all the blood. Part of his shirt was torn away, probably by claws, and deep wounds were carved in the man's gut. His neck was a mangled mass of blood and flesh, but his face was curiously untouched. I focused on that. Ruddy complexion, blue eyes, brown hair, heavyset. I studied him carefully to make sure the shock of seeing him in this situation didn't cloud my memory, but I ended up absolutely sure I didn't know him.

"Tim, I've seen him before. He was outside the MacGregor's house in Wyoming. He shot me, actually—that's probably why I overreacted," Eliza said.

At her words, I stepped closer to the man and gazed down at him. This man was the one stalking us in Greybull? Was he the same one who rammed my car? Did he follow us from Wyoming or somehow pick up our trail here in Vegas?

"I've never seen him," I said.

"And he has no ID." Tim sat back on his heels. Unlike Eliza, his clothes sported only the smallest of blood spots.

At some later point in time, I would have to think about the fact my new friend had such a capacity for carnage. Right now, I just said, "Eliza, do you want to go wash off?"

"Yes," said Tim decisively. "Bring your clothes, the washcloths, and the towels you use back here."

Eliza handed Tim the towel, detoured to her suitcase, and disappeared into the bathroom. We heard the water running for quite a while.

Sheila still stood by the door with Carson. She hadn't said one word and I wondered how much she regretted her impulse to get on that plane to Las Vegas.

I smiled at her, weakly, and walked over to retrieve Carson.

Squeezing her arm, I asked quietly, "Are you all right?"

"Me?" She cleared her throat as her voice squeaked. "I'm fine. I wasn't the one attacked or..."

Killed. The ending of the sentence echoed in my head.

"I know." I nestled Carson into me, a rush of gratitude for his safety threatening to overwhelm me completely. I had *not* fainted this time and I would *not* cry. Deep breaths.

I shook my head. "I just don't understand. Is it Carson? Why Carson? Why would these people want Carson? Yes, he's a full moon Were and a strong one. But he's a baby. He's helpless; he can't do anything with his powers yet."

Something clicked in my brain.

"That's it, isn't it?" My voice rang flat in my own ears. "They want him because he's helpless. Because he can't fight back. Because he's strong—or he'll be strong—but he's not a threat. They want him. For something."

"But for what?" Sheila's question voiced what we all wondered. And we had no answers. Dammit.

****

After midnight, we finished cleaning up the mess, both literal and figurative. Tim wrapped up the body, along with all the soiled clothes and towels, in the motel blanket. A scratchy, dirty shroud for our enemy, which I thought grimly fitting. With the help of the man's own car keys, Tim and Eliza had thoroughly searched his car. Not the blue sedan that forced me off the road, by the way, but a full-size black sedan with dark, tinted windows. The scariest—and most infuriating—thing they found was a stash of three baby blankets, a pack of diapers, and a case of formula in the trunk. Yes, he had definitely planned to kidnap my baby. The bastard. I had quickly moved from being completely nauseated to feeling like perhaps ripping the guy's throat out had been too quick a death. Um, except when I actually thought about the mess made of the guy, I still felt the earth reel beneath my feet. I feared I'd see those images for quite a long time in my dreams.

The car had no paperwork indicating insurance or registration. Tim would ask a contact in the DMV to trace the license plate, but he was convinced he'd get no useful information. The man's gun was a .22, a Beretta model 87 Cheetah, according to Tim. Knowing approximately nothing about guns, I believed him.

I found it harder to believe the conclusion he drew.

We gathered in Sheila's room, before Tim went on a grisly errand to ditch the car and the body.

"Looks like organized crime," Tim announced in his mild voice. "Everything about this guy's setup, from clothes to weapons to vehicle, points to the mafia."

A beat of silence reigned in the room as everyone digested this idea.

Then we all talked at once. "The mafia knows about Werewolves?" Eliza said. "How can we fight the mafia?" Sheila said. "The fucking mafia is after my baby?" I said. I have an issue with anger and swearing.

"Calm down." Tim raised his hand. "Listen, knowing it's organized crime doesn't change anything. We still search for a well-prepared group of multiple humans in league with at least one Were. The larger ramification of ties to the mafia is something for the council to deal with: how widespread is the knowledge, how can it be contained, how are they trying to exploit our existence? I'll alert the council to this possibility immediately and tell them we—I—will continue to investigate. We don't need to deal with any of that. We need to protect Carson, rescue Kayleigh, and identify at least some of the key players in this group."

Gee. When he put it like that, it seemed so simple.

"Do you think it's safe to bring the council into this?" Eliza asked. She had spent the last two hours scrubbing the carpet in our hotel room, apparently using some special solvent and soap meant to take out bloodstains. I tried not to think about how Tim knew exactly where to purchase such supplies. I thought the room might pass a cursory inspection, but I certainly hoped no evidence prompted a thorough forensic investigation. At least if it was the mafia, they weren't likely to notify the police their hired goon was missing.

"At this point, I don't think I can risk not telling the council. After all, if this truly is the work of the mafia and knowledge of Werewolves has become at all widespread…Well, it could be a huge threat." Tim fiddled idly with the dead man's car keys.

"But if someone on the council is in league with them? And knows that we know?" Sheila leaned forward urgently, her blue eyes full of concern.

Tim sighed. "I'll be circumspect. I'll report to my supervisor and relay concerns that someone inside the council may be part of this. I think it's time for us to change location and not tell anyone where we're staying. Even my contacts at the council."

We all nodded in agreement.

"All right, then." Tim stood and ran his hands over his tight curls, weariness showing in every action. He seemed so mild and unassuming, but able to make such quick command decisions—I hadn't quite figured him out. "I'm going to take care of the car and the body."

"What are you going to do?" Sheila said, stifling a yawn.

I rubbed my eyes. Damned contagious yawns.

Tim shrugged. "I'll drive out into the desert, find a remote place with some sort of cover, then torch the car with the body in it. I figure if it works for the mafia, it'll work for us. Maybe they'll assume a rival family did it."

"How will you get back?" I wondered aloud.

"I'll shift and run back. It might take me a while, depending on how far I have to go. Don't look for me before noon or so." With that, Tim said farewell and left.

"All right. So I guess we'll stay here until Tim gets back, then move." Sheila yawned again and pushed back her heavy blonde hair. Here it was, way past midnight on a night full of violence, terror, and blood, and Sheila still looked gorgeous. How did she manage? I wish I could have chalked it up to witchcraft, that's for sure.

I looked down at Carson, sleeping on me in his sling, and sighed. I was definitely not letting him out of my sight anytime soon. If ever again.

Chapter Fourteen

Even Carson was exhausted, so exhausted he slept until almost nine the next morning. Or technically that same morning, I guess. We crashed hard after Tim's departure, Sheila and I on the two double beds in her room—me, with Carson practically attached to my body. Eliza curled in wolf form on the floor. She claimed she was just as comfortable when furry, and also her senses remained more acute, just in case another threat arose. Personally, I probably would have slept through anything short of an earthquake. A strong earthquake, at that.

When Carson roused and made his little mewling noises, I groaned and Sheila flung her hands out.

"Can't you tell him we still need our beauty sleep?" She turned over. "Talk about a long night."

Eliza, on the other hand, sat up quickly, shaking herself almost as if still in wolf form.

"Time to get up, folks. Tim should be back soon and Kayleigh's still in danger."

She was right, of course. Somehow, the aftermath of last night and my intensified worry about my baby forced Kayleigh's situation to the back of my mind. I took care of Carson while I thought about the next steps.

Actually, that's a bald-faced lie. I thought about coffee. Lovely coffee. Piping hot black coffee. I thought after coffee, after several mugs of coffee, I would be able to think about the next steps. But first, coffee.

Half an hour later, we were basically awake and sitting in a restaurant down the street that did, indeed, serve the requisite morning coffee. Even good coffee, though I would have been happy enough with anything purported to contain caffeine. I poked the last remnants of eggs around my plate and smiled in gratitude at the waitress who continued to promptly refill my mug. Needing a mental break from tales of murder, kidnapping, and the mafia, we'd kept the breakfast conversation light by unspoken accord. Eliza devoured a stack of pancakes and mopped up some spots of syrup with the last bit of her second helping of bacon.

"What," she said to me. It wasn't quite a question.

I started slightly. "What?"

Eliza set down her fork and fixed her attention on me. "You've been surreptitiously staring at me throughout breakfast. I think we should just talk about it."

"Talk about what?" I lifted my coffee and took a large sip.

"All right. If you're not going to say it, I will. 'Eliza, have you killed a man before? Eliza, do you often go crazy and rip people's throats out? Eliza, how can you just sit there and eat breakfast, as if you didn't maul someone twelve hours ago? Which tastes better, bacon or human flesh?' " Eliza's voice was low, but nearly shaking with anger.

I didn't know what to say. Those were my exact thoughts, but it sounded so vicious uttered aloud.

"Now, Eliza." Sheila's warm drawl broke the tension. "We're all sure bacon tastes better. I know that I, for one, am just happy to have the bloodthirsty, crazed monster on our side." Sheila winked at Eliza and nonchalantly spread strawberry jam on a piece of whole wheat toast, hold the butter.

Eliza sighed and dropped her head into her hands briefly. Then she sat up and addressed us both.

"Sorry. I'm a little sensitive. I didn't actually mean to kill that man, but when I saw him threatening you, Julie, and Carson, and I realized he was the same man I'd fought in Greybull, well, I acted irrationally. I guess I'm angry with myself—I shouldn't project it onto you two."

I chose my words carefully. "To be honest, Eliza, everything that happened last night shocked me. I know you wanted to protect us and I am very grateful. But this was the first time I've really been exposed to the…potential for violence…Werewolves have. It shook me. But it doesn't change my basic opinion of you—you're still Eliza, I'm still glad to have you here. I still want to be your friend." I shifted uncomfortably in my seat.

"Thank you," Eliza said quietly.

"Cheers, then." Sheila lifted her cup of tea—crazy girl, not liking coffee—and leaned forward. "To the three of us. Friends and accomplices, no matter what."

We joined her in the toast and, corny as it was, I felt a glow of warmth not entirely explained by the caffeine coursing through my veins.

"Okay, then, troops." Sheila broke through our smiles. "I'd like to run to the store and get some supplies. I think I might take some time this afternoon to make some protective charms for the three of us—actually, the five of us; Carson and Tim, too. And I had another idea. If we haven't made any progress finding Kayleigh by nightfall, I'd like to try to dreamwalk and talk to her. Perhaps, she can give us some clues as to where she's being kept."

I nodded enthusiastically. "I'm glad someone has some positive ideas."

"I think someone should wait at the hotel when Tim returns," Eliza said, "because we want to check into a new place as soon as we possibly can."

In the end, we decided Sheila and I would go shopping and Eliza would wait for Tim. Even in broad daylight, I didn't feel comfortable staying alone at the hotel with Carson, just in case someone else continued to stalk us. I didn't trust myself to protect him alone. We'd still be sans Werewolf, but I felt safer surrounded by other people in, say, a department store. Eliza asked us three times if we felt safe without Were protection, but she also seemed happy to have some time to herself. I think she was still working through her own actions the previous night. While I could admit I, too, was still taken aback by the vision of Eliza tearing out the throat of our assailant, I also hoped she wouldn't start second-guessing herself in a way detrimental to our mission. More than likely we'd need her capacity as a—what had Sheila said—a bloodthirsty, crazed monster in the next few days. Ah well, she was our monster, anyway. I gave her a big hug, and we dropped her off at the motel.
****

Sheila and I must have met our capacity for stress and worry, because we tacitly avoided talking about anything involving the mafia, murder, Werewolves, or

Witches during our shopping jaunt. We went back to the large store where Sheila had shopped the night before to pick up her supplies for dreamwalking. We chatted for a few minutes about Sheila's latest dating exploits—Bryan was already history—and dropped a couple of quarters in the slot machines. Yes, the store had slot machines. Only in Vegas. Sheila complained good-naturedly about some of her summer session students, who had apparently registered for her classes thinking Rhetoric and Persuasion meant an excuse to argue. She often complained about teaching, but it didn't fool me: she thrived in the classroom.

I laughed nearly uncontrollably at Sheila's story of a seventeen-year-old student hitting on her—he'd thought it was a turn-on to unbutton his shirt while asking if she was a "cougar"—when my phone rang.

I grabbed it from my pocket, then relaxed as I saw my mom calling.

"Hi, Mom," I said and waved Sheila to silence. She proceeded to dance around, making funny faces, and causing Carson to scream with laughter, almost as disruptive as a crying fit. I didn't mind, though, because after a short and stilted conversation with my mom, I made my excuses and hang up.

Nonetheless, my happy-go-lucky mood had been disrupted by the juxtaposition of my mother asking normal parental questions while I continued subterfuge and pretended I wasn't stalking the mafia around Las Vegas and my bloodline didn't somehow contain Were ancestry.

We paid for our purchases and walked out to the car. I was still in deep thought and Sheila sensitive to my mood—or lost in thought of her own.

As we drove down the street back toward the hotel, I saw something that made me pull over quickly and stop the car.

"What are we doing?" Sheila asked.

"A library," I said, already opening my door. "Let's just go in for a few minutes and see what kind of information we can dig up on the Las Vegas mafia."

Sheila unbuckled Carson and followed me dubiously.

"Sheila." I looked at my friend in exasperation. "We might learn something helpful."

Within five minutes, I had Sheila parked in front of a computer scrolling down webpages about the Vegas mafia as I hurried to grab a few books off the shelves. Carson happily waved a little slip of scrap paper around, which was fine with me as long as he didn't try to eat it.

While I perused a short stack of books, Sheila kept up a running—whispered—commentary about what she found on the internet.

"Wow, look at this, an abstract of a paper about women in the mafia: 'Wom/in: Gender Difference in the Mafia.' Huh, it analyzes a few movies, one of which takes place in Las Vegas..."

"Sheila. Focus. We're not researching for a conference paper, you know."

"Right," she said, but she continued skimming the article.

I flipped through my own finds: *Casinos, Money-Laundering, and The Mafia, Rise and Fall of the Lansky Family*, and *The Stardust: From Mob to Money-Maker*. It didn't take long before I'd gleaned the salient points.

"Well." I pushed back from the table and plucked Carson from Sheila's lap. "According to the FBI, there's much less mafia activity in Las Vegas since 1994 or so. At least, the last big roundups they discuss were in the 1980s, when they arrested a number of family heads in the Midwest—Cleveland, Chicago, Milwaukee, Kansas City—affiliated with the crime in Vegas. Whatever's going on now seems more underground, not like the good old days of mob-operated casinos and money-laundering."

"So what does that tell us?" Sheila asked.

"Well, if the mafia is low key, then it's improbable they have the police completely in their pocket. Meaning we don't have to worry about police investigating the...murder...of that guy last night and tracing it to us. It's also interesting so many of the mafia families are national. I never thought about mob families from places like Milwaukee being involved in the scene here."

Sheila nodded. "Did you find anything about the Japanese mafia? The Yakusa?"

"Nope. Nothing. Looks like, if anything, we're dealing with plain old homegrown organized crime."

I frowned as a thought occurred to me. "It seems odd the mafia would be quiescent since the mid-1990s, when Las Vegas used to be such a profitable base."

I met Sheila's eyes. "Maybe this," I gestured vaguely, "is part of a new power play by one of the families."

Sheila nodded, slowly, and we filed back to the car.
****

I must admit my body tensed as we approached the motel. I tried not to imagine all the things that could have gone wrong while we were away. We didn't even have a chance to knock on the door, because Eliza opened it as we approached.

"Super Were senses strike again?" I joked in relief.

"You know it, human." Eliza grinned. She continued in a near-whisper, "Tim's back and taking a power nap."

"Oh," I said. "Should we go into the...other room?" The murder room? The bloody room?

Sheila seemed to share my thoughts. "Actually, Eliza, how about Jules and I go pick up some sandwiches for lunch? Then we can check into our new hotel and I can get to work."

"Hey, Eliza," I said, "how strong is Tim, anyway? I've been meaning to ask for a while."

She shrugged. "Strong enough. Waxing moon, mid-range for that. Not as strong as me, of course."

Of course. Sheila smiled at her in shared kinship. I tried not to roll my eyes at either of my supernaturally-oh-so-powerful friends.

We dilly-dallied during the lunch errand, trying to give Tim enough time to recuperate, and returned with a box full of sandwiches, chips, and pickles. Tim sat up as we entered the room.

"Do I smell roast turkey?" he asked, through a slight yawn. He looked a bit worse for the wear, his baby-face droopy with fatigue.

"Sure thing, handsome," said Sheila, plopping the box of sandwiches down on the bed. "We got turkey, ham, and roast beef. Take your pick."

Diving into the food, Tim emerged with a foot-long turkey sub, a bag of cheddar-flavored chips, and a soda.

He barely waited to unwrap the food before biting into it.

"What, no rabbits last night?" Eliza took her own sandwich.

Huh? Oh. More wolf jokes.

Tim didn't dignify her with a response, but tore another mouthful off his sub. Sheila watched him and I had a hard time reading her expression. Perhaps, incredulity regarding his lack of table manners? Or maybe she just wondered how the night's exploits went, because she proceeded to ask, "Did everything go okay? Car and body disposed of?"

Tim nodded, then swallowed before speaking, "Yes. I took them about twenty miles out of town, into an area with multiple gulches—dry gulches at this time of year."

"And you ran back twenty miles?" Sheila's eyes remained fixed on him. He glanced at her and nodded with a shrug.

As Tim finished his food and then some, and the rest of us ate our sandwiches, we filled him in on the rest of the day's plans.

"So," I said. "I guess the next question is: where should we stay? Do you know of any other decent motels?" I directed the question to Tim.

"Actually," and Tim smiled with a rakish grin completely at odds with his normal expression, "we're moving to the Bellagio."

As the three of us stared at him blankly, he explained his logic. First, as an upscale, tourist hotel on the Strip, the Bellagio was the opposite of the places we'd stayed up to this point, which might throw our enemies off the scent. Uh, literally. Second, we needed to stay somewhere where a casual scenting of our group wouldn't automatically scream, "Here are the council investigators." If we stayed at the Bellagio, anyone noticing us would naturally assume we were there to enjoy Las Vegas, not to hunt rogue Weres and the mafia. Third, the Bellagio was the type of high-class hotel where we could come and go as we pleased without worrying about bellboys or others gossiping about us. We'd be just one more group of tourists at the casino and, after all, what happens in Vegas stays in Vegas.

I must admit the idea of staying someplace like the Bellagio greatly appealed to me. Aside from the monetary aspect of things. But when I brought up the issue of money, Tim waved his hand and said, "Don't worry about it. I'll expense it."

I looked at him askance. "Even for us? Even though the council doesn't even know we're helping with the investigation?"

He nodded and I decided not to question him any further. Hell, it was the Bellagio.

****

So, that's how our mongrel group of two Werewolves, a Witch, a human, and a Were pup in the midst of throwing a I'm-too-tired-but-I-don't-want-to-nap fit ended up checking into the Bellagio. Tim booked us into two adjoining suites, under assumed names of course. To call the Bellagio a "hotel"—or any other word applicable to our previous rooms—was to confuse filet mignon with ground chuck. From the time we drove up to the entrance and viewed the famous dancing fountains, to the time I gawked at the marble entryway, the huge Chihuly blown-glass flowers on the ceiling, and the sweeping interior staircases, to the time I threw open the door to the first suite, I felt like I stepped farther and farther into a fairytale. In a totally different way than finding out about Werewolves.

"Wow," I said, profound as usual. Our suite—the one for me and Eliza—had two bedrooms and a large living room complete with leather couches, entertainment system, and a fully-equipped kitchenette. The bathroom, practically as big as the living room, contained a huge sunken tub and a separate glassed-in shower with slate walls. And about ten million huge, soft, white towels that, I swear, smelled slightly of cinnamon. In terms of square footage, it probably put my little house in Jacksonville to shame.

A door in the living room—a beautiful door partially concealed by all sorts of moldings—led to the suite next door and so I knocked. Sheila opened the other side and quirked her mouth to one side.

"Jules," she said, "do stop drooling and pretend you've stayed in classy hotels before." She raised her eyebrows in mockery.

"Ha, ha. Anyway, are you sure you'll be all right staying in the other suite with," I lowered my voice, "Tim?"

"There *are* two bedrooms, you know," Sheila said, with a teasing note in her voice.

"That's not what I mean—"

"I know. But, seriously, at this point I think we have to trust him. If he were out to betray us, he could have done it several times by now. Instead, he's been nothing but helpful."

"Yeah. You're right."

"So," Sheila shifted tone yet again, "time for me to work."

****

Carson conked out for a nap almost instantaneously, so I left the adjoining door open and gathered with the others in the second suite. Sheila knelt on the floor to set out the items we bought earlier on our shopping jaunt. She commandeered a glass coffee table as her workspace and, so far, had created a circle of stubby white candles. In the center of the circle, she set the same metal bowl she'd used last night and filled it halfway with mineral water.

Sheila set about tearing the petals off the potted geranium we'd bought. Its white and pink varicolored flowers looked very pretty as Sheila dropped them into the water. Our Witch next took a coil of copper wire, heavy gauge we'd bought at the hardware store, and laid it in a circle surrounding her candles. She crossed the ends of the wire carefully and joined them with a quick twist of her wrist. Next to her setup, she carefully placed five safety pins.

I snorted. Since one of the pins was for Carson, Sheila had been adamant we buy those childproof ones with the plastic tops shaped like animals. When I questioned her choice, she'd replied haughtily her spells would work on anything. We just needed a focus to attach to ourselves.

"Okay, folks." Sheila pulled her hair back and tucked it behind her ears. "This won't be much of a show, but I do need to focus so your silence is appreciated."

The rest of us settled back comfortably and waited. Sheila struck a match and lit the candles, starting at the twelve o'clock position and moving clockwise until all six were lit. Then she picked up a wooden chopstick and stirred the mixture of geranium petals and water. Three times clockwise, one time counterclockwise. Over and over, she repeated the pattern until I lost track of the repetitions. Then she set down the chopstick—outside her copper circle, of course—and leaned forward to blow. Instead of blowing on the water itself, as she had last night, she blew forcefully from the center of the circle out, several times in various directions. She blew well above the candles, of course, so although their flames danced slightly, none guttered. She tilted her head back and blew three times toward the ceiling. Then, she laid her hands on either side of the copper circle, like a set of parenthesis. She closed her eyes and the room was perfectly silent for several minutes. I looked at Tim and Eliza, watching this performance with equal fascination. Eliza caught my gaze and smiled, moving her shoulders as if to say, "Your guess is as good as mine."

Sheila sat back, eyes open but still intent upon her geranium stew. Daintily and with seriousness that utterly belied the ridiculous look of the safety pins, she picked up each pin, turned it in her fingers, and dropped it into the water. Picking up the chopstick, she stirred again, this time starting with a counter-clockwise motion and ending with clockwise. After doing this a number of times—again, I lost track—she put down the chopstick and blew out her candles, starting with the last lit and proceeding to the twelve o'clock position.

"There," she announced, relaxing back on her heels. "Now, each of you needs to pick up your own safety pin from the water. Try to touch only the pin you take. Here, I'll go first." She deftly reached into the water and snagged a safety pin with a big, white sheep on the end. "Don't dry it off, let it air dry."

Eliza went next, peering into the bowl and picking a pin that sported a brown dog's head. Tim followed suit and ended up with a pink pig. My safety pin had a Holstein cow—actually, it looked a lot like Carson's car seat cover. One yellow ducky pin remained in the bowl and I queried, "So, Carson needs to pick up his own pin?"

Sheila frowned. "Well, yes. Or at least, that would be best."

"What if he spills the whole thing, does it matter?" I frowned at the bowl dubiously.

"Well..." Sheila pursed her lips. "I forgot about the four-month-old factor. Since you're his mother and you share blood and body, it will probably be okay for you to take it for him. That's better than the bowl spilling, anyway. I need to dump the petals and water into the earth."

"Into the earth? Are you kidding?" I said. "We're in Vegas, on the Strip. There's probably not a square foot of non-concrete-covered dirt within blocks of us."

"Not so," Sheila said, triumphantly. "There's a botanical garden right here in the Bellagio."

Geez. Only in Vegas.

For the safety of the ritual bowl, I pulled Carson's pin carefully from the water. I didn't pin it on myself, per Sheila's instructions, but after it dried, I put it in my pocket to pin onto Carson's outfit as soon as he woke up. I pinned my own cow on to the underside of my shirt, near my neck.

"Hey, Sheila, how exactly does this work, anyway? In what way will it protect us? Repel bullets, make us invisible?" I asked.

Sheila rolled her eyes. "It's subtle, not something as dramatic as that. Mostly, it'll serve to distract the eye or attention of anyone wishing you harm. The charm may interfere with their aim, if they shoot at you, but it certainly won't actually repel a bullet. It will also increase your...I guess you'd say your ability to attract good luck, which can definitely be useful in a dangerous encounter."

"Huh." The little safety pin didn't look capable of doing any of that. Frankly, I'd rather have a force field that stopped bullets, but I guess you take what you can get.

Eliza looked at her little pin with more respect and attached it to herself, as did Tim.

"Well," Sheila picked up her bowl, "I think I'll go and empty this in the botanical gardens. Jules, do you want to come with me?"

I hesitated for a moment, thinking of Carson, but realized Eliza and Tim could watch him just as well as I—actually, probably better. I wanted to see the rest of the Bellagio. Besides, maybe I'd drop a quarter or two into the slot machines; test this little safety pin's luck.

Sheila and I set off for the gardens, with strict instructions for one of the Weres to call my cell phone if Carson woke up or if anything else happened. Frankly, we all felt equal parts exhaustion after our rough night and impatience to do something, to take action that would allow us to find Kayleigh. We had agreed, however, that without any other clues, we'd never find Kayleigh by driving around randomly.

Waiting for Sheila to talk to her tonight was our best recourse.

The gardens were beautiful. If I'd been trying to dispose of some magical water in such a place, I probably would have skulked in with the bowl hidden and tried to empty it behind a tree or something. Because of my attempt at surreptitiousness, I would probably have been confronted by some employee of the Bellagio and thrown out of the hotel. Sheila, on the other hand, waltzed into the gardens with the bowl held front and center, dazzled everyone with her smile, and then held the bowl up high before slowly, dramatically pouring out its contents. Her performance garnered confused looks, a few smiles, and even applause from one attractive man who then moved in quickly to chat her up. She talked to him for a few minutes, tossed her hair back and laughed at some not-so-clever joke, and then took her leave with a squeeze of his arm and a wink. A master of friendly rejection that was our Sheila.

"So," I said after she returned to my side, leaving her bemused would-be swain staring after her, "should we play the slots for a minute? You know, now that we're so lucky?" I raised my eyebrows at her.

"Jules," her tone was stern, "that's not the purpose of the amulet. Don't abuse it, unless you want it to fail when you *do* need the luck."

Huh. That was the first time I'd heard a safety pin called an "amulet."

"But," Sheila's eyes sparkled, "if you're up for it, can we go outside for just a few minutes and watch the fountains? I've seen them in movies and such, but I'd love to watch them in person."

"Sure." After all, we deserved a few minutes of fun.

Walking through the swanky hotel, we saw an interesting cross-section of America. Drunk college kids, middle-aged couples with kids in tow, and, of course, some high rollers. I kept expecting to see George Clooney or something, but such was not my luck. Even with a Holstein cow-adorned amulet. I will admit my jaw dropped when we saw one room with hundred dollar slot machines. Truly. Slot machines that took tokens worth one hundred dollars each. Who had that kind of money? I wasn't so sure about the whole Vegas thing. Here was this beautiful hotel and casino that, on one hand, I could luxuriate in and appreciate. Yet, on the other hand, I found the whole town a slap-in-the-face indictment of capitalism and the culture of excess: people throwing away their money, other people continually building the biggest and best and newest attraction, the entire city siphoning off water for miles and miles around.

Sheila and I joined the group of people waiting for the fountains to perform. The show was worth waiting for. The fountains started dancing, sending their jets skyward in time with the music, and Sheila and I found ourselves oooh-ing and aaah-ing with the crowd like at a fireworks show. The water cycled through several songs, then lapsed into quietude again. The crowd gave a collective sigh and many people moved off toward other attractions, though a few diehard fans looked ready to camp out for the next performance.

"Well. Back to the room, I guess," I said.

"I just wish we could *do* something, instead of just waiting for nightfall."

"I know."

Sheila leaned on the stone wall and studied her fingernails. "I need a manicure."

"My treat, when we get back to Oregon."

"Jules, this is your first time in Vegas, right?"

"Right. If only I was an old-Vegas hand and knew all about where the mafia had their lairs."

"Hmmm." Sheila grinned. "I was thinking more along the lines of seeing some of the Vegas sights—just for half an hour or so, since Carson's safe and there's nothing productive to do."

"That sounds great, actually. I'll call Eliza and make sure it's okay with them."

Eliza reported Carson was still asleep and gave us the green light to spend half an hour walking around the Strip. It wasn't much time, but—then again—half an hour sounded like enough, considering the heat. Sheila pulled me down the walk toward the main sidewalk. She craned her head this way and that before pointing.

"Caesar's Palace is right next door. Across the street and that way," Sheila gestured to the left, "is the Venetian. Are you up for a bit of a walk? I'd really like to see the Venetian."

"Sure."

I fell into step beside Sheila and we moved into the flow of pedestrians, crossed the Strip on an overhead walkway, then headed past a number of casinos: The Flamingo, The Imperial Palace, Harrah's. Each one was a variation on a theme—the theme being "How Can We Entice People In to Gamble and Shop." We passed three women handing out small pieces of paper the size of baseball cards. Perplexed, I took one, only to realize they advertised escort services and exotic dancers.

Sheila walked on a few steps, before she noticed I'd stopped.

"What is it?"

"Nothing. Just...this is a crazy city." The front of the card had a picture of a naked woman—Amber, if the print was reliable, which I found dubious at best—with her significant bits and pieces covered by black stars. The back listed pertinent details about "Amber" and gave a phone number. I handed it to Sheila, who raised her eyebrows.

"I should take a bunch of these and analyze them in my rhetoric course. Or with my women's studies students." Sheila picked up a bunch of discarded papers others had thrown to the sidewalk. "Look how many of these are women of color, mostly Asian women, and how young they look. They *might* be eighteen, but they're sure made to look younger."

"Yuck."

We continued down the street, Sheila stuffing the cards into her red lizard purse. I pulled out my phone and glanced at the time. "No way we're going to make it to the Venetian and back in half an hour. We're almost there, but it's already been fifteen minutes."

"Okay, well, call Eliza and tell her we'll be a little later. I guess distances are deceptive on the Strip."

I did so, and we proceeded.

The Venetian truly was spectacular. The inside gallery resembled the outdoors—in Venice, of course. The high ceilings were painted a cloud-dappled blue, airy piazzas featured street performers posing as marble statues, and the shops looked like freestanding stores. And a canal—an actual canal ran through the middle of the casino—complete with gondolas. I'd heard about the Venetian, but it surpassed expectations.

We walked around for a few minutes and gawked at the scene. As we navigated the crowds, I looked for suspicious people, but found only the usual tourists. Nevertheless, I continued to check behind us, as I grew more and more uneasy. Sheila kept making jokes about people buying purses that cost more than her yearly salary from Southern Oregon University. Actually, she wasn't really joking, but we acted like it was funny, anyway. At Sheila's insistence, we stopped for gelato— dark chocolate for me, strawberry for her—and sat on a bench near the canal to eat it.

"What is it?" Sheila asked.

"What is what?"

"Why do you keep looking around like that? Just restless?"

"No," I said, slowly, putting it all together. "I think someone is following us."

Sheila bolted upright and turned in a full circle.

"Who?"

"I don't know. I just feel...like someone is watching."

"Okay. Okay. Well, it's been a stressful couple of days. Are you sure it's not your imagination?"

"No," I said, "I'm not sure. I'm just the human."

"Okay." Sheila scanned the moving crowds. "So...what do we do?"

I shook my head. "Start back toward the Bellagio and see if we can spot anyone following us? Maybe I'm just being jumpy?"

"That's your plan?"

"Do you have a better plan?"

"No. Do we call Tim and Eliza?"

"Absolutely not," I said. "Not until we know if it's true. I want them with Carson; *he's* the real target."

Chapter Fifteen

Of course, if I had Were senses, I'd know if someone stalked us. The thought looped through my mind as we threaded between shoppers and out of the Venetian. The back of my neck tingled and I had to fight the urge to turn around every other step. Once on the sidewalk, I watched the windows as we passed to see if I could get a glimpse of someone behind us. Sheila stopped and pointed to something in a store; we both used it as an opportunity to search the sidewalk behind us.

After several such stops, I said, "That guy in the green t-shirt, is he watching us?"

"With the jean shorts?"

Sheila and I stood close together. I heard the tension in her voice and saw it in the set of her shoulders. The guy *did* seem to watch us. When he saw our attention turned toward him, he gave Sheila a slow up-and-down look. An ogle, practically. Okay, he was just one of Sheila's many admirers and not a mafia thug. Unless it was a cover. Was it a cover?

"What do you think?" I asked.

"I think he's harmless. And not my type."

"Okay." I scanned the rest of the crowd, aware we'd been standing in one place for long enough any real tail would have had a chance to hide. "Let's keep going."

We continued down the Strip, consciously alternating our pace from fast walking to a slow amble. I resisted the urge to rub the back of my neck, to smooth down the hairs that felt so prickly. When possible, I angled my body to Sheila as if in conversation, while stealing sidelong glimpses of the sidewalk. Nothing. But I still felt...

"This sucks."

"Have you seen anything? Anyone?" Sheila asked.

"No." I rubbed my eyes. "If only—"

Sheila waited for a minute, then prompted. "If only what?"

"I wish—" I made a futile gesture and shook my head. "I just wish I knew if there *was* someone watching us, following us. I wish I could sense more."

Sheila said nothing.

"Or, you know, or hide us. Or get us out of here."

"Jules."

"What?" I felt defensive.

"Julie Hall. I know what you're thinking and you might not even become a Were. You might die. Have you really thought about that? That you might *die*? Do you want Carson to grow up without a mother? His father is already dead."

"What are you talking about?"

Sheila glared at me, and my anger rose in return.

"I didn't mean—Goddammit, Sheila, that's not what I meant." I lied.

"Oh?"

How did she do that? How did she load such meaning into a single syllable?

"I didn't mean that. I meant—I wish I knew if I was imagining things or not." I sounded grumpy even to me, which only made me grumpier.

We walked a few more paces in silence, and Sheila, apparently, decided to let the subject drop.

"Let's detour through the Flamingo before we cross the street to the Bellagio," she suggested. "If there is someone still nearby, we can lose him in the casino."

Following her lead, we ducked through the door of the Flamingo. Once inside, we proceeded to wind our way through the crowds, trying to stick to areas of dense congestion and make sudden turns. At one point, I stood and watched a craps game for several minutes, while Sheila continued on, doubled back, and scoped out the vicinity. When she returned to my side, she declared herself fairly convinced no one followed us.

"Unless they're very skilled," she added as a caveat.

I didn't mention the obvious: if the mafia stalked us, they *would* be very skilled.

Instead, I nodded agreement and we decided to return to the Bellagio—via the side door of the Flamingo and down a different street, then positioning ourselves as much as possible in the thickest clusters of tourists. By this point, I couldn't even decide if I still felt like we were being watched; my instincts and paranoia fused.

With no further events, we arrived at the Bellagio, back at the dancing fountains where this whole misbegotten excursion began. I leaned on the stone railing, craning my head up and down the Strip, looking back at all the various resorts. No one. It must have been my imagination after all. Then I did a double-take, my eyes backtracking and searching the crowds. Even after I caught glimpse of what had attracted my attention, it took me a beat to realize what I saw.

"Sheila, it's Ian and Dave." I pointed halfway down the block.

Sure enough, the lanky forms of Ian MacGregor and his best friend Dave Blithe walked up the Las Vegas Strip.

"Who?" Sheila asked, blankly searching the crowd.

I realized with a small shock Sheila didn't know them and explained, "Ian MacGregor, Mac's younger brother. He's seventeen. And his best friend Dave. They're both, uh, you know, dog-lovers and from Wyoming. But what the hell are they doing here? They're putting themselves in danger."

"Yes," drawled Sheila, "people without credentials or experience should definitely not put themselves in harm's way, right?"

Okay, so she had a point. But still, at least we had a bit of age and experience on our side. Plus Eliza and Tim. These boys were in way over their heads, if, in fact, they were here alone to investigate the murders.

I made my decision quickly.

"Ian. Dave." I yelled as the two drew closer. I repeated myself a few times before they seemed to hear me, then waved my arms wildly as they looked about. Dave saw me first and elbowed Ian, who startled visibly. The two of them had a quick exchange of words and detoured up the walk to the Bellagio.

"What are you doing here?" Ian asked. "I thought you and Eliza headed back to Oregon."

"I could ask you the same question. Do your parents know you're here?" I said, careful not to snap at him. Or, that was my intent.

Dave looked at Ian, who directed his gaze to the pavement. His shoulders slumped and he muttered a reply.

"What?"

"I said," Ian's voice raised with a note of anger, "no, they don't know we're here. They think we're out camping and hunting for a week."

"Ian——" I started.

"No." He snapped his head up to look at me. "No, you're not my mother and I have every right—more right than *you*—to be here. He was my brother, not my, what, lover? Sex toy? Disposable boyfriend? *Baby daddy?*"

I literally took a step back from him, wounded by the anger in his voice. Tears rushed to my eyes though luckily, luckily not down my face.

"Sorry, punk." Sheila stepped toe to toe with Ian, though he had her by about five inches. "You do not talk to my friend that way. She loved your brother— loved him. The only reason they broke up is because *he* wouldn't open up to her. She's been spending the last year pining after him and finding out he's dead broke her heart all over again. So you," she poked him in the chest, "are going to apologize."

"Now," she added, when he didn't immediately move or speak.

"Ian," Dave spoke, "she came all the way here to figure things out. Or avenge him. Or something. Even though she's *human*." It sounded like a swear word, coming out of his mouth. He jerked his chin at Ian.

195

"Dude, you're seriously overreacting. Listen to the Witch."

Ian unclenched his fists and mumbled, "Sorry."

I blinked hard and made a show of cleaning my glasses.

"So," I said brightly. "Now that we're all best friends again, should we go inside and talk about this? You know, instead of providing free entertainment?" I gestured to the people surrounding us, all of whom had been listening eagerly and all of whom now started to talk avidly amongst themselves as if they had not noticed the four freaks making a scene in front of the Bellagio fountains.

"You're staying at the Bellagio?" Dave asked, his expression one of envy.

"First rate all the way, boys," said Sheila. Linking her arm through mine, she drew me through the doorway and across the foyer. Dave and Ian followed, hesitating only briefly for a shared look.

Chapter Sixteen

Sheila knocked on the door before then using her card key to open it. The door swung in to reveal Tim, mild look gone from his face, standing as if ready to spring. The muscles in his arms and neck tensed as he took in our group.

"Tim," Eliza sounded exasperated, "I told you, I know them. They're not enemies, they're my pack. Ian MacGregor and Dave Blythe."

Dave and Ian had frozen in place, but all three Weres relaxed as the truth of Eliza's words made itself apparent to Tim. Eliza came closer to the door.

"In, in, in, folks," she said, "and shut the door."

"Is Carson still sleeping?" I queried, to which I received a curt nod.

I knew Eliza and Dave were both full moons, but the dominance in the room clearly belonged to our girl. She was not happy to see the two teens. As soon as the door closed fully, she strode up to the taller Weres and gently, firmly, mock-playfully pushed them both, thumping them each with her hands on their shoulders.

"What the hell are you two pups doing here?" Although they stood a couple of inches taller, she somehow seemed larger.

Ian opened his mouth and then closed it again, looking at Dave with wide eyes. Dave took half a step backward and stopped with his back against the wall.

"We came to see if we could figure out what's going on. The council and their investigators"—if Ian hadn't sounded submissive, I would have said he sneered the words—"don't seem to be doing their job."

"You two took it upon yourselves to come here, with no permission and no guidance, walking blindly into a situation that killed older and better Weres?" Eliza's dark brown eyes narrowed in anger.

"*Better* Weres?" spat Dave.

Ian's defiance surfaced and he retorted, "Just like you. Why are *you* here, when everyone believed you were going to Oregon? *You* aren't trained council investigators, either."

"First of all," Eliza stared at Ian until he dropped his gaze to the ground, "you have no way of knowing we're not here as part of the council's response to these killings."

She reached up and grabbed his chin, forcing him to meet her gaze.

"However," she continued, "You are correct. The council doesn't know we are here. But I am second only to our pack Full, and Julie is answerable to no one. We are adults taking responsibility for our actions, even when they lead us into danger. I intend to take the consequences with our pack, as well. Do you?"

Her speech widened to include Dave. "You two pups," the exaggerated scorn in her voice was unmistakable, "are not yet adults. You do not have full standing in the pack. You lied to our pack about your whereabouts. You put yourself at risk, carelessly, thoughtlessly at risk. This is not a video game, pups. And you—" She smacked Ian again in both shoulders. "You should know better. How do you think your parents would react if they lost both their sons? Do you really think you'd fare any better than Mac—Mac, who was older, wiser, stronger—if you actually fought our enemies? Or would I need to call your parents and tell them you were dead? Can you imagine the look on your mother's face as she buries her last son?"

Ian closed his eyes and wilted. "I'm sorry, Eliza," he mumbled.

"I can't hear you."

He let out a big breath. "I said I'm sorry. You're right. I don't want—I wasn't thinking about my parents. I just thought..." His voice broke with raw emotion. "I want him caught. Him, them. Whoever. The people who killed my brother. I couldn't stand sitting in Greybull, waiting, day after day, hearing nothing, hearing people's excuses, hearing about more people being killed. Kidnapped. Dammit, why isn't anyone doing anything?"

His fists clenched again, and I was surprised he didn't punch a hole in the wall. His angst clearly visible in the way he held his body and his face.

Dave bumped his friend with his shoulder.

"We can be careful and everything," he said to Eliza. He looked around the room at each of us in turn. "I know I'm not as strong as you, but I *am* a full moon."

He seemed caught between bitterness and respect for Eliza as a stronger full moon Were. And he definitely pronounced the last part of his declaration with pride.

"Yes, well," said Tim quietly, "I'm a waxing moon, not quite as strong as young Ian here. Yet, I'd bet on myself in a fight against you any day. As Eliza says, you're a pup."

Dave seemed to swell with anger and I thought he might attack Tim right then and there to prove himself. Tim took four steps forward to stand directly next to Eliza. He didn't swagger or glower. He just stood with Eliza, matching her height almost exactly, and gave Dave a slow smile. The hairs on my arms rose and I found myself holding my breath, hoping Dave would be sensible. Indeed, he shook himself vigorously and shrugged.

"Maybe we'll find out someday," he muttered.

Tim and Eliza let his comment pass, obviously secure in the knowledge they'd firmly established dominancy over our teen Weres.

The baby monitor squawked, and I left the scene to retrieve Carson. My little boy—who, heaven help me, would someday be a teenaged Werewolf—was wide awake and chortling. I loved it when he woke up in a happy mood, and I spent a few minutes tickling him and kissing his chubby belly. While I was at it, I also attached his safety pin amulet to the waistband of his stretchy shorts. I figured if I put it there, even if the supposedly childproof pin came undone, it would be as likely to poke his diaper as his flesh. Although, hopefully, a lucky protective pin wouldn't spring open and stick my baby, since I'd have to question the whole "lucky" and "protective" bit if that happened.

When I came back into the other suite, the Witch and the Weres had settled down in the living room area. Ian lounged on the armchair, long legs sprawling, while Dave had flopped down on the floor. They both drank sodas, apparently from the mini-bar. Tim and Sheila sat more conventionally on the sofa, while Eliza stood, looking out the window. I lay a blanket on the floor and put Carson down for tummy time.

"Did you catch everyone up to speed?"

Eliza answered me. "There's not much to tell, since Ian and Dave will not be involved in Kayleigh's rescue."

The two teens looked sullen, so I assumed I'd missed what must have been a lovely discussion.

"I still say you might need us," Dave said, but without much energy. "And I've been to Vegas before, last winter break. I know the city. I've met some people. That might be helpful."

"Well, not to change the subject, because, really, it's been a downright pleasure hearing you Weres argue," said Sheila with a smile, "but I'd like to scry for Kayleigh once more before nightfall, just to see if there have been any…changes."

We all knew her thoughts. I empathized with Ian and Dave, feeling like they wanted to *do* something. Everyone in the room was impatient to figure out a way to help Kayleigh. We tried to contain our restlessness until we had a plan that might be reasonably helpful. After all, Tim had checked out all the leads on the ground before we even arrived in Las Vegas. We'd spent the time since then kidnapping a Were—who turned out to be an ally—killing a man, cleaning up the crime scene, and hopefully hiding traces of our location. Plus doing a bit of magic. When put that way, I guess it wasn't like we'd been watching soap operas and eating bonbons, yet I knew if Kayleigh was dead— if we didn't to reach her in time—I'd feel an immense burden of guilt.

Declaiming loudly the lot of us couldn't be quiet enough Sheila went into the other suite in order to scry. I noticed she used a swig of water to swallow a few ibuprofens before she left the room. Hopefully, she wouldn't overtax herself.

****

Twenty minutes later, Sheila returned to us, although she looked as if she'd passed an entire sleepless night. Slightly pale, with dark circles standing under her eyes, she heaved a sigh and sank deeply into the cream-colored leather couch.

"Well, she's alive," Sheila reported in a flat voice.

"And?" I prompted.

"She looks in pretty bad shape. I think she'll heal, given what I know about Werewolves, but she has heavy bandaging around her hips, here." Sheila gestured to the top of her hip bones. "I saw those bandages even through the hospital gown. She may have had some other injuries, it's hard to tell. There were a number of bruises, all over really, and some scrapes and scratches like she'd been struggling against someone. She was curled up on the mattress again, alone—I wish I could catch a glimpse of her *with* someone, but it takes a lot of energy for me to watch through the scrying dish.

"She remained tied up with silver chains and—this is the weirdest part—she was hooked to an IV."

"Oh!" Sheila bolted upright. "Here's the good news. The curtains on her window were open a bit, just enough for me to get a glimpse. She's in an area of rundown houses, small houses crowded together, and I saw one other thing. On the corner of the street, a red neon sign said 'Fish Fry.' Luckily, it's starting to get dark enough that the sign was clearly visible."

"Could you see the restaurant's name?" Eliza asked. Tim already started opening drawers in the desk, searching for a phone book.

"No." Sheila grimaced.

"That's okay, Sheila, you did a great job. Fish Fry will be enough for us to find her, right Tim?" I looked at Tim hopefully.

He riffled through the restaurant pages, his usually placid face creased by a frown of concentration. "Why are there so many restaurants in this damn town?"

"It's Las Vegas, Tim." Eliza moved to stand beside him. "Here, this part is by type of restaurant. Seafood...seafood... Okay, let's cross-check with a map, we don't need to look anywhere high class."

After quite a while, we'd compiled a list of over forty possible restaurants that mentioned fish or seafood.

"Now what?" I asked.

"Now I take a drive and look for a flashing red Fish Fry sign," said Tim. "Surely there's not more than one—or two—of those. And you," he pointed at Eliza and me, "stay with Sheila and wait for her to get any more information. At the very least, she can make sure Kayleigh knows we're on our way."

"Are you sure you should go alone?" Sheila looked at him for a long moment, clearly anxious.

"I can go," volunteered Dave, met with a resounding "No" in unison from me, Eliza, Sheila, and Tim. He rolled his eyes at our immediate response and continued to plead his case. "Really, I could be helpful. Read the map or something. We're not going to rescue her this minute, right? We're just going to find her and case the joint?"

I rolled my eyes, at Dave's obvious attempt to use detective language.

"They're not going to let you go," Ian said. "Save your breath."

Dave huffed and flopped back onto the floor. "It's stupid. Just because we're not eighteen."

Eliza's voice was sharp when she said, "Because I don't want to be the one to call your parents, Ian, and your sister, Dave, with news of your deaths. I don't want to explain to Full we allowed you pups to put yourselves in danger."

"Fuck that," said Dave, sitting upright again, "I am not a *pup*. Seventeen, eighteen—I'm smarter and faster than any human, regardless. Human laws of…age or whatever shouldn't apply to Weres." Again, he spat the word human like an epithet. Anger spilled off Dave and permeated the room.

"Stop it," snapped Eliza. "We've been through this. My answer will not change."

"Give it up, Dave," Ian said, wearily nudging his friend with a foot.

Dave made a frustrated sound. "Let's go for a walk or something. I'm not just hanging around here."

"No. No walks. You're not going out by yourselves."

I looked at Eliza, worried she might push him too far and have a fight on her hands. Instead, Dave just balled his fists and groaned again.

"Under fucking house arrest."

"Could be worse, bro. They've got cable," Ian said, defusing more of the tension with a casualness I began to appreciate.

Sheila made a show of clearing her throat. "As I was saying, Tim, will you be safe going by yourself?"

"Yes," he answered curtly. "I prefer knowing Eliza is here to protect you, Julie, and Carson. With the boys as backup, of course." A slight salve to their wounded pride, there.

He added, "Sheila, if you discover anything while dreamwalking, call me on my cell right away."

She nodded and excused herself to start preparing the supplies she'd need for her next spell.

As for me? Feeling like the practical yet superfluous human, I decided to order room service, since it was quite late and we hadn't eaten since those long-ago subs. Besides, I knew Ian and Dave would soon deplete the mini-bar if I didn't do something.

Before Tim left, I watched him check his gun and slide it into a holster under his arm. Somehow, that gave me pause. It's not as if I didn't know this was life-and-death serious: Mac had been killed, after all. Beheaded. Carlos, too. I'd witnessed a scene of carnage last night, even if I didn't like to think about Eliza ripping that guy's throat out. Yet seeing Tim prepare his weapon so matter-of-factly, as if he completely accepted he might have to use it, just another tool of his trade—well, it put everything into perspective. I hoped we could rescue Kayleigh, find out more about our enemies, and turn it all over to the council. Without anyone else getting hurt.

Chapter Seventeen

After Tim left, Eliza stayed with Ian and Dave while I went into the bedroom with Carson in tow to help Sheila get ready to dreamwalk. She already made some preparations and now used ashes to draw a circle under the head of her bed where her pillow lay.

"How is everything out there, still civil?" she asked.

"I guess. So, you don't need quiet to prepare?"

"No. I need to invoke my will before I fall asleep."

"What are those ashes from?"

She quirked a smile. "The bay leaves and ferns I just burned."

"Huh. This magic stuff is very particular, isn't it?"

Sheila continued arranging ashes in a thick circle. "Yes. I'm about out of tricks. I've wracked my brain to remember anything else, but these are the only spells I use with any frequency. If I'm going to continue hanging around with Werewolves, I need to study hard when I get home."

I didn't want to say the obvious "if any of us get home," so a moment of quiet took over. Carson chewed on his own fist like it was the best invention ever. Which, come to think of it, is kind of true: opposable thumbs and all—go evolution.

"Granny and I used to dreamwalk all the time," Sheila continued abruptly. "She'd enter my dreams and we'd have a great time—Unicorns, huge amusement parks, the beach, outer space. When you're dreamwalking, you can shape the environment, so you can imagine how much fun we had."

She reached up to rub her eyes. "I am sorry I never told you. It's a huge relief, talking to you about my craft."

"Well," I said after a moment, "I'm still a little mad—or hurt—you didn't tell me before. But it's hard to believe, even after everything I've seen. Werewolves. Magic. My son changes into a wolf and my best friend casts spells. I probably wouldn't have believed you. When this is all over and when everyone's safe, I want to hear more about it, more about your granny Emma, your witchcraft, the other Witches you know. Their libraries. Maybe I can even help you organize your, uh, spellbooks. Help you do some research."

Sheila nodded, then let out a deep breath. "Thanks, Jules."

"Anytime, BFF."

I worried I might step on thin ice, but had to ask anyway. "Sheila, you never watched my dreams, did you?"

Sheila straightened. "No! Never. That is completely unethical, like reading someone's diary. In a case like this, when Kayleigh's life is endangered, I have no qualms about finding her dreams. But other than that—and, well, some rather unfortunate and questionable choices with a few high school crushes—I would never watch someone's dreams without permission. We have our own code of ethics, you know."

"No, I don't know. Are Witches as organized as Werewolves?" I groaned and mock-held my temples. "Did you hear that question? Can you believe I just asked that question? Where is my normal life?"

Sheila reached out and squeezed my arm. "This is life, Jules. You've been thrown into the deep end of the pool and I think you're doing well. Treading water at the very least.

"Some Witches work in covens, but, no, we don't have actual leaders, or a strict code of conduct, other than what's necessary for self-protection and secrecy. It's more like schools, various philosophies of witchcraft handed down within family lines or from teacher to student."

I started to ask another question, but Sheila waved her hands at me. "Can we talk about it later? Right now, I need to focus on Kayleigh."

"Oh. Right."

Sheila moved in silence again, carefully spritzing her ash circle with water. I wondered what the cleaning staff would think of all of this, but figured they'd probably seen worse. It was Vegas, after all. She wrapped one of Kayleigh's blonde hairs around one of her own gold hoop earrings and then placed it in the center of her ash circle. At my glance, she explained gold stood in for fire with this spell—gold and the spark of fiery spirit in the dreamer herself.

When she had everything arranged to her liking, she said, "All right, then. I'm ready. Please make sure everyone stays quiet, okay? I'll wake myself in about an hour. It will take me a little while to find Kayleigh, since I've never dreamwalked to her before. I hope she's asleep—even if she's not actively dreaming, I should be able to push her into that state."

With a hug for good luck and my assurances we wouldn't disturb her, I left the bedroom as she placed her pillow over the ritual items and lay down.

Later, Sheila described dreamwalking to me. She said, when the spell initiator fell asleep, her consciousness woke up in a dark place, directionless, full of changing colors and an ever-shifting wind. The colors were somehow indicative of dreamscapes, although no direct relationship existed to geographical proximity or anything else tangible. Sheila wasn't sure what the wind represented and mentioned it only in passing, with a high degree of anxiety: she said her granny had absolutely refused to discuss the wind and forbid her to even speak of it. Anyway, when entering this place, Sheila appeared with the token—in this case, the earring wrapped in Kayleigh's hair—held tightly in hand. By focusing on the token, she could somehow shift her surroundings until she approached colors that more closely matched the aura around her token, thus indicating her approach to Kayleigh's sleeping self. If the object of her search were already dreaming, she would see bright flashes of light, echoed in the token. She could focus on the light until it became a specific point, then move closer until she'd fall into it, like a sun or a bright black hole. At that point, she'd find herself in the other person's dream, able to shape the dream and communicate directly with the dreamer.

Sheila never told me what Kayleigh had been dreaming about. With a flat voice, she said merely it had been a nightmare—a nightmare Sheila quickly resolved into a normal, pleasant scene. Sheila spent some time convincing Kayleigh she was a real person, a dreamwalking Witch, trying to communicate with her. I supposed that made sense: if someone popped into my dream, changed everything, and then sat down to have a conversation, I'd be unlikely to believe she wasn't just another vivid figment of my dreaming imagination.

After Kayleigh understood Sheila was real and the genuine possibility of rescue existed, Sheila said her relief and gratitude were so intense the entire dreamscape morphed—flowers blooming on carpets and walls and silly stereotypical things like that. Sheila added she felt almost guilty, like she should have stressed the fact we were a ragtag group of untrained rescuers, with the exception of Tim. In the end, she decided Kayleigh needed hope more than anything, so she merely said we were a group of Weres and Witches already in Vegas to track her. Kayleigh didn't have much to say about her current location. She revealed she'd been jumped right outside her car, ironically next to a police station, and had been knocked out almost immediately with some sort of drug in gauze over her face. Of course, since she was a Were, she metabolized the drug uber-quickly, but had woken to find herself bound with duct tape on the floor in the back of a vehicle. Note to self: even Were-strength struggled against good old duct tape, if enough was used. Who knew?

Kayleigh said she'd only seen one Were and described him as blond with a beard, matching the description Suzy Zhang had given of "Taylor Dunn." Kayleigh said his first name was Ken and she'd never seen him before. She said a number of other humans were involved—more than she could count—and, after

Sheila asked, she agreed with Tim's assessment they were organized crime. She added in an uncertain voice she'd scented someone or something else, not quite human and not quite Were, during her incarceration.

We learned all of this after Sheila woke up, about two hours after she'd gone to sleep. It took longer than she anticipated, since she'd never dreamwalked to Kayleigh before. When she came into the living room, Eliza and I spoke quietly while the boys watched TV at low volume, some movie about pirates.

"There's something really weird going on here," said Sheila. While we gave her our full attention, she explained the basics of what Kayleigh said. Then she continued, "The part I really don't understand is Kayleigh says there's some medical aspect to it all. There's a doctor and he subjected Kayleigh to some sort of procedure with her bone marrow."

"Bone marrow?" I repeated. I looked at Eliza, but her face appeared blank.

"Yes, they've been putting her under and pulling bone marrow from her hip bones, her breast bone, and her shoulder blades. About ten times a day—that's why she has the IV and that's why she has the bandages."

"What the hell? Why would anyone want her bone marrow?"

No one had an answer for me.

"Let's think about this," Eliza spoke, the gears of her mind almost visibly turning. "What do any of us know about bone marrow?"

Ian and Dave both shrugged. Sheila shook her head in bewilderment.

"No, seriously. Even the most basic information. What do we know about bone marrow?" Eliza prompted.

"You use it to treat things like leukemia, right?" I hazarded. "Because it has lots of stem cells or something?"

"You have to match to be a donor. Like with blood types, but I think it's more complicated," contributed Ian.

"Okay." Eliza turned to Ian. "You and Dave go to the business center here in the Bellagio and research bone marrow on the internet. That's your way of being helpful."

"Okay." Ian stood up and stretched, then extended a hand to pull Dave to his feet. "We can do that. I'm not sure what we're looking for, though."

"Sheila, you get some more rest. You look exhausted, and we may need your talents later," Eliza said, continuing to direct. "I'll stay here with the non-Weres and we'll wait for word from Tim." She omitted the obvious: Carson and I might need her protection.

Chapter Eighteen

Dave and Ian left quickly, apparently grateful to have a productive task. Sheila crashed in the other suite, and Carson fell asleep on a mat of blankets I'd set up next to one of the beds. I returned to the living room and found Eliza watching a re-run of a cooking show.

Noting my surprise, she quirked a shoulder. "There's nothing on. This seemed mindless and non-violent, anyway. Feel free to change the channel."

"This is fine," I said, settling next to her on the couch.

We spent the next half an hour watching chefs struggle with strange ingredients. Or, at least, we divided our time equally between watching the TV, glancing at the clock, and staring at the phone as if willing it to ring with news of Kayleigh's whereabouts. As the crowning dishes graced the judge's table, Eliza straightened and strode toward the door.

The knock came just as she reached for the handle, and Dave nearly fell forward into the room. He held a sheaf of pages in his hand and started talking almost immediately.

"Well, I'm not sure how much good any of this—" He broke off in mid-sentence and looked around. "Where's Ian?"

"What do you mean? He was with you," Eliza said.

"But…" Dave's head swung from Eliza to me and back again. "He left about ten minutes ago to come back here."

After a split second, Eliza whirled and pointed at me. "Wake Sheila up. Lock the door after me and don't let anyone in. *No one* besides me." She grabbed Dave by the arm and pulled him out the door with a curt command.

I stood and watched as the door closed behind them before dutifully locking it with the double-bolt and swinging across the metal arm. I performed all these actions without thought—without allowing myself to think. Then, I went into Sheila's room.

"Sheila?" I spoke softly but she nonetheless woke up with a start.

"What's going on? Did Tim find Kayleigh?"

"No. Dave came back without Ian. Something's wrong." Panic started to mount as I uttered the words.

Sheila was fully alert by this point, eyes wide, and she swung her feet over the side of the bed.

"Where's Ian?" she said.

I shook my head. "Dave thought he came back here, but he didn't. Eliza went with him to look."

"Maybe he went to play slots?" Sheila offered, but we both knew he hadn't.

"Shit. That damn kid. Erin's going to—" I cleared my throat. "Sheila, can we go sit next to Carson?"

She nodded and grabbed my hand, squeezing it tightly.

We had no sooner started across the room than a quiet knock sounded on the front door of the suite. Heart racing, I peered through the peephole, saw Eliza, turned the locks, and opened the door. She stormed into the room, Dave pulled along in her wake. I shivered, rubbing my forearms, and took an involuntary step back at the look in her eyes.

"Ian's been taken," she said flatly and crossed to pick up her cell phone.

"No," I cried. "What happened?"

"It's my fault," Dave said, sliding down the wall to sit heaped on the floor. "It's all my fault. Dammit! It's my fault."

"What's your fault?" I knelt beside him. "What happened?"

"He was coming back here to update you, and they grabbed him. Shit, they grabbed him and they took him and this was *not* supposed to happen. It's my fault."

"Dave." I gave him a little shake to stop him. "It's not your fault. We thought we were safe in the hotel, that Ian would be safe. Goddammit, maybe it's my fault. Maybe someone *was* following us, earlier."

Dave didn't listen to me, but buried his face in his hands, muttering under his breath.

"Okay. No more talk about fault. We need to focus on getting Ian back." Eliza's voice cut through Dave's rambling. "Tim's on his way back. Dave, you stay here, right here in this room, and protect Julie, Sheila, and Carson." Eliza crossed the room, fixing her eyes on Dave, pulling him to his feet with the fierce power of her will. I had to avert my gaze from the expression on his face.

"Dave, under no circumstances are you or any of the others to leave this room. If someone besides me or Tim tries to get in, you call the police." Eliza's voice acted as an anodyne, and I found myself straightening my shoulders.

"The police?" I repeated, startled.

"The police. Call 911. This is not a time to worry about pack law—this is a time to survive. If it comes to that, we'll deal with the aftermath later. Tim called in an emergency council team, too." Eliza held our gazes until Dave, Sheila, and I all nodded.

"This time it's different," she continued grimly. "This time, we've got a scent trail and we're going to follow it. We're going to get Ian back."

I nodded, not trusting my voice.

"Okay," she said, then opened the door and left.

Released from the spell cast by Eliza's intensity, Dave fell back against the wall, eyes closed. His voice was hoarse as he repeated, "It's my fault. This was *not* supposed to happen."

"Dave." I nearly shouted at him. "Of course, it's not your fault. Of course, it wasn't supposed to happen. You heard Eliza; we're going to get him back."

He looked at me, seemingly without comprehension, and then my words sank in.

"Yes," he said. "Yes. We'll get him back. Of course, we'll get him back. I'll get him back." He set his jaw and stared at me.

"Okay. Okay, now," I said in a soothing voice, as if to a wild animal. I backed away a step, disconcerted by the fervor in his voice.

Sheila moved to stand beside me and held out a hand to Dave. "Come on, Dave, let's sit down for a minute. Eliza and Tim know what they're doing." She shot a quick glance at me and suggested, "Jules, why don't you go check on Carson?"

I escaped the room gratefully, feeling the tension defuse as Dave sank into the couch.

Carson was fine, still sleeping, and I tried to calm my own breathing by watching him for a few minutes. I leaned over to soak up his baby scent, to give him a kiss, and to make sure his little pin was still affixed securely to his pants. Taking one more deep breath, I rubbed my hands on my jeans to wipe off the sweat and walked toward the living room.

Dave spoke into his cell phone.

"No," he said. "No, this was not the way—I'm telling you—No, I was going to—Yes. Yes, tonight. I *can*, if you—Okay then." He put down his phone and caught sight of me.

"Eavesdrop much, *human*?" He nearly snarled.

"Calm down, Dave." I held up my hands and met his eyes as calmly as possible, though much of me wanted to turn and flee.

"We're going to find him." I repeated several times, and Dave gave a huge sigh. He rolled his shoulders and some of the tension left my own body in return.

"He's my best friend," Dave said, with tone of compounded misery and stress.

"I know."

"I'd do anything for him," he continued, half to himself.

"I know."

"I'm going to get him back."

"Yes, we're going to get him back." I nodded in agreement.

After a moment, I asked, "Who were you talking to? Did you call someone in the pack?"

Dave's head came up and his eyes narrowed. "Am I not allowed to talk to my own pack, human?"

I resisted the urge to step back and instead said, lightly, "Of course you are, Dave. I just wondered." Yeah, I wondered what Eliza would have to say about it. But I was not about to provoke our angst-ridden, anger-laden teen Were.

Changing gear, I said, "Where's Sheila?"

"She's scrying for Ian." Dave jerked his head to indicate the other room.

"Oh, good idea." I walked to the door and poked my head through quietly. Seeing Sheila utterly absorbed, I withdrew to sit on the couch. Dave paced back and forth.

Several minutes later, Sheila came back into the room.

"I saw him," she said without preface. "He's in the back of a car. He's okay, not hurt. They're moving right now; I don't know the area well enough to know where they are."

"Can't you keep watching and find out where they end up?" I asked.

"It's not like that. I can't just keep watching like it's a television—every moment I'm scrying drains my energy."

"Dammit! It's never this hard in a mystery novel. Aren't the bad guys supposed to be really stupid? To leave all sorts of clues? To sit there and reveal all their plans while you're scrying?" I knew I wasn't being rational, so I ended my angry tirade with a shake of my head.

"Right. And Witches should be all powerful and Werewolves should never be taken by surprise. Yep, if you and I ruled the world, Jules, that's how it would be." Sheila sighed and stretched, working out knots in her neck. "Plus, the mini-bar would be free. I know it isn't, but I think I need some chocolate anyway, what do you say?"

Sheila and I split a fancy chocolate bar and watched Dave pace until I worried about the durability of the Bellagio carpet.

It seemed like hours, but realistically only twenty minutes or so passed before another knock on the door broke the silence. I started as if it were a gunshot, and Sheila pressed my arm with a sympathetic hand.

Dave reached the door before I'd even stood up. He yanked it open, not bothering with the peephole, and said, "Tim!"

Tim strode in, took us all in with a searching glance, and said, "Eliza's got Ian, they're coming right up."

"But how is that possible?" Sheila asked. "He was in a car, I saw him."

Tim looked at Sheila and flashed an incongruous smile, before continuing. "Apparently, they dropped him off, a ways down the Strip. He made his way back here as soon as the sedative wore off, and Eliza found him coming up the front walk."

I shook my head, bewildered. "That makes no sense. Why would they drop him off?"

Tim held out his hands and shrugged. "Sheila, tell me what you saw."

He dropped down next to her on the couch, and they conferred in low voices. I joined Dave near the door, fidgeting. Before there was a knock, Dave moved to open the door. We both stepped back so Eliza and Ian could enter. Ian still looked a bit confused, and Eliza had one arm around his shoulders.

"Ian." I gave him a big hug, then stepped back to examine him better. "I'm so glad you're okay. What happened?"

"You scared us, bro." Dave downplayed his relief.

"Yeah, scared myself, too," Ian said. He shucked off Eliza's guiding arm and crossed the room to drop into a chair.

"Tell us what happened," Eliza instructed.

Turns out, Ian left the business center to bring us some of the preliminary information on bone marrow. He explained to us non-Weres that sometimes in a big crowd, he tuned out his senses so as not to be overwhelmed. In this instance, by the time he scented a fellow Were, it was too late: someone had followed him around a corner and jumped him, holding gauze to his mouth and nose. He tried to fight back, to no avail, as the Were slammed his head against a marble pillar. Ian surmised the group ushered him out by pretending he was a drunken comrade. He regained consciousness in the backseat of a car, on the floor, and someone quickly gave him a shot that knocked him out again.

He wasn't sure how long he was unconscious, either time, but by the time he came out of it the second time, he found himself lying on the sidewalk with tourists gingerly skirting the area. He promptly threw up, confirming everyone's assumption he was drunk, and woozily made his way back down the Strip toward the Bellagio.

He had no idea what prompted them to release him. Neither had he gotten much of a definitive look at any of our enemies. He reported the Were was blond, bearded, and not strong—maybe a crescent moon.

After hearing his story, we sat in silence for a moment. My mind whirled with unanswered questions.

"Well," Tim said, finally, "I'm going back out and search for our famous Fish Fry, because we can't count on our enemies suddenly releasing Kayleigh, too."

"You," he gestured to the rest of us, "need to check into yet another hotel."

****

I don't think I was the only one sorry to leave the Bellagio—and not only because Carson had been sleeping so nicely. He did, in fact, wake up while we checked out, but at least he didn't throw one of his screaming fits. Eliza and Tim drove us around in circles for about ten minutes, before we checked into a second-rate hotel near the Strip, with three adjoining rooms to accommodate the addition of the teens to our team. They had a room in some seedy hotel, but Eliza forbid them to return to pick up their belongings. She got them each a toothbrush from the front desk and told them to consider themselves lucky. Surely, Ian, at least, did. After we'd checked in safely, Tim left to scope out red neon signs.

"I still don't understand why they let Ian go," I mused, dancing in place with Carson in his sling, trying to get him to fall asleep again.

"I know. Both of the pups need to calm down. I can hardly get a read on them, they're so agitated," said Eliza, as her cell phone rang. She crossed the room to get it and answered it quickly.

"Tim? Did you find her?" Upon hearing his answer, her mouth set into a grimly satisfied line. "Okay." She scribbled on a piece of hotel stationery, underlined it twice with a heavy hand. "Give us twenty minutes."

I felt adrenaline pour through my veins. Fight or flight was right. I wasn't one hundred percent which I wanted to do, but I knew we only had one option to save Kayleigh's life.

Eliza hung up the phone and faced the rest of us. In that moment, she was the picture of animal grace, composed and eager.

"He found her. Or, at least, he found the Fish Fry and it looks like the right place. He's not going to get much closer until we're all there as backup."

"Okay." Sheila stood and pulled her hair back into a ponytail, securing it with an elastic band from her pocket. "Let's go." Her voice was firm.

"Julie?"

I nodded at Eliza's prompt, not quite trusting my voice not to sound nervous. I hesitated for a moment, then looked at Ian. "Ian, will you watch Carson while we...go? I don't want to bring him with us. I know you'll take good care of him."

I did think Ian would take good care of his nephew. He was a strong Were, plus I remembered that day at breakfast when the two of them happily played at the kitchen table. He might be too cool to act enthusiastic about a baby, but I trusted deep down, he had those care-taking instincts. While I swallowed hard at the thought, I knew if something happened—something dire happened—he'd take Carson back to his parents. Carson would be okay.

Panic welled up in me at the train of thought. The thought of my baby being without me—the thought of something happening...

"Jules," Sheila said quietly, "Maybe you should stay here with Carson? We'll be fine without you. Depending on what kind of guard is on the house, we might not be able to do anything right now anyway— we may have to wait for more council backup."

"I'm going," I said. "Ian?"

Ian shrugged. "Yeah, of course. I'll watch Carson. If you're sure we can't go?" He'd dropped the defiant attitude and instead asked the question sincerely, his eyes trained on Eliza.

"I'm sure."

I sat down to feed Carson quickly. He was sleepy enough I risked putting him down on the bed. Miracles upon miracles, he turned his little head to the side, closed his eyes firmly, and was fully asleep in about two seconds. It couldn't have occurred at a better time, that was for sure. I showed Ian and Dave how to use the baby monitor, made sure Carson's little ducky pin was still fastened on his pajamas where I'd put it earlier, and knelt to give him a kiss. I breathed in deeply, relishing the scent of my baby, and stood. I hoped no one noticed my clenched hands, nails digging into the palms.

Everything would be okay. I wasn't going to let everyone down now.

****

When I went back into the other room, Eliza and Sheila were ready. They had changed into dark clothes, and Sheila handed Eliza a gun.

Sheila handed Eliza a gun?

My surprise must have registered clearly.

"Jules, darling," drawled my best friend, "do shut your mouth. They're Tim's. He showed me earlier.

There's one for you, too, and one to leave with the boys. The man travels well-armed, I'll say that much."

"Do you know how to fire a gun?" Eliza asked.

I hedged slightly. "Well, I've done it before. Sheila, I didn't know you had experience with guns?"

She smiled. "I have three older brothers, as you know. One of them is a cop who feels strongly that everyone should know how to use a gun. He started taking me to the shooting range when I was about fifteen. I'm out of practice, though."

Not so out of practice from what I could see. She handed me a gun, showed me quickly how to turn the safety on and off, showed me it was loaded, and demonstrated a proper shooting stance, reminding me to be careful of the recoil. Uh-huh. I made mental notes on all of that, desperate not to make a mistake, but dearly hoping I wouldn't have to use the gun. Not, uh, to shoot an actual person or anything.

With that, we were off into the night.

Chapter Nineteen

Walking through the lobby of the hotel with a gun stuck into the pocket of my jean jacket, through a bank of slot machines hosting carousing gamblers and stuffed visitors to the all-you-can-eat seafood buffet was perhaps the most surreal experience of my life. I felt sure the sheen of sweat on my forehead—mostly due to nerves, but also slightly due to the fact I wore a jean jacket in Las Vegas in the summer—was a giveaway and we would have a horde of security guards swarming over us. But somehow no one gave our group a second glance. Except for the men we passed, most of who were incapable of not noticing Sheila. Eliza strode beside me, seeming calm and competent. Sheila looked rather exuberant, though I thought it was just her natural way of dealing with the same anxiety I felt. Her eyes were wide and dazzling, she had a crooked smile on her face, and she walked with purposeful energy. I tried to muster the same feeling—that "game on" feeling—and envisioned what it would be like if we were in a movie. The three of us. Were, Witch, and human. Three powerful women taking matters into our own hands and seeking justice. Except, well, I wasn't so sure I was powerful. Being a dark moon wolf meant nothing. Two powerful women and one woman filled with determination more aptly described us.

Mac, I reminded myself. To steel my nerves, I thought about Mac, all the qualities I'd loved, those I'd hated, all taken away from me and from Carson—little Carson—by this ruthless group of...whoever they were. Well, we intended to make sure they didn't get Kayleigh, too. We'd find them and set the whole weight of the council after them.

Unless the council was in on it, but now was not the time to think about such things.

Ordering us to wait in the lobby, Eliza brought the car around, then slid to the passenger's seat and gripped the directions firmly in her hand. I pulled the car out into traffic and, just as quickly, found myself stymied by what looked like a parking lot. A parking lot of cabs full of drunken people. The restless energy we felt made being stuck in traffic even worse than usual.

"Dammit," I said, hitting my palm on the steering wheel. "Don't they know we've got places to be, people to rescue?"

"Calm down." Sheila reached up and put a reassuring hand on my shoulder. "It's not going to help anyone if we get in an accident. Actually, since we're all carrying illegally concealed weapons, please, please don't get in an accident."

"Turn right as soon as you can," said Eliza. "It's fine. I'll call Tim and tell him we're running later than we thought, so he doesn't worry."

While Eliza talked on the phone with Tim, we managed to crawl about a block, and I made a quick and dirty right turn onto another street. I followed her prompts and we were soon well on our way to meeting Tim.

****

It took us another fifteen minutes to reach where Tim waited. His car sat in the parking lot of a strip mall about two blocks away from the infamous Fish Fry sign. The red neon blinked at us, looking to my high-strung nerves like a warning. Or a blood stain.

Tim sat in his car and he lowered his window as we pulled up beside him. His amiable mien was in direct opposition to the seriousness of our mission.

"Okay," he said without preamble, "Sheila, from your description, I guess the house Kayleigh's being held in is either down this street or that street." He gestured.

When none of us disagreed, he continued, "Eliza and I will drive down both streets. She'll cloak us in darkness, and we'll see if we can find the exact house. There should be signs, both scent and sight. Sheila and Julie, you stay here and lock the car until we return. If we don't come back within fifteen minutes, I want you both to go back to the hotel and leave Las Vegas immediately. Don't go home—and don't tell me where you might go. If it comes to that, you can leave this," he handed over a piece of paper, "at the front desk. I left a voicemail for my council contact instructing him to go there for a message if he hasn't heard from me by tomorrow."

Sheila and I nodded. I, for one, didn't know if I trusted my voice at that moment. Eliza slipped out of our car and into the front seat of Tim's. Sheila moved up to the front and gave me a tight smile.

"Okay," said Tim, "We'll be back within fifteen minutes." Eliza waved and I lifted my hand in return.

Sheila and I both looked at the clock, nine thirty-three.

When I raised my head to watch Tim and Eliza leave, I didn't see their car and I panicked slightly before realizing Eliza must have pulled darkness over them. Hopefully, they'd be on the lookout for other cars, since drivers couldn't see them.

I drummed my fingers on the steering wheel.

I pushed my curls behind my ears, hard, wishing my hair didn't always fall in my face.

I took off my glasses and cleaned them carefully on my t-shirt.

I chastised myself for using my t-shirt when I should use the special glasses-cleaning cloth.

Nine thirty-six.

"This sucks," I said to Sheila.

"Aptly put."

Nine thirty-eight. Five minutes had passed.

Every time a car passed on the road, I tensed slightly, hoping no one thought it weird our car was parked here.

At nine forty-two, my cell phone rang and I nearly jumped out of my skin. The incongruity of my ringtone—Big Bird singing "Somebody Come and Play"—set Sheila into a wild fit of giggling. Catching my breath, I saw the call came from an unknown number with a Wyoming area code.

"Shut up," I hissed to Sheila, who continued laughing. "Hello?"

"Julie?" Ian said.

"Ian, what's wrong?" Breath left my lungs.

"Nothing—I mean, I don't know—I mean…. Is Dave with you?"

"What? No, Dave's not with us. What the hell are you talking about?"

Ian paused and then spoke so quickly I hardly understood him. "He was right here, he was right here, still sleeping, everything was fine, he was right here on the bed, and I went to the bathroom, and I was only gone, like a second or something, but when I came out, he was gone and Dave's gone, too, and I didn't know where they went or if Dave followed you or what? Or why he would bring him? Or if someone—"

"Ian!"

Ian stopped talking.

"Are you saying Carson's gone?"

"Yes, Carson and Dave!"

I barely noticed the phone dropping from my hand. I heard Ian's voice and then Sheila's, but I sat there, frozen. In the back of my mind, I vaguely noticed myself thinking, "Oh, this is what happens when someone goes into shock," but I couldn't connect that thought to myself or to my body, which seemed to have gone completely cold. All I heard was the roar of blood in my ears and my heart beating incredibly loud and fast.

"Julie! Julie!" It took me a second to realize Sheila had been calling my name and even then, I couldn't respond, couldn't remember even how to respond. Then Sheila shook me, her hands on my shoulders, shaking me hard and I fell against her and realized I was screaming.

"Julie." She held me against her and hugged me tight, saying over and over again, "It's going to be okay, he's going to be okay; we'll find him."

After several minutes, I pulled back. "Oh my God, Sheila." My voice sounded pleading, but I'm not sure what I thought she could do. "Oh my God, Carson. My baby, my Carson, Sheila!"

"I know, I know." She gripped my hand and ignored the fact I spoke like a crazy woman on a soap opera. "Jules, look at me."

I barely saw her through the tears streaming down my face, but I tried to meet her eyes.

"Julie Hall, I promise you, I *promise* you we will find him. We will find him."

She repeated the mantra, holding my gaze, until I finally nodded. I wiped my face with the back of my hand—tears, snot, and all—then blew my nose as Sheila handed me a tissue.

"My God, Sheila," and I truly meant it, truly meant to reach up in prayer to beseech God, any god, all the gods, "Carson."

As if I thought the words formed a complete sentence, but I knew Sheila understood.

"We'll find him," she said one more time, nodding at me firmly. "I told Ian I'd call him back in two minutes, after we had time to think."

"Okay. Okay."

I sank back in my seat. My head felt like it might explode with pain and pressure—the pain of such a violent crying jag; the pressure of emotions I didn't know how to possibly express. Fresh tears ran down my face but I tried, I really tried to compose myself. To think productively. To do something.

I looked at the clock.

Nine fifty.

It took a beat for me to realize what that meant: seventeen minutes since Eliza and Tim set out. We'd promised to leave after fifteen minutes. Mute, I pointed at the glowing green numbers.

"Nine fifty," said Sheila, matching me for the ability to state the obvious while somehow sounding surprised. We stared at each other.

From the parking spot next to us came the sound of a car door opening, and I closed my eyes in relief as Tim's car appeared.

Eliza popped open my car door almost in midsentence. "We found her, I'm sure of it—" She jerked to a halt. "What happened?"

I opened my mouth and then closed it again, not able to utter the words.

"Ian called," Sheila said, as Eliza's eyes widened in alarm. "He went to the bathroom for a quick minute and both Carson and Dave disappeared."

"What?" Tim and Eliza exclaimed.

"There were no signs anyone had been in the room," Sheila continued. I schooled myself to listen carefully, since I hadn't had the presence of mind to get the full story when Ian called. "He didn't scent anyone. Dave didn't say anything about leaving the room. Ian actually checked the restaurant, thinking perhaps Dave had taken Carson down there for some reason. But neither of them had been there."

Everyone remained quiet for a moment before Tim spoke, saying out loud our collective thoughts. "Dave kidnapped Carson."

I made myself stop shaking my head. "It just doesn't make sense."

"Sure it does," Tim said. "If Dave's our traitor, it makes perfect sense."

A minute later, something clicked.

I bolted upright in my seat. "He traded him for Ian."

"What?" Sheila and Eliza said in unison.

"Dave. He traded Carson for Ian. He's been in league with them all along. He called them on the phone—I heard it—I just didn't know it at the time. He said they'd done something wrong, it wasn't supposed to be that way, he promised something about tonight. That's what it was, that's what he promised. He promised them Carson."

"But Dave is pack," protested Eliza hotly, before stepping backward and throwing up her hands. "Damn that pup. What the hell is he doing?"

To that, we didn't have a clear answer.

"You even said you couldn't 'read' him," I reminded Eliza. "That both the pups were extremely agitated. He's been lying to us this whole time, somehow."

"Ian is really scared," said Sheila, directing her attention to Eliza. "He's alone and he's frightened, and his best friend may have kidnapped his nephew. I think he needs us—we shouldn't leave him alone right now."

Eliza rubbed her face. "If he gets hurt, Erin will kill me."

Taking that as assent, Sheila said, "I need to call him back. Should I tell him to hop in a cab and come here? Or should one of us go back for him?"

"You go," I nearly shouted, as inspiration hit. Sheila raised her eyebrows in alarm, obviously wondering if I'd gone off the deep end. "No, Sheila, you go back, go to the hotel and get Ian, and while you're at the hotel, scry for Carson. Find him. Find out where he and Dave are. There are tons of his things all over the hotel room and you know him well, it'll be a piece of cake. Right? Please?"

Sheila nodded. "Of course, Jules. I'll go right now and scry for him and call you right away."

"Be careful, Sheila. If Dave is in league with these people, they may know about our new hotel. Do your thing and get back to us." Tim's mild eyes were unusually intense. To my surprise, he reached over and squeezed her arm.

"Right. Then Ian and I will meet you, where? Back here?"

"Back here in an hour," instructed Eliza. "Unless we call you first. The three of us will stake out the house where Kayleigh is being held. We'll find out how many people are in there and figure out the situation."

I agreed. As much as I wanted to be back at the hotel, the last place Carson was, I knew I would collapse when confronted directly with his absence. Sheila would find him. She promised.

Chapter Twenty

So that was how I found myself in the backseat of Tim's car, listening to two Weres argue. We parked on the street two doors down from the house holding Kayleigh. With our car wreathed in darkness, the two Werewolves discussed, in very heated voices, whether or not one of them should get out of the car and snoop around the property. Actually, even though I'd pointed out either one of them would be easily sniffed out by the enemy, they weren't so much arguing about the "whether or not" of the plan, they argued over "who." Eliza thought she, as full moon, should venture near the house. She claimed she was more likely to keep full darkness about her and she could call the moon in other ways—I assumed by creating more crazies—if threatened by discovery. Tim argued he was the official investigator, highly trained for these types of dangerous situations, and, in fact, in charge of our group. Eliza didn't seem cowed by any of that, either because she was indeed the stronger Were or because Tim was so mild-mannered it was hard to take him seriously sometimes. I stayed quiet for about five minutes of their spat, then abruptly opened the car door.

"If you two can't decide, I'll go." I had no patience for them. We needed to rescue Kayleigh and Carson, and we needed to do it right then. Since Kayleigh was closer, we'd free her first so we could focus on Carson.

Dammit. The plan was obvious. Why were they delaying?

"Julie, get back in the car," Eliza snapped.

"Wait." Tim said, eyes narrowed in thought. "No one would expect a human to walk into their safe hold. Maybe, there's a way this works."

"Are you crazy? What can Julie do?" Eliza demanded.

"Thanks for the support."

Tim said, "We know Kayleigh is subjected to medical procedures, multiple bone marrow withdrawals. It would make sense for a medical professional to check on her, make sure her accelerated healing keeps up with the loss of bone marrow." He looked at us. "Right?"

"Rrrright." I thought I knew where he was going.

"What if you pose as a nurse, Julie, and enter the house to check on Kayleigh? A direct entry, knock on the door and everything."

"How am I going to pose as a nurse?"

Tim studied me. "I think what you're wearing works—it wouldn't make sense for you to arrive in scrubs since this is covert. And I have a black bag in the trunk you could carry. It's for my extra clothes and things, but it looks a medical bag. At a quick glance and if you hold yourself properly…."

Uh-huh. So jeans, my yellow t-shirt, and a black overnight bag would make me look like a nurse?

"Actually," Eliza said, "I don't think that's a bad idea. Here." She plucked Tim's cell phone charger from the car floor. "Drape this around your neck and it will look like a stethoscope. Just make sure to keep the ends tucked into your jacket."

Right. Better and better.

"What if they won't let me in? What if they won't leave me alone with Kayleigh? What if..." I ran out of words. Too many what-ifs circled in my mind. Besides, I'm the one who first decided I should check out the house.

"It's up to you, Julie," Eliza said in her most serious voice. "If you think you can pull this off, it's probably our best way to get someone inside the house covertly. If you don't want to do it, then I—or Tim— will check the perimeter of the house and once we know what we face, we'll decide if we should make a frontal assault."

The idea of a frontal assault sounded horrible. I considered, then slowly nodded.

"I can do this." I lifted my chin and met Eliza's questioning gaze.

"Good girl," she said and I snorted. "We'll be right here, wreathed in darkness. If you need me, just yell. Better yet, try to get near a window or something and then yell, so I can find your precise location."

This plan contained so many flaws I decided the best thing was not to think about it any further. Hell, at least while I risked my silly life, I would have something else to think about besides Carson.

Carson.

Besides, if something happened to Carson, I wouldn't care what happened to me anyway.

****

Less than five minutes later, I knocked on the front door of 1107 Deerhollow Road, with a cell phone charger draped around my neck and a small black bag in my hand. I sucked in my stomach, squared my shoulders, and assumed a slightly-bored expression.

"Yes?" The door opened a crack and a man's voice greeted me.

"I'm the nurse, here to see the patient," I said.

A beat passed before the voice spoke again. "Who sent you?"

I raised my eyebrows. "Are we in the habit of using names now, in open air, right here on the doorstep?"

When an immediate answer didn't come, I sighed, made a show of taking out my cell phone and snapped, "Fine. If you choose not to let me in, it's on your head if she's not ready for tomorrow's procedure. What's your name? So I can report you."

The chain on the door slid back slowly and the door opened slightly farther. The man was big. I don't mean big as in tall; big as in brick-wall, his width seemingly equal to his six-foot height. His shoulders were barely contained by a light-weight jacket which also strained over his biceps. His jaw was broad, his eyes small and gray, and I wanted to run away from him screaming.

Instead, I thought, *Carson*, set one foot forward, and demanded, "Well?"

"How come I haven't seen you before?"

"Obviously," I looked him straight in the face, "because I haven't been here before. Did you think you knew everyone involved in this entire…operation? That all personnel were at all times involved in this particular venture? Or have you considered the possibility there are those of us involved in other ways and means?"

"Right," said Steroid-Man. "Well, I guess the others are busy tonight."

Please, let the others be busy tonight.

"They fill you in?"

"I've been briefed, yes," I said, coldly.

"Right. She's up the stairs on the left."

With those words and a pointed finger, he stepped aside.

I took three steps inside the door and then turned back to him. "I assume she's fully restrained and incapacitated?" My tone indicated I had a hard time assuming competency of him or anyone else involved.

"Of course. You want a guard?"

"That will not be necessary. If you have done your job correctly, that is."

I made it in the house.

****

My heart pounded loudly, seeming to say, "You're a stupid idiot, a stupid idiot" as I walked through a very ordinary living room in the direction Steroid-Man pointed. Sure enough, I came upon a stairway leading to the second floor. I tried to contain my nerves well enough to take note of everything: dining area and kitchen straight ahead, stairway on the right, hallway to the left that looked to contain a door to the garage and probably a bathroom, another door off that hallway…an office? In the kitchen, three men sat around a table that had seen better days. They looked like thugs. Thugs playing poker who seemed to think their fellow at the door must have cleared me adequately. One of them— sandy hair, squinting eyes, cigarette in his mouth— leered at me slightly. Ewwww. I tossed my curls and turned my back on him, walking up the staircase. I felt partial relief when I rounded the corner of the stairs because I didn't have to worry they stared at my back. Although I found it disconcerting to think I didn't know *what* they were doing below. What if they called someone to check on this so-called nurse?

Shut up, heart. I could barely think over its thumping.

The upstairs hall saw a continuation of the ugly light blue carpet from below. Who the hell carpets their house entirely in light blue? Resale value, people. Five doors led off the hallway, three of which stood open. Biting my lip, I tiptoed down the hall to peek into each room: two bedrooms and a bathroom, none of which were occupied, all beyond filthy. Like, beer bottles, cigarette butts, dirty clothes filthy. And I won't describe the bathroom. Suffice it to say, I felt a fresh surge of sympathy for Kayleigh. Of the closed doors, only one was on the left side, Kayleigh's location. But...

I walked over to the other door, the closed door on the right. Standing right outside it, I held my breath and leaned my ear against the door. Nothing. I reached a somewhat shaky hand and tried the doorknob. Finding that it turned freely, I pushed ever-so-gently on the door.

"Hey!"

I swiveled around, hand flying to my chest.

"I said the left door. I forgot to give you the key. Here."

How the hell had Steroid-Man climbed the stairs so quietly?

"Don't go in there, *he's* in there."

"Oh." I reached out and took the key from him. "Thanks. Sorry about that, I always confuse my right and left—kind of dangerous, being a nurse and all, always worrying I'll get something wrong during surgery." I laughed nervously.

Shut up, Julie.

"Yeah." Steroid-Man looked like he also thought I should shut up. "Hey, what did you say your name was, again? I gotta log it."

"Jane Halloway," I said in a steady voice. "Thank you for the key and for the warning. I wouldn't want to wake *him* up." I used the same emphasis the guard had. "Now, if you'll excuse me, I'll get to work." I made a little shooing movement with my hands and turned my back on Steroid-Man to walk confidently across the hall to the other closed door.

Yes, the only door with a lock on the knob. Very observant, spy Julie Hall should have noticed that right away. Actually...I nearly missed the lock with the key as I realized in retrospect one of the doors downstairs also had a lock on the outside. Curious.

My shaking fingers inserted the key and I risked a look over my shoulder to make sure Steroid-Man had left. With a small sigh of relief, I turned the key and twisted the handle.

Before I'd even opened the door half an inch, an immensely loud and angry growl greeted me from inside the room. I jumped again and quickly pushed the door all the way open. Sidling inside, I closed it firmly behind me and scolded, "Shhhh! Quiet down, don't wake him up, whoever *he* is."

The growling subsided, but perhaps out of puzzlement as much as anything else. My own mouth dropped open from shock as I saw Kayleigh.

First of all, she was gorgeous. Now, I often described Sheila as gorgeous and she is—eye-catching, poised, dramatic, full of charisma. Eliza had her own quiet beauty and grace. Even though I hated my freckles, I knew I wasn't too awful to look at. But Kayleigh Anderson? She looked like a model, a flippin' supermodel. Even wounded, growling deep in her throat, appearing feral with a bared-teeth grimace, and covered in a hospital gown. Actually, that might have been why she looked like a supermodel, given the weird aesthetic of fashion photography. Kayleigh Anderson: thin, toned, breasts I feared might not even be implants, wavy blonde hair that fell nearly to her waist, huge blue eyes murderous at the moment, perfect pouty rosebud lips, honey-colored tan. Oh yes, the exact California bikini beauty my mind associated with a name like Kayleigh. Plus she'd known my Mac. The inevitable questions rose to my mind. How well had they known each other? I ruthlessly stamped down the jealous beastie in my chest. Of all times. *Focus, Julie*.

Kayleigh lay on a mattress on the floor. In contrast to the rest of the house, this room was actually clean, mostly because of its Spartan nature. One white sheet covered the mattress and another bunched around Kayleigh's feet. A hospital gown that incongruously sported a pattern of pastel polka dots covered her, barely. Her hands and feet were bound with duct tape threaded with silver chains. I saw the chains had left burn marks in several places—I'd have to find out more about inimical silver was to a Werewolf, in order to make sure Carson wasn't over-exposed.

Carson.

I wrenched my mind back to the task at hand, needing all my attention on the present moment.

Kayleigh's beautiful hair hung in lank tangles and her cheek marred by a large scratch, probably a gash at one point but now healing. Bruises covered her: cheekbone, both shins, collarbone. One of her wrists was completely yellow-green, still decorated with faint purple splotches. As Sheila had described, I saw bandages beneath her gown, jutting off her hip bones, her shoulder blades, her breastbone. The IV in her left arm attached to a bag dripped down from one of those metal IV-bag hangers just like in a hospital.

She lay there, growling at the back of her throat, her eyes fixed on me and her hands and feet scrabbling futilely. I double checked the door behind me, making sure it closed tightly, and crossed to her.

Staying carefully out of reach, I set the black bag on the ground and hissed, "Kayleigh. Calm down, I'm with Sheila, the Witch from your dream, we're here to rescue you."

"Then get me the hell out of here," she said in a sweet, breathy voice.

I stifled a hysterical laugh.

"We will, we will get you out of here."

We hadn't made enough plans; I didn't know what to do. My attention had been so focused on getting into the house, on fooling the guards, on finding out how many people were there. Why hadn't we figured out what to do if I'd actually reached Kayleigh, if I had a moment alone with her?

Making a split second decision, I unzipped Tim's black bag and riffled through the items he'd given me. Getting tangled in the stupid cell phone charger aka stethoscope, I ripped it off my neck and threw it on the ground. Finally, I found the Swiss army knife. Trying to hurry, I sawed through the tape at Kayleigh's wrists and unthreaded the silver chain, which I shoved in my pocket. When I finished, I handed her the knife and went to the window to plan our escape.

I didn't realize the window was barred until then. What kind of house had a barred window? In what type of neighborhood did people not notice a bedroom with a barred window? I mean, yes, the window faced the backyard, peeking through other yards until the faint flash of the Fish Fry was just visible. And, yes, the bars were painted white. But, seriously. Bars on the window?

"Fuck!"

Kayleigh finished shaking and rubbing her wrists and now hacked at the duct tape wrapping her ankles. I noticed she took extra care not to touch the silver chain and I hurried over to help her again. I unwrapped the chain and fiddled with it in my hand as she ripped through the rest of the tape. She chafed her ankles, bending and flexing her feet, working the blood back through. I noticed she'd ripped quite a bit of skin off her ankles, but she barely seemed to notice.

Kayleigh reached up and pulled out her earrings. Oh. Massive silver earrings. Then, she gritted her teeth, grabbed the IV line entering her arm, and gave a hard tug. The IV needle came out, along with a substantial chunk of the flesh from her arm. A gobbet of flesh. Blood poured out of her left arm, but with a grim face, she merely used her right hand to hold it, tight. I imagined edgy fashion magazines lined up to capture the pictures of the gruesome scene.

"Holy crap," I said.

"No big deal," she said in her bubble-gum voice. "I healed around the needle. We do that. The bleeding will stop in a second as it knits back together. Especially now that I don't have silver all over me."

"Hey," I said, as a thought occurred to me, "the guard said I should be careful not to wake *him,* somebody across the hall."

"Yes, probably the Were, that Ken guy." Kayleigh showed her teeth in something resembling a smile. "Don't worry, I can take him."

From the looks of her, she'd relish every minute of it, too.

"Well, there are at least four heavily armed thugs out there, too, so let's try to get out of here without fighting the big bad Were?"

"Not so big, not so bad. Truly."

"Uh, okay. I know you heal from bullet wounds pretty well, but me? I'd rather get the hell out of here."

Kayleigh's eyes widened in surprise, as if she'd forgot the weaknesses of mere humans.

"By the way, I'm Julie. Julie Hall." It seemed ridiculous to hold out my hand for a shake, but I did it anyway.

"Mac's girlfriend?" Kayleigh's voice jumped another octave in surprise.

"Yes! You, you know about me?"

"Mac mentioned you last time we worked together, yeah." She assessed me with a newly critical eye. "He didn't tell me you were a superspy, though. I didn't even know you were in this line of work."

"I'm not. Or at least, I wasn't until they killed him."

"I see. Out for revenge? They'll get theirs, Julie, never fear. If not this minute, then soon. Soon." She gave a truly wicked grin I couldn't help but return.

The smile froze on her face a second later, as she stiffened; her whole body at attention. "Someone's here."

"What?" I whispered.

"Someone just knocked at the front door." Kayleigh cocked her head, looking for all the world like some sort of golden retriever.

Chapter Twenty-One

I jumped up and ran to the barred window, while Kayleigh paid careful attention to something only she could hear.

"Can you break these bars?" I hissed.

"I can try." She took a step toward me before her eyes suddenly widened in alarm. "Shit, Julie, they're coming—the guard said something about you." She stood poised between the door and the window, not able to fully commit to either path.

"Who is it? Who is it?"

I heard the pounding of footsteps on the stairs and I took another step backward, my spine pressing against the wall beside the window.

Fuck.

As another thought crossed my mind, I randomly grabbed the IV pole, swung it, and smashed it into the window. Glass shattered and I yelled, "Eliza! Eliza!"

Only seconds later, the door burst open and everything happened at once. Steroid-Man and two of the other thugs burst into the room, with another man behind them, this one not built in the thug mode, but appeared absurdly like a preppy outdoors model. Then I saw a blur of tawny fur and realized Kayleigh had shifted. The wolf flew at the throat of Steroid-Man who fired a hasty shot that cracked into the ceiling. A blur of motion. I dove for the floor, rolling next to the closet,

246

and flung open the door, hoping it would provide a modicum of cover. I didn't go so far as to crawl *into* the closet, mostly because I didn't think I could live with myself if my friends got hurt while I curled in a ball on the floor of a closet. Mostly covered by the door, I peered into the room.

It felt like watching a badly cut action movie; I only absorbed quick images. Kayleigh shook her head, blood flying from her tawny muzzle; Steroid-Man staggered backward, his hands flying to his neck; the reflection off a gun held by my sandy-haired thug admirer, whose eyes narrowed as he searched for a shot. Then I heard a groan from the window and the white-painted bars flew through the room, hit one of the guards in the midsection and sent him flying into the hall. Eliza jumped into the room, her buff-fur standing on end. I only briefly saw her before I lost track of her, my gaze sliding away from her like oil as she pulled on the shadows in the room to conceal herself. Another wolf entered the room and I had time to wonder, Tim? Ken? before the wolf sprang at Kayleigh and the two tumbled into a whirl of fur and growls of rage.

Suddenly, I remembered I, too, had a gun and fumbled desperately at the back of my jeans where I'd stuck it, thinking it looked too obvious in my jacket pocket. I had a hard time grasping it and then realized my fist was still clenched around the silver chains from Kayleigh's ankles. I shoved them in my pocket with the others and finally pulled out the gun. I pointed it at the door, hoping I could hit one of the other guards, held my breath, and squeezed the trigger.

Then I removed the safety and raised the gun again.

Dammit, what if I hit Eliza? Where was she? I hesitated.

Through the chaos of the room, I heard a crash from downstairs. Kayleigh and the gray wolf combatted in the middle of the room, though Kayleigh's teeth were closed around the other wolf's neck and he was keening. Both wolves were flung about by the wild movements of the enemy wolf I assumed was Ken/Taylor Dunn. Steroid-Man appeared dead, judging from the condition of his throat. The remaining guard tried to find a clear shot at Kayleigh. Then, he was knocked off his feet by a blur of teeth and fur, as Eliza dropped her cover and rushed past him. She crashed into the man I'd seen arrive behind the guards. That man thumped to the floor so hard I heard his head hit, despite the ugly blue carpet. Eliza crouched at his throat with a growl that raised the hackles on my neck. And I wasn't a wolf. I didn't even have hackles. Her threat rumbled through the room.

Everyone froze.

The man, the one resembling a wholesome model, said quietly, "If you harm me, you're dead."

Insane laughter bubbled up in my throat, and I swallowed it down.

"You, put your gun down," Tim said from the hallway. His gun was trained on the sole standing guard who, in turn, lowered his weapon slowly. "Kick it here."

The guard complied and put his hands on his head. His face revealed no emotion, and I didn't want to be near him when he reclaimed his gun, that was for sure.

"You." Tim swiveled to face the stand-off between the two wolves. The Ken/Taylor Were lay on his back, with Kayleigh poised above his jugular. "Change."

A long pause ensued before the wolf-form writhed into the shape of a man. A slower transformation than I'd seen from any of our Weres, almost as if every step had to be conceived separately. Certainly nothing like Eliza's fluid shifts. I watched as his form lengthened, twisted, and became that of a blond, bearded man. Sweat poured down his face, joining blood from bites on his shoulder and arm. One of his legs was curled strangely.

"Kayleigh." Tim's voice held a note of warning and the trembling wolf whined softly. She took a half step away from the man, but then, with a sudden lunge, she flung herself on him with a snarl. Before any of us could react, she tore his throat out with one white flash of her teeth.

Blood poured out of the body, which arched once before collapsing.

Kayleigh savaged his body, snapping and tearing at his flesh until he was unrecognizable. Finally, she pulled away from him and sat back on her haunches.

As she relaxed, our shock released the rest of us. The guard sank down on his knees and crawled backward as far as possible from Kayleigh's blood-covered form. The oh-so-composed preppy model type turned an awful gray color as he stared at Eliza's fangs so close to his own vulnerable neck. Eliza seemed to draw back slightly as if to make sure she wasn't also tempted to some act of carnage, though she didn't ease her guard on the man. The only one who seemed relatively nonplussed was Tim. His mild face stoic, neither his attention nor the point of his gun ever wavered.

Me, I turned to the side and heaved violently. Again and again, unable to control my body's revulsion. At least I didn't inadvertently fire my gun or anything; even in the midst of my misery, I had the presence of mind to lay the .22 carefully by my side.

"Kayleigh." Tim's voice rang cold and sharp as ice, and acted as smelling salts to my raw nerves.

The tawny wolf shrugged, actually shrugged, which I didn't know was possible for a canine. Then she rose to her feet and stretched, a long and leisurely stretch, licked her chops, and changed into the supermodel. This time, she was probably beyond even the tastes of modern fashion: covered in flecks of blood, streaks of it matting her hair, looking like a murder victim herself.

"Sorry," she said in her sweet, breathy voice, not sounding sorry at all.

Tim let out his breath in a hiss. "We'll talk later. Go tie up the guard in the hall, he's still unconscious."

Guards. One, two, three… "Tim, there was another guard in the kitchen when I got here," I said, sounding slightly hoarse. I wiped my mouth on my sleeve.

"Taken care of." His voice gave no indication of the details.

Kayleigh flounced past Tim, leaving drops of blood in her wake. From the hall, came dull thuds as she none-too-carefully rearranged the unconscious thug and then I heard the unmistakable ripping sound of duct tape.

"Now this one," instructed Tim.

When Kayleigh re-entered the room, the kneeling guard shrunk back. The vision of the tough blond thug nearly cowering in front of the gorgeous woman would have seemed humorous in other circumstances. Given what had just transpired, however, his reaction was pure common sense.

The sleek werewolf secured the guard firmly, trussing his hands behind him and binding his legs at ankle and knee. When she finished, she slipped the roll of duct tape onto her wrist like a bracelet and rose fluidly, waiting for further instructions from Tim. She didn't spare a glance for what remained of the blond Were's body, even as my gaze was drawn back to it, only to be jolted afresh by the sight. Afraid I might vomit, again, I rose shakily and pulled on a corner of Kayleigh's former sheet to cover the lumpy shape of the body. The metallic smell threatened to overwhelm me, but I felt a bit better once I couldn't see the mess. Even when blood started soaking the white sheet almost immediately.

Tim raised his brows.

"Sorry," I said, swallowing thickly. "I'm fine." I didn't turn my gaze in Kayleigh's direction, though I swore I sensed amusement in her silhouette.

Tim nodded once. He still held his gun pointed at the slim man on the ground next to Eliza.

"Eliza," he said, neither voice nor weapon wavering, "back away."

The buff-colored wolf obeyed. Her teeth remained barred, her back legs ready to spring.

"Stop." Tim raised his voice and at first, I thought he addressed the man. I realized in the next instant Kayleigh had taken an eager step forward and froze again at Tim's command. She tossed her blonde mane and slumped against the wall of the room.

"Eliza, change." Obviously, Tim would prevent Kayleigh from approaching this captive any closer than necessary.

Between one heartbeat and the next, Eliza straightened to human form. Her fawn-colored hair was barely out of place, still secured in a straight ponytail down her back. She held out one hand toward Kayleigh who snorted and tossed over the duct tape. After securing the man, Eliza sat back on her haunches and fixed her gaze upon him.

"If I harm you, I'm dead, huh?" She echoed his earlier words. "Who are you, my friend, that your blood is so valuable?"

"Jimmy Bianco." Tim answered the question.

When no other information came, I asked the obvious, "Who the hell is Jimmy Bianco?"

"His father is Joe Bianco, Joey White-hand. Brother-in-law to John Romano, head of the Romano family, based in Chicago. With a foothold in Las Vegas, so it seems.

"The question is," Tim continued, as he stood over Jimmy, "who else is involved? How far up does this go?"

For a man lying on his side with his hands and feet joined by duct tape, Jimmy Bianco showed remarkable poise. With no wolves threatening to rip out his throat, he'd regained some color. He had wavy dark brown hair that managed to fall perfectly across his forehead, shadowing the palest brown eyes I'd ever seen—like frothy milk touched with a taste of coffee. His forehead was broad, his jawline strong and set in pleasant determination, his khaki pants creased sharply, and only after Eliza forced his arms backward did his pale green golf shirt come untucked. He still looked handsome. In fact, in other circumstances, I'd probably flirt with him.

"The real question," my voice shook with fear and anger, "is where the *hell* is my baby? What have you done with him?"

Jimmy looked at me, really looked at me for the first time. As the least threatening form in the room, I don't think I merited his attention before.

"You know," I continued, "my baby Carson, the Werewolf? The one your men have been following around the country and trying to kidnap?" My voice rose as I didn't elicit a response and I stood over him, hands clenched, eager to kick him or something.

"I don't have your son," he said. "I don't know where he is."

"The hell you don't. Dave Blythe took him, and I know he's working with you."

Kayleigh spoke up, her incongruous voice startling me once again. "Have you been in the basement yet?"

Tim, Eliza, and I turned to look at her.

"What's in the basement?" I asked for all of us.

"I'm not sure," Kayleigh said, "But I think we need to see it. Or them."

Chapter Twenty-Two

After Kayleigh's cryptic comment, Tim dragged Jimmy near the remaining guard and set Eliza to watch them both. Perhaps he didn't trust Kayleigh with them; I know I didn't. She seemed perfectly normal right now, but I couldn't forget the sight of her savaging Ken's body even after he was dead. Tim, Kayleigh, and I went downstairs, me trailing behind. My anxiety about Carson spiraled up my spine, now that I wasn't distracted by life-and-death danger.

Kayleigh led our small group down the hall, toward the other locked door I'd noticed. I realized there was not one dead guard in the kitchen, but three. Killed cleanly, from the looks of things; a couple of gun shots and what appeared to be a broken neck. I looked at Tim with new respect. Not bothering to find a key, Kayleigh merely twisted the door knob and the lock broke with an audible ping. Then she flicked on the light and went downstairs. I followed the two Weres, rubbing my arms hard as energy mounted in the air. I realized with a start they both growled deep in their throats, so low I felt it in my chest as much as I heard the noise.

"What *is* that?" Tim asked sharply.

"I'm not sure," Kayleigh said in response. "That's what we need to find out."

As we descended into the basement, I saw the space had undergone a recent remodel—hasty at that. A rough cement block wall stretched across the room, its gray expanse broken only by a heavy metal door. On this side of the new wall, the basement looked bizarrely like a cross between a hospital and mad scientist's lab. A metal table stood just off-center, with several movable lights. Thick leather restraints outfitted the table, and coils of silver chain lay beside it. A glass-fronted chest glinted with various metal instruments, several IV poles dotted the side wall, and other bits of unintelligible medical equipment caught my eye as the Weres crossed quickly, very quickly to the metal door.

Tim raised his gun and thumbed off the safety. He cocked his head at Kayleigh, who lifted her chin in assent. Then, after checking the door handle, he threw his entire weight at the door.

The hinges snapped, door flinging violently into the dark space, and Tim ended in a crouch that put him well below instinctive target height. Kayleigh let out a cry somewhere between a roar and a howl and darted through the opening.

A cacophony of noise rose like a solid wall. I stood, covering my ears against the growls and howls and screams. One voice rose loudest and the others responded, quieting into whines and scuffling noises.

Slowly, Tim stood to his full height. "Mother moon," he breathed more entreaty than curse. "What have they done?"

I took unsteady steps to join him.

The area behind the wall was dimly lit. As a human, I couldn't see as well as the Weres, so I reached out a hand in slow motion to flick a switch. Overhead lights flooded the area. A hall ran the length of the concrete block barrier, facing the cells. Or pens. Five of them. Each containing one or two…creatures…the stuff of nightmares. The things in the pen were neither human nor wolf, but something somewhere in the middle, something horribly, horribly in the middle. They were all different, like lumps of wax half melted between shapes, combining various aspects of teeth, hair, limbs. Each had the same eyes, though. Eyes full of horror and hatred and anguish and anger, reflecting the electric lights like cats caught in the middle of the street.

Kayleigh stood in the hall, still as stone.

We fell silent, just as the creatures had ceased their noise, though they continued to watch us while pacing and shuddering in their cages.

In a flurry of movement, Tim turned on his heel and stormed back up the two flights of stairs, leaving Kayleigh and me to follow him, dragged in his wake. When he entered the room with our captive, Eliza sprang to her feet, looking at me wildly.

"What. Have. You. Done." Tim punctuated each word with a sharp kick.

Jimmy didn't cry out. Even after he'd regained his breath, he didn't speak. Tim kicked him again, harder, right in the ribs.

"Were those…things…Weres?" I asked Kayleigh. She shook her head, mute.

"Fine." Tim turned his back on the still-silent Jimmy. "Perhaps you're not ready to talk." With one quick motion, he threw the bound guard over his shoulder and set off through the house. I quickly followed him.

Back in the basement, Tim threw the guard roughly on the cement floor in front of the cages. The nearest creature slunk to the bars and tried to stick its muzzle through, sniffing and drooling.

Tim sat the man up, holding his head until he looked directly at the creature. The guard blanched.

"Do you remember what Kayleigh did to your friend Ken?" Tim's voice was mild, oh so mild. "Do you have any doubt these creatures would do the same or worse, were I to open the cages and have you join them?"

The man tried to avert his gaze, tried to look at me, perhaps thinking I was the weak and squeamish link. I thought about Carson, and clenched my hands.

"Is your loyalty to little Jimmy worth such a death?"

The man's mouth worked several times before he managed to make sound. "It wasn't supposed to happen that way. They were mistakes. Jimmy and Dr. D was gonna fix 'em."

"*What* wasn't supposed to happen that way?" Tim's voice rang through the tense room.

"Changing them, making them change. They was supposed to be strong and real, like Ken. That's why they volunteered. But he's going to fix 'em, that's why we needed to try another Were. And it's working—look at that one." The man jerked his chin in the direction of another cell, "He's better now. Almost."

The creature in question retained human legs and hands with his otherwise wolf-form. His face looked like lump of clay squeezed by a child's fist. His eyes, one high, one low near his foreshortened stump of a muzzle, and mismatched: one a tender brown and the other green. Both shot with blood. He keened, pommeling his front legs at the bars of his cage. His

257

fingernails were caked with blood that streaked his hands and the fur of his legs.

The man winced. "Jake," his voice was gruff and broke slightly, "you'll be okay, man. You're getting better."

My gorge rose again.

"These... You knew these people? These were people, you knew, that you... Were they all dark moons? Is this what happens when you change a dark moon?" I looked at Tim in desperation.

"No." Tim's face remained impassive. "When you change a dark moon, if it's successful, there's no difference between that Were and a born Were. If it's not successful, the dark moon dies.

"My guess is these were ordinary people—regular humans—someone tried to change. With bone marrow transplants, yes?" Tim toed the guard.

The man sighed and closed his eyes for a moment before looking up at Tim. "Yeah. That's right. Ken said the Weres just weren't strong enough, though. Or maybe it was the blood-type. I'm no doctor."

"But typing for bone marrow is a lot more complicated than blood type, isn't it? I think it's really hard to find a match." I searched Tim's face as if he had the answers.

"Where's the doctor who did all this?" Tim asked. When the guard didn't answer, he knelt down in front of him, holding the man's chin and forcing their gazes together. "Do you think your friends—are you confident Jake is still Jake? That he still knows you? That he bears no grudge for the fact he is in there, like that, while you continue to help Jimmy mutilate and torture others, in a vain attempt to create Weres? Mafia Weres? What would happen, if I put you in his cage?"

The guard shot a quick glance at the-creature-who-had-been-Jake. A shudder crept over me.

"I dunno, man. I dunno where the doctor's at. He comes in the mornings to start the procedures. You gotta believe me, I'm just the muscle here. They don't trust me with nothing."

Tim flung the man down, and I winced as his head hit the cement. A thin trickle of blood made its way from his blond hairline and all of the creatures scented the air with sudden avidness. Tim walked over in front of the cage holding Jake and investigated the lock with studied nonchalance.

"Really, I don't know nothing! Ask Jimmy where Dr. D is, Jimmy would know." The guard babbled on for several moments that stretched and stretched, as Tim remained facing the cage doors, holding the bars, ignoring the man's words and then pleas.

With a disgusted look on his face, Tim turned around, picked up the guard, and left the basement. He motioned for me to precede him. Before leaving the room, he faced the cages once more.

Speaking clearly and with utmost formality, he said, "By mother moon and her silver light, I promise you I will return and I will see you either rehabilitated or granted the mercy of death." He bowed his head to the misshapen creatures and closed the door firmly.

****

On our way up the stairs to the second floor, my cell phone rang. I jumped, understandable given my taut nerves. Were I a violin, my strings would snap.

When I fumbled the cell phone out of my jacket pocket, I saw Sheila calling.

Carson.

"Did you find him? Sheila?"

"Jules, he's fine. I scryed for him and he's fine. He's with Dave, and he wasn't even crying and we're going find him, okay?"

"Where the hell are they? Where are he and Dave?"

"They were in a car—"

"Dave took my baby in a car? Without his car seat?" I found myself shouting into the phone and took a deep breath. Perspective. Must maintain perspective. My baby had been kidnapped by a rogue Werewolf and car seat safety was not the straw to break this camel's back.

"I'm sorry," I said, much quieter. "Go on."

"Okay...They were in a car, a cab, and I watched them pull up to a house, a fancy single-story ranch house right off a golf course. I even saw a sign for the Painted Desert Golf Club."

I repeated the name once aloud and several times to myself.

"Where are you guys? What's going on now?"

"Uh, long story. We rescued Kayleigh and captured Jimmy Bianco, who's apparently the son of the brother-in-law of some head mafia guy named John something. We also have one of his guards as prisoner. Also, uh, several dead guards. We found eight...creatures. Half-man, half-wolf creatures. Apparently, they are regular humans the mafia tried to turn into Weres by giving them bone marrow transplants."

Silence on the other end of the phone and I imagined Sheila trying to digest the news. I heard Ian asking her if everyone all right, so I answered the second question and told her we were all fine.

"Okay," said Sheila. "So now what?"

"Now I'm coming back to the hotel, and we're going to find Carson. That's what."

I ended the call and walked into the bedroom where everyone congregated. Tim had dumped the guard on the floor about six feet from Jimmy. Jimmy sat up and provided monosyllabic answers to the Weres. At the moment, I cared about none of it.

"Sheila found Carson. I'm going back to the hotel and then I'm going to rescue him. Are any of you coming with me?"

"I am," said Eliza, immediately.

"I'll come, too."

At Tim's answer, Jimmy's eyes visibly widened.

"You're going to leave us here, with *her*?" he asked.

Kayleigh smiled, a feral movement of her lips, and said in her breathy voice, "We'll have a good time, Jimmy. You and me. Just like the last few days. Although," she made a slight moue, "a little different."

Her wink might have been a gunshot, judging from Jimmy's reaction. His gaze swung wildly to where Ken's body still lay, barely covered by the now red-soaked sheet.

"I can be helpful," he said, sitting as upright as possible given his bonds.

"You haven't proven so," said Eliza matter-of-factly.

"If you harm me, my father—and Romano—will kill you. They will hunt you down and kill you."

"Now, that's not helpful talk, is it?" Tim directed his next question to Eliza. "Shall we?" He motioned to the door.

"Dammit, Jimmy, that bitch is going to kill us as soon as they leave. Answer their goddamn questions," the guard shouted.

I had the feeling the guard wasn't used to yelling at his boss.

"I'll answer your questions, really. Just don't leave me alone with her," Jimmy said, his eyes wild with terror.

"I tell you what," Tim walked over to Jimmy, "I'll stay for a while, for as long as you answer our questions. If you stop cooperating, I *will* leave Kayleigh to guard you."

"Tim, call us on Julie's cell," Eliza said over her shoulder as she and I hurried out the door.

Chapter Twenty-Three

Twenty minutes back to the hotel. Twenty minutes of me quietly ripping my cuticles to shreds. The last ten minutes were just on the damned Strip which needed about ten lanes if it was going to hold all the damned cars. Dammit. Eliza drove, a good thing, because if I'd been behind the steering wheel, I was pretty sure I'd have driven on the sidewalk. If the cops came after us, I was also pretty sure we had assorted bloodspots on our clothes that might be hard to explain.

We didn't engage in small talk during the drive. Or big talk, either.

When we finally arrived at the hotel, we drove up to the door and I hopped out, leaving Eliza idling the car. Sheila and Ian stood close inside the front door, pretending interest in someone's slot machine. Sheila saw me in an instant, elbowed Ian, and strode toward the door. I realized Eliza was going to blow a gasket if Ian came with us, but came to the almost instantaneous conclusion I didn't care. Ian was one more strong Were on our side, he was Carson's uncle, and I would take all the help I could get.

When Sheila reached me, she held out her closed hand. I extended mine and she dropped Carson's ducky pin into my palm.

"Found it on the floor," she said.

I closed my fist around the pin, wishing it would spring open and impale my hand, wishing I could have some physical injury to take my mind off the pain I felt.

I'm not sure if it was the set of my jaw, the mulish look on Ian's face, or the innocent expression worn by Sheila that elicited Eliza's quiet "Damn you all" as the three of us slid into the car. She either decided we had no time to waste or decided she didn't want to argue, because she pulled the car out of the drive without another word.

As we turned onto the Strip, she said, "Ian, if you get hurt, I'll kill you. Julie, if he gets killed, *you* are telling Erin." That out of the way, she asked Sheila, sitting in the navigator's seat, "Which way?"

Sheila looked at her cell phone and proceeded to give precise directions to the Painted Desert Golf Club. Luck was actually with us as we took the most direct possible route and managed to locate the precise house Sheila saw in her scrying.

"There," Sheila said, followed by, "No, don't slow down."

Eliza drove on for a block, made the first right, and parked the car.

"That one, part brick, white siding, number 578."

"Okay," I said and pulled out my phone. "Shit, I don't have Tim's number. Why don't I have Tim's number?"

Sheila rattled off the number.

"Uh, Sheila?" I raised my eyebrows at her. "Why the hell do you have Tim's phone number memorized?"

After a moment of hesitation, Sheila turned and beamed a smile into the backseat. "Why Jules," she said, "you know how numbers get stuck in my head."

Actually, I knew no such thing, but I wasn't going to argue. Instead, I had her repeat the number more slowly and dialed Tim. When he answered the phone, I asked, "What did you learn from Jimmy?"

"Well, first, I learned he lives at 578 North Painted Desert Drive."

"Oh."

"His friend and co-conspirator, a guy named Joey Daniels is there. He's Dr. D. Three or four mafia goons will likely be in the house.

"From what our friend Jimmy says, there is a lot of infighting between the different mafia families in Vegas right now, hence the heightened guard. The plan to create Werewolves serving the mafia was Jimmy's bright idea to ensure his future—and his father's, but he hasn't shared the plan with his dad yet. He wanted to make sure the procedure worked first."

"Okay," I said, "so, the doctor and three or four guards." Yes, I cared about the big picture, but I focused on essentials and right now getting to Carson was the only thing that counted. "Dave will be there, too, we can't forget Dave. But no other Weres?"

"No. Ken was the only Were working with Jimmy. There were two others—both lone wolves, one from California and one from rural Nevada—but they're both dead. Killed by the doctor's experiments. They weren't strong wolves to begin with. Ken, full name Ken Martinone, was actually a dark moon wolf, turned by a bite. He was the one who brought all of this to Jimmy, the mastermind behind it all, if you will. Ken met Dave when he was in Vegas with his sister during the winter holidays and I guess he convinced him. Anyway," Tim stifled a sigh, "I've learned all I'm going to from our friend Jimmy Bianco. I'm leaving Kayleigh here; I think I've impressed upon her the need for restraint. I'll join you as soon as I can."

I summarized the information for three in the car and then said, "We can't wait for him, though. He might be half an hour—I'm not waiting half an hour."

No one contradicted me.

"All right," said Eliza, "Ian and I will go in, either through the front door or a back entrance, we'll figure that out on the ground. I'll cloak us in darkness, but Dave will scent us through that. Ian," she turned to search his face, "I know Dave is—was—your best friend. We may have to fight him. He might get hurt or even killed. Are you sure you're up to this?"

I saw a muscle move in Ian's jaw, but his eyes and voice were steady as he answered, "Yes."

Eliza gave one decisive nod.

"Julie and Sheila, you come in behind us. Stay out of any direct fighting as much as possible. We'll try to disable or distract as many guards as possible—after all, we'll heal from bullets—"

"Unless they're silver."

Eliza continued over my interruption, "*Even* if they're silver, unless they hit something vital. Just takes longer." She pointed at me. "Julie, your sole mission is Carson, find him and get him out so he can't be used as a hostage."

Good, my mission accorded with my actual plan.
****

Sheila and I waited near a large hedge and tried to judge when we should follow the two Weres. Every atom of my body craned in the direction of Carson.

"Let's give them two more minutes," I said, looking at my watch. Sheila nodded, with her head twisted to see the house.

After not quite two minutes, I decided I couldn't wait any longer, but Sheila didn't quibble. We checked our guns, neither of which had actually been fired since I hadn't managed to participate in the fighting earlier. I felt as confident as possible. Which meant not very confident, but I hoped I faked it well. I watched a lot of crime shows, after all. I read a lot of mysteries. Some with Werewolves.

Given the late hour, or maybe super early morning, we didn't have to worry about nosy neighbors and we crept to the back door of the house. We hadn't quite reached the stoop when we heard a crash, followed by cursing and Dave's voice yelling, "I told you that Witch bitch would find us."

The kitchen door stood ajar and, with a gesture of my head to Sheila, I bumped it open with my foot, gun held at the ready. The kitchen was empty, except for a dead body I attempted to ignore after a cursory glance. I motioned Sheila to follow me. When she came abreast, she whispered, "You know, *I'm* the one who knows how to shoot. I'm going first."

We followed the sound of fighting toward the living room. As we stalked down the hall, pieces of the action came into view. A pair of legs jutted from behind a plaid couch, legs with jeans and cowboy boots, so not one of ours. Eliza faced the downed person, a snarl twisting her mouth, and, just as we arrived, a clap of thunder and a red bloom suddenly appeared on her right shoulder.

Immobile silence, like the shock after a camera flashes. Then Eliza crumpled to the ground, forcing my lungs to convulse in a gasp before she twisted into her wolf-self and disappeared from my sight as she called the moon. The next thing I saw, she flew through the air, a vengeful wolf, lunging at the shooter, whom I only saw for a split-frame, his own face morphing from satisfaction to terror.

She was going to be okay, our girl. She'd heal. I repeated the thought, then realized I had spoken aloud as Sheila responded with a fierce, "Yes."

Yips and growls and crashes sounded from the other part of the room, the part still hidden by the wall, and I was about to peer out when I heard the other noise. My whole self was pulled straight and taut, as if by a dog whistle.

Carson, crying.

Looking at me in alarm, Sheila started to mouth, "What?" before she heard it, too. Her eyes narrowed. "Go," she said, "I'll help out here. Go!"

I didn't need to be told twice. Actually, I didn't need to be told at all. Without pausing to let my fears catch up with the rest of me, I darted straight through the living room and down the other side of the hallway. Carson cried hysterically with a note in his voice that said I-need-mama-right-now and I trembled, literally trembled in eagerness to reach him, pulled by a magnetism that had reset my compass on the day of his birth.

When I reached the closed door that kept me from my screaming baby, I still didn't pause for thought. I smashed open the door, gun held in my hand but certainly not at the ready, more likely to bodily jump any goon in the room than have the presence of mind to take aim and fire. I was only momentarily disoriented by the scene, a low-lit bedroom obviously meant to soothe. Not some mafia thug, but a round-faced woman, hair pulled into a bun, gray hairs sticking out randomly from among the black, her face creased with worry, crooning at Carson and doing the two-step baby bounce. At my entry, she stopped moving and held my baby—*my baby*—close to her chest, as if to protect him. Protect him from *me*.

"Give me my baby," I yelled and stormed forward.

"No, no!" The woman's eyes focused on my gun first, then rose to my face. "No. Who are you people? Leave our sweet baby alone.

"Dave." She cried, "Mr. Dave. Someone is trying to take your brother, help, help."

"Give me my baby. Dammit!"

Carson screamed loudly, that baby scream where his lips turned blue and his face turned red and mottled. The woman hugged Carson to her, sidestepping me and dodging around a rocking chair.

I screamed. Yes, I threw my head back and screamed, pouring my rage and desire and frustration into a scream that left me hoarse and panting. The woman's eyes widened and she crossed herself, praying quietly under her breath. Abruptly, Carson fell silent, perhaps awed his mama made that sound. Something to which he could aspire.

In the relative silence after my explosion, I looked the woman dead in the eyes, raised my gun, and fired a shot into the ceiling. The percussion made us jump, all three of us, and drywall fell down in a small landslide.

I said, "Give. Me. My. Baby."

She did.

In romance novels, the author often uses phrases like "the world stopped" or "her heart only then began to beat" when the male and female lead characters first see each other. I don't know about that kind of love, if it really exists, if it's any truer than the love where you work together, where you accept each other's annoying habits, where you roll your eyes inwardly at your partner's occasional stupidity. I mean, I loved Mac, but I never felt he was the whole reason for my existence, that his appearance was like rays of sunlight piercing the clouds or any such thing. Our relationship was much more complicated.

But this? This. Taking Carson into my arms made me whole. He still gave those little shuddering sighs that end a fierce crying jag, and my heart shook, gasping along with him. He was so small, so small I could envelop him entirely, cradle him against my chest, smell his head, that sweaty-sweet baby smell, breathe in his little breaths. His cheek was so soft. Leaning my face against him felt like touching nothing at all, like putting soapy fingers through a bubble. My baby, my Carson, little Carson. He had been gone forever, the absence inside me had swallowed me alive, yet it had only been hours, a few scant hours. My whole life.

The woman in the room moved and my attention jerked, a spasm of alarm, but, no, she just sank down into the rocking chair.

"I don't understand," she said, "Mr. Dave, he said their parents were dead."

"Mr. Dave said a lot of things, I'm sure. Look," I said, clear this woman wasn't involved in the greater plot points. "This is not a very safe place right now. If I were you, I would leave as soon as possible, go home. And don't mention anything about any of this to anyone."

"I never talk about Mr. Jimmy's business," she said and I wasn't sure if she reassured me or felt affronted.

"Good, then."

Ninety percent of my brain soaked in Carson, through every possible sense. The other ten percent decided my job—my only job at this point—was to get him out of the house to safety. I wasn't likely to be any help in a fight, anyway.

I might need both hands, though. In the absence of my sling—why hadn't I brought the sling—I grabbed a throw from the top of the chest footing the bed. Sage green chenille and would do in a pinch. I wrapped Carson to my body and tied a knot at my left shoulder. Fashioning a temporary sling made me feel fairly competent for the first time tonight. I fished out a spare pacifier from my pocket and gave it to Carson, hoping to soothe him until he could nurse. I kept my left hand on Carson's back, unwilling to give up that touch even as his body nestled against me, and kept the gun in my right hand.

When I crept into the hall, I didn't see anyone, friend or foe. I heard fighting in the living room and I sent a fervent prayer into the universe. I told myself over and over I couldn't help and, in fact, Carson and I would be a huge liability. Nothing assuaged the guilt I felt as I walked to the front door. The hall was empty, as were the front steps, and I stepped out into the night feeling an absurd letdown. I hesitated on the front walkway, then turned to wait near the same hedges where Sheila and I had lurked earlier.

Carson stirred and I sat down in the midst of the brush to comfort him. Probably my most surreal parenting experience ever: shouldering aside prickly branches, untying my make-shift sling, setting the gun down within easy reach. This neighborhood was definitely pricey, large well-irrigated yards, cultivated trees and bushes for privacy. Which I guess was just as well, since a bunch of Werewolves and mafia fought in good old Number 578. I couldn't hear the battle from where we hid.

When Carson finished feeding, his body was limp and soft with sleep. I carefully bundled him up again and tied him against me firmly. I weighed my options, wait longer? Go back into the house? Then a car turned onto the road, a car I recognized, Tim's car. I rose slightly as he continued down the road and parked farther from the house. He stepped out of the car, closed the door firmly but quietly behind him, and slipped into wolf-form. He loped toward the house and flicked an ear as he caught my scent, quickly detouring to my side.

When he reached me, he didn't change form, but poked his nose into my hand. Taking this as a normal wolf-greeting and a prod for information, I updated him as best as I could: some guards down, still fighting inside, Eliza shot but healing, I'd grabbed Carson, obviously, and headed out to wait for them.

"Do you—should I come in with you?"

The wolf shook his head adamantly, a human gesture that looked odd on a wolf but intelligible. He pawed the ground near my feet, glanced upward to make sure I understood, and turned to dart toward the back of the house. I watched his gray tail flick around the corner and bounced on my toes in that automatic baby-soothing motion.

Then, I heard a muffled crack. I ran to the back of the house, gun in my hand. After I'd taken half a dozen steps, my mind finally categorized it, "Gunshot, silenced," and I extended both arms, holding my weapon, and darted closer to the side of the house. I hesitated at the corner, then bit my lip, exhaled, and rounded the corner, gun first.

Tim lay crumpled on the ground, close to the back steps, in human form. A clinical voice in my mind said, "That doesn't bode well," while the emotional voice said, "Shit, shit, shit, shit," and focused on the man approaching Tim's downed body. The half-moon illuminated him briefly and glinted off the weapon in his hand, the gun pointed steadily, oh-so-steadily, at the fallen Were.

I'm not sure if I made a noise or not, but I remember the man jerked his head in my direction, right before I shot him. I remember his head in the next instant, jolted back with the impact of the bullet, blood and bone and other things spraying out the back of his skull. I stood there, paralyzed as if I had been the one shot. Instead of the shooter. Holy fuck.

My gun had no silencer, and I noticed a light flick on in the neighbor's house. Carson also began crying in protest and I had the horrible fear I'd somehow deafened him.

My mind blurred, but later, when I reflected back on the night, I felt overwhelming gratitude the recoil from the gun hadn't harmed Carson. I managed to keep the gun steady without jerking into my baby—perhaps even in such a moment, my instinct to protect Carson outweighed anything else. Sheila couldn't get over the fact I'd shot the man in the head. The next day, she repeatedly asked, "Don't you know you're not supposed to aim for the head?" Even once I explained I hadn't aimed for his head, I'd been trying for something down on his torso; she just shook her head at me. Hell, maybe the lucky cow pin helped after all.

But at that moment, my ears still ringing, I found myself unable to construct any clear thoughts at all. I bounced Carson, soothing him automatically, and stared at the two crumpled bodies in the grass: Tim and the man I'd shot.

Sheila ran out the back door first, and gave an inarticulate cry as she skidded down on her knees next to Tim. The next second, she yelled, "Eliza, Eliza!" The buff-colored wolf launched from the back steps. She landed in human form, kneeling next to Tim, and my breath caught at her gracefulness.

"Who's out there? I'm calling the cops."

The voice echoed from the neighbor's partly open window, and I heard a muttered curse from Eliza. Darkness seemed to rise from the ground like fingers of fog, encircling all of us, flickering. I hadn't been on this side of the moon-calling before. I hadn't actually realized she could call shifting darkness over this large an area, this many people. Carson seemed soothed by the moving darkness and fell quiet again.

When I reached Tim's side, he was breathing, albeit with a rasp and a gurgle. Eliza bent her head to his chest wound and for a horrified second, I thought she might lick the blood.

"Silver," she snapped, "still embedded."

Her ponytail lashed the air as she disappeared back into the house and reemerged with a knife, an ordinary carving knife from the kitchen.

"Hold his shoulders. Sheila, hold his shoulders, I need to get this out."

As soon as Sheila placed her hands on Tim's shoulders, Eliza said, "Tim, stay with us. You're going to be okay." She plunged the knife into his chest, widening the wound, causing a fresh gush of blood to stream thickly down his side. Her taut expression reflected her concentration and I focused on that, rather than Tim's chest. She turned the knife, twisting and probing and I saw her eyes narrow as she found the bullet. After a very long minute, she coaxed it out of the wound and sat back, relief coloring her cheeks.

"Definitely silver and nicked a lung before getting hung up on his ribs. Probably would have killed him if I hadn't gotten to it. I think he'll be okay now, though."

"You 'think'?" Sheila's voice came as barely more than a whisper, and her hands still lay on Tim's shoulders.

"Well, as you noticed, we're not exactly in an operating room. I definitely worsened the wound just now, but he should start healing." Eliza wiped her hands on the grass, leaving long tracks of blood.

"Where's Ian?" I asked.

"He's inside, watching Dave, who is unconscious at the moment. For a pup, he put up quite a fight." She moved her lips in what might have passed for a smile in other circumstances.

"What about the guards?"

"Also taken care of. Two guards and the infamous Dr. D are tied up in the living room. I see, uh, you took care of this one." Eliza jerked her head in the direction of the fallen man, and I nodded stiffly.

The blood flowing out of Tim slowed, and his breaths sounded clearer. Sheila watched him, as if will alone could heal him. I sat down on the grass next to Eliza, my back to the other body. The body I hadn't let myself think about too much, yet. Carson sighed in his sleep and I breathed him in, deeply.

"So, we won, didn't we? Didn't we? We won." The whole evening seemed like a blur to me. "Now what?"

Eliza answered after a moment. "I think we contact the council and let them take care of clean up. They'll question everyone involved, especially the doctor. And it'll take the power of the council to cover up all of...this." She gestured widely.

Tim made a small sound and his eyelids twitched once, twice. One of Sheila's hands flew to her mouth, not muffling the sob that shook her. Her other hand moved to stroke his slightly shaggy hair, brushing the short curls.

"Shh, shh, you're okay, you're going to be okay, now. Tim, you're okay," her bent head murmured over him.

Several heartbeats later, his eyes opened and gazed up at her. "Sheila?"

Sheila laughed, brushing away the tears that fell on Tim's face, and she bent down to kiss him, first on the cheek and then on his lips, gently, but with an undercurrent of frantic passion. Tim raised one hand, in the direction of Sheila's cheek.

I closed my mouth and turned to Eliza, who met my gaze with a bewildered shake of the head. Abruptly feeling like a voyeur, I turned away from the murmuring pair and Eliza did the same.

The day's emotions rushed over me, a hangover of fear, disgust, and violence roiling in stomach-turning confusion. I felt relief, jealousy, and bone-deep fatigue. In fact, such weariness, my eyes started to close of their own accord. I sank down onto the lawn. The grass was soft against my face, the night quiet now. From what seemed like a great distance, I was aware of Eliza prodding me, saying my name in a sharp voice, but I brushed her away like a troubling dream. Then she disappeared and I slipped farther away, farther and farther.

Something hit me, hard, across the face and I startled half awake, mumbling in protest. It came again, a sharp smack across my cheek and I opened my eyes to find Sheila, her hand raised.

"What?" I tried to say through my thick tongue.

"Get up, Julie. What are you doing?"

I started to say sleeping, of course, but then wondered why was I sleeping? Was I…lying on the ground? With Carson still attached to me in his sling? Alarm rang through me and I would have sat upright, if my muscles had responded. As it was, I sat up slowly, carefully, and looked around as full memories of the evening surfaced.

My first coherent question was, "Where's Eliza?"

"She ran that way," Sheila pointed toward the front of the house, "changing form as she went."

"Why?"

"I'm not sure. She tried to rouse you, then jumped up and said, 'Dave' and took off."

Since I was more or less myself again, Sheila resumed her former place, resting Tim's head in her lap. Tim's eyes were open, though still clouded with pain. No fresh blood showed, so I assumed his wound had started to heal.

He spoke quietly, taking shallow breaths after every few words. "Dave called the moon on you— probably tried for all of us. He must have made an escape."

"He made me fall asleep?"

"Called you into oblivion." Tim's breath hitched and he paused for a moment. "One of the hardest powers. Easier on a human than on another Were. Or a Witch, maybe. He really is strong, that one."

"So Eliza went after him. Should we try to go help?" I asked, mostly a rhetorical question.

"Ian." Tim closed his eyes, but the one word made me jump to my feet. I swayed, but most of the fuzziness had dissipated.

"Right," I said, "you guys stay here." My comment was mostly for show, since I didn't think Sheila planned to leave Tim's side anytime soon.

Since Eliza had taken off around the side of the house, I assumed Dave wasn't inside, but I still entered cautiously. No surprises, no mafia thugs jumping out at me, no loose Werewolves. In the living room, I found several bound people—I assumed the guards and the doctor—and I checked briefly to make sure they remained secured. Then I moved to my main target: Ian. He wasn't moving, but I didn't see a lot of blood, so I was hopeful. But when I reached him, my stomach jumped and I instinctively wrapped my arms around Carson.

Ian's neck lay at an unnatural, contorted angle, his head misplaced on his spine.

As I gasped, he blinked and moved his eyes in my direction. After a moment's pause during which I tried to conceal my horror and shock, I knelt at his side.

"Ian, can you hear me?"

"Yes." His voice came out through clenched teeth.

"Are you going to be okay?"

After a silence, he said, "I think so. But not if my neck heals crooked like this. You need to straighten my spine."

My mouth went suddenly so dry I cleared my throat several times before my voice sounded. "All right."

Hands shaking, I found a safe spot on the floor for Carson and loosened the blanket binding him to me. I snuggled him into a cozy position and tucked the blanket around him tightly. Then, as much as I wanted to find some other reason to procrastinate, I turned back to Ian.

"I'm not sure how to do this," I admitted.

"Me neither. Is Eliza around?"

"No, she took off after Dave."

Fury flashed in Ian's eyes, but he took a shallow, shuddering breath and re-focused.

"With my spine aligned, everything can heal correctly. So, it should just be like, uh, setting any other broken bone?"

I had never had a more surreal conversation, which spoke volumes, considering the last two weeks of my life.

I looked at Ian clinically, trying to remember my days of CPR, correct positioning of the neck and all of that. Kneeling behind his head with my hands under his shoulders, I first hefted his torso to ensure a straight line from his hips. Then, I cradled his head in one hand, placing the other at the base of his neck. Taking a deep breath, I pulled his head up and out, into alignment, trying to ignore the grinding noise and the small pops that resulted. I held his head firmly in both hands, running my fingers down his neck.

"That seems okay, now. I think."

"Thank you."

I swallowed firmly, feeling my stomach roil in aftermath.

"How long will it take for this to heal? For you to move and everything?"

"I'm not sure." Sweat stood out against the pallor of Ian's upper lip.

"Can I get you anything? A glass of water?"

"No, but can you move those guys? I'm not a freak show." Ian darted his eyes in the direction of the tied-up guards and the doctor.

"Oh." The three prisoners or hostages or whatever they were had been so quiet I'd pretty much forgotten them. Maybe that's what they hoped—we'd forget all about them.

As I stood up to walk over to them, Sheila and Tim came into the room. Tim walked quite slowly and leaned a bit on Sheila, but his mobility this soon after taking a bullet in the lung amazed me. Lots of benefits to being a Were.

"This is the doctor?" Tim looked down at one of the bound figures, the man with jeans and cowboy boots I noticed earlier. He looked like he'd lived in the desert for too long without ever using moisturizer or sunscreen. His brown hair grayed at the temples.

I shrugged.

"You," Tim toed the man none too gently, "Are you Dr. Daniels?"

After a moment, the man sighed and said, "Yes."

"You're the doctor responsible for mutilating those people?"

Funny. Tim, barely able to walk, with his baby face, rumpled clothes, and scruffy hair. Yet, somehow, the tone of his voice made Dr. Daniels blanch under his tan.

"I would not expect you to understand the cost of medical experimentation," the doctor said stiffly. "Each of those men volunteered."

"A volunteer who expected—who had been promised—supernatural powers. Who had been told by *you* he would be transformed like Ken. Even though you knew Ken was a dark moon and these others were not." Tim accompanied his words with a short kick in the doctor's ribs before continuing. "Did you show the later volunteers what happened to others? Did they know?"

Spots of color appeared on Dr. Daniels' cheekbones and the haughty look fixed on his face. "All scientific innovation has costs. People risk much to gain the abilities you were born with, Were. With each new set of bone marrow, with each group of stem cells, I got closer to the answers. If I only had access to stronger Weres, I know I could be successful."

"Each new set of bone marrow?" My voice was shrill, and I shook. "That's all they were to you, sets of bone marrow? These were people—people you killed.

Including my...including Mac, my...People you killed when they were no longer necessary to your...your fucking experiments." I spat the last word in rage. "That's why you wanted my baby. My *baby.* The strongest, most helpless Were you knew about. To suck out his bone marrow and create monsters."

Such rage gripped me, I actually understood why Kayleigh had lost it, why she had torn that traitor Were to shreds.

"You're the monster," I finally said. "You asshole."

Pulling my rather tattered dignity around myself, I turned my back on him and walked back to pick up Carson. I sat next to Ian, focusing on him and the baby and trying to calm down.

From the other side of the room, I heard Tim questioning the guard. He started by explaining, very carefully, Jimmy Bianco and their safe house were under our control. Then he informed the captives he had called the pack Council earlier in the evening and an emergency team of Weres would arrive within two hours. He engaged in drawn-out speculation about the treatment of the captives by the Weres, about the reactions of the council upon seeing the malformed creatures at the safe house, about the chances the captives would ever be allowed to live now they knew Werewolves existed. Tim delivered all this in the mildest of voices, as if he made conversation at a barbecue. But by the end, all three captives spilled their guts, trying to outdo one another by sharing details about their doomed venture, hoping their lives would be spared. The doctor rambled about bone marrow, about stem cells reordering DNA, about Were healing powers overcoming normal complications like "type" or "rejection." I didn't listen to it all. I couldn't bring myself to care. I just sat and watched Ian heal and Carson sleep.

My semi-trance broke when Tim stopped in the middle of a sentence and turned his head in the direction of the front hall. Ian's eyes opened wide and a snarl twisted his mouth. His body twitched. A moment later, the front door opened with a bang that would have alarmed me, but for the warning. Eliza walked in the front door, dragging Dave behind her. Literally. She held him by one ankle, and pulled the tall teen behind her with no apparent care for his wellbeing, evident in the way his head crashed up the steps, into the doorframe, and on the wall. Eliza must have knocked him unconscious in their fight and, from the repeated blows his skull took as she dragged him in the house, he would remain so for at least a little while.

"Everyone okay here, then?" Eliza asked, with a searching glance around the room. "Ian?" Her eyes stopped on him and something in her face eased as she realized, although grievously injured, he was healing.

"We're all fine, somehow. Maybe the lucky pins helped?" Tim shot a look at Sheila and a sudden smile shot across his face. She flushed. "The council's team should be here in two hours."

"Good." With a thump, Eliza dropped Dave's foot. "They can take care of this one, then."

"I'll take care of him," muttered Ian.

"You, idiot pup, will be lucky if your mom doesn't take care of you first." Eliza dropped lightly onto the couch.

"Will he stay unconscious for that long? I mean, until the council's people get here?" I asked.

Eliza frowned. "No, probably not. I guess we should tie him up."

"With silver," said Ian.

Eliza sighed and rubbed her eyes for a minute, then went over to Dave and got to work with the duct tape.

"Why is there always a roll of duct tape hanging around, anyway? Is it some sort of mafia accessory?" No one responded as I wondered aloud, though Eliza quirked a smile in my direction.

"More to the point, does anyone have silver chain of any sort?" Eliza sat back on her heels. "I didn't bring any from the other house."

I handed her the chains I'd pocketed after freeing Kayleigh. She hissed as the silver hit her fingers, looped the short chain around his wrists, and said, "We'll have enough notice if he wakes up. Besides, I wouldn't mind an excuse to bash him in the head again."

"I'll help," Sheila and I said at the same time.
****

When Dave roused, however, we weren't quite so quick to knock him unconscious again. He groaned and tried to move before realizing he was bound. Apparently, the fact his hands were duct taped behind him brought back the night's events in full, because his eyes opened with a start and he swung his head around, assessing the situation. Immediately, Eliza and Tim were on guard, hovering over him.

"Try anything and I'll slit your throat," Eliza said grimly. "Not with silver, mind you, I don't want to deprive the council of a full trial."

Ian remained on the floor, though he'd gained enough mobility to roll onto his side and look at Dave. The positions of the two teens were oddly mirrored, lying on the floor facing each other. Ian's expression gave no clues to his thoughts as he stared at his friend. Dave returned the look for a brief moment before closing his eyes, throat moving convulsively.

"You nearly killed me." Ian said, voice devoid of emotion.

When Dave didn't answer, Ian continued. "You were my best friend. You nearly killed me. You killed my brother—not directly, but you're in league with *them*. You might as well have killed him yourself. You were my best friend." Ian's voice rose and broke, the emotion suddenly pouring through. I clenched my hands at the raw pain on his face, while I struggled in turn with my own anger and grief over Mac's death.

"You—you—you—" After a moment's pause, Ian voice dropped again, to a near whisper. "You were my best friend."

"Ian." Dave opened his eyes, and I saw anger and sorrow warring in them. "Ian—I didn't mean to hurt you; you have to know that. I didn't want it to be like this. It wasn't *supposed* to be like this. I saved you—I got you back when they took you—they weren't supposed to take you, but they didn't know, and I got you back and I didn't mean to hurt you."

"If you didn't mean to hurt me, then why did you bring me to Las Vegas?" Ian said. "Tell me that. You brought me here to give me to them, didn't you? *Didn't you?* You certainly didn't come here to help me avenge my brother."

"I brought you here so you would understand, so you could join us."

Ian recoiled at Dave's words.

"No, listen," Dave continued, urgently. "It's not their fault they had to kill Mac. That wasn't the plan either. Mac wouldn't listen—he could have been helpful; he could have part of my pack—"

"*Your* pack?" Eliza's voice cut in, dripping with scorn. "Is that what they offered you? Leadership over a pack of mongrel—"

"We weren't making mongrels." Dave's eyes shone with fervor. I sank down on the couch as he continued. My stomach hurt.

"Don't you understand? We were making Weres. Making those pathetic, weak, useless humans into *Weres*. Once we did that, once we allied with the families—once we took control of the others—think of the power we could amass. The pack and the mafia together? We wouldn't need to live in secret, wouldn't need to hide our existence from these pathetic humans, we could rule openly, take control."

"Dave. You almost killed me. They killed Mac. And Carlos," Ian sounded bewildered, "What the hell were you thinking?"

"They wouldn't have had to kill Mac if he'd been reasonable and agreed to help. His bone marrow was useful; Dr. D was so much closer to finding the answers. But Mac wouldn't bring us other Weres. He didn't understand. He wouldn't listen. They tried so hard to make him understand the potential—Ken spent time with him, Dr. D, Jimmy—he wouldn't listen to any of them. They had no choice; he *made* them kill him." Dave talked fast and loud, as if he honestly thought he could convince us—convince Ian—he had made the right decisions, that any of this could be justified. "Carlos was on our trail; he'd tracked down Dr. D and nearly killed him in the park. We were lucky Ken was close by and he had time to intervene. Even though they didn't have a chance to get a sample from Carlos."

A sample. I opened my mouth, then closed it and shook my head futilely.

"But those people…" Eliza's voice trailed off for a moment. "Dave, those things aren't Weres. They are monsters."

"Those were the first ones and the process almost worked. Dr. D refined it." Dave's earnestness was more painful than anger would have been. "They were only humans, anyway. There were bound to be mistakes."

"Eliza," Ian said, "Take him away. Please, get him out of here. I…"

Eliza drew back her foot, as if to kick Dave in the head, but then stopped. Her mouth tightened and she said, "Don't try anything, Dave."

"I won't. When I explain it all to the council, they'll understand. I know they will."

None of us said anything more, as Eliza dragged Dave into the other room. There didn't seem to be anything left to say.

Chapter Twenty-Four

Nine Weres headed by a full moon named Chris Usher, who could have passed for a mafia goon himself, poured through the doors an hour later and took control.

"This is him?" Chris gestured to Dave with one meaty hand.

"Yes. Dave Blythe. He's strong. He'll need a full contingent of guards," Tim said.

"No problem." Chris dismissed the challenge and surveyed the rest of the prisoners. After his assessment, he looked at Sheila and me through narrowed eyes.

"I need a full report on these," he said, jerking his chin in our direction. "Do we silence them now?"

Tim and Eliza stepped forward in unison. While several other Weres prowled around and managed the scene, Tim explained my relationship to Mac and Carson, my vested interest in keeping pack secrets, and the crucial role I played in cracking the case. He also credited me with saving his life, which I suppose was true. He made me sound a lot more heroic than I felt. Since Sheila was a Witch, he continued, she could be trusted to keep the evening's events quiet as well. She wouldn't want her own abilities revealed. Eliza allowed Tim to make the official report, though her silent support spoke volumes. After several minutes, Chris shrugged, ran a hand over his close-cropped hair, and declared the council could decide to silence us later, if they decided it necessary.

Lovely.

As Chris talked to Tim, the other Weres circled around taking charge of prisoners. At one point, Chris ordered four of them to the other scene, where presumably Kayleigh continued guarding Jimmy Bianco. Unless she'd slaughtered him. Minutes after those Weres left, Chris dismissed Sheila and me from the scene. He made it more than clear the two of us—as non-pack members—were no longer welcome. He also dismissed Ian, a minor who shouldn't be further involved, and told the teen to drive Tim's car back to the hotel. Chris was adamant all three of us return to the hotel, not leave without permission, and talk to no one.

Tim and Eliza were detained by the other Weres for further questioning and, possibly, to assist the clean-up effort. Since catching a few hours of sleep was just about the only thing on my mind, I didn't balk at the orders. Thankfully, Sheila volunteered to drive, since I thought I might fall asleep on the road.

I snapped Carson into his car seat and slid into the front seat next to Sheila. As we coasted down the finally-nearly-deserted Strip and approached the hotel, I looked over at Sheila.

"So," I said, "you and Tim?"

She shrugged one shoulder and smiled. "Yeah. I think so."

"When the hell did that happen?"

"Right away, really. At least, the draw and the tension were there right away. I'm surprised you didn't pick up on it. I mean, he's so..." She trailed off and shrugged again.

"He's so what?" And when she didn't answer, I fumbled on. "I'm just really surprised. He's so...ordinary."

Sheila threw her head back and laughed; a full-throated laugh that caught me by surprise. I found myself giggling with her, but at the same time, I wasn't a hundred percent sure what she found so funny.

Wiping her eyes, she said, "Jules, if you think a Werewolf hit man is ordinary, your new perspective on life is totally warped." And she erupted in laughter again.

"All right, all right," I said, as we caught our breath, "But you know what I mean, don't you? You walk down the street and have every eye on you. Tim's so...he's so...well, he's almost negligible. You know. If you didn't know he was a Werewolf hit man."

Sheila shook her head. "I think his façade is very consciously cultivated."

"Yeah, maybe." After a minute, I asked, "So, is this a serious thing? Like a real relationship? Or is it a typical Sheila six-week affair?"

She shot me a dirty look. "We'll see, I guess," she said in an unusually quiet voice.

****

Even after I'd seen the Werewolves in action, I was surprised how efficiently our night's work was obfuscated. Tim told us the malformed half-Were creatures had been granted mercy killings. As for Jimmy Bianco, Dr. Daniels, and the guards, Tim very carefully didn't reveal their fates, but I had my suspicions. I didn't think the council could allow people with knowledge of Weres to survive and plot against their kind again. Tim remained close-mouthed about the rest of the night, but Eliza revealed both she and Tim had been berated for involving non-Weres in pack business. She told me there was further debate among the Were team about taking permanent action to ensure silence from me and Sheila. In the end, however, the more dubious members of the team had been convinced I—as Carson's mother—had vested interest aligned with the pack. Sheila, as a Witch, didn't pose quite the same threat a regular human would. She, too, was a complicit partner in keeping such realms of activity private. Hopefully, the council agreed when they received the report.

As for Dave? His fate hung in the balance. A very sober Eliza explained he would have a full trial by the council. Most likely, his Were powers would be permanently stripped, a punishment meted out by nine full moon wolves ritually calling the moon. Or he might be executed. I wasn't sure which Dave would think worse.

I searched the Las Vegas papers for the next two days, thinking I'd see some sort of reference to our escapades, but found nothing. I wasn't quite sure how the council managed it, but they must have connections in high places.

****

Our goodbyes were hard. Sheila and Tim stood off in a corner talking in low voices, holding hands. She gazed at him as if trying to memorize every feature and build a holodeck or something. He looked rumpled and affable as usual, but something in his stance matched her intensity.

Eliza, Ian, and I stood near the doors. Ian held Carson. Since That Night, which had somehow become capitalized whenever we referred to it, Ian hadn't spent nearly as much time sulking and peering through his bangs. He dropped the I'm-too-cool-to-dote-on-a-baby act, as well. I think he spent a lot of time reassessing things. He'd been generally quiet and wouldn't talk about Dave. I didn't know enough about teenagers—heck, or about Werewolves—to push him, so I focused on playing a supportive surrogate big sister role, letting him know I was there; ready to listen when he wanted to talk. I did a lot of talking, myself, convinced it was good for him to hear my own thoughts and confusion about everything. The terror I felt over Carson. The anger and the pity I felt for Dave. The horror I felt killing a man, even though it saved Tim's life. The grief I still felt about Mac. I had a hard time coming to terms with it all, and I thought the least I could do was to show Ian some of my own process. He turned out to be a good listener.

"So, you're going to come and visit us in Oregon, right? Both of you?"

"Damn straight," said Eliza. "Next time, no crazy stalking killers."

Ian snorted. "I'm sure my mom will have us all visiting you so often you'll think twice about inviting us."

Silence took over as we all thought through the ramifications of my jaunt to Greybull.

"Unless I move to Greybull like your dad said I should. Right?" I meant it as a joke to lighten the mood.

Eliza's voice turned serious, ignoring my wishes for levity and a smooth parting. "Actually, Julie, you should think about it. There will come a time—soon—when Carson needs other Weres. What are you going to do in two weeks when he changes again? Or, maybe you can handle things next month, but what about in a year or so, when he needs to explore and learn how to hunt?"

"God, Eliza. Let's take things one step at a time, okay?"

I was not moving to Greybull, Wyoming. No way, no how.

"Besides," I added, smiling weakly, "Maybe Tim will relocate to southern Oregon, given the way the lovebirds over there are carrying on."

Eliza let the subject drop, though I understood it as a momentary reprieve from what would be a long-standing topic of discussion.

"Sheila," I called. "We should get moving."

In response, Sheila flung herself into Tim's arms. Eliza and I spent some time making faces at each other before I loudly ahem-ed several times and Sheila resurfaced. Tim smiled in a bemused fashion and ran a hand over his hair, causing several curls to stand up straight with his attempt to smooth it.

After a chorus of goodbyes and plenty of hugs, I snapped Carson into his cow-print car seat and joined Sheila in the front. With a deep breath, I started the car. Somehow, it felt like surfacing after a long underwater swim, back into real life. Back to Jacksonville, Oregon, where surely things would settle back into something approaching normality.

As we pulled out of the parking lot, Eliza waved frantically and I rolled down the window.

"Julie," she yelled.

"What?"

"Make sure he doesn't bite you."

293

It took me a minute to understand her meaning, but then I shot an alarmed glance at the backseat, at my peaceful little baby who had no teeth. Yet.

A word about the author...

Sarah's love of reading, writing, and all things fantasy started with her explorations of Narnia, Middle Earth, and Pern. She is a huge enthusiast of all fantasy, paranormal, and science fiction. Flying her geek flag early, she started D&D with the good old boxed sets (and still plays today). Her stories focus on strong women, strong friendships, magic, and love.

She lives with her partner Gary, their three kids, and three cats. She's also an artist and a boardgame geek.

http://sarahestevens.com